There were few men who had the power to turn Amanda into a submissive love slave but Roger was one of them.

'Come here,' he said, his eyes boring into hers. 'I want to see your body again. All of it.'

His hands slipped down to her waist and bunched the material of her thin sweater into soft folds. In one smooth movement he pulled the garment over her head, tossing it casually to the floor.

As usual Amanda wore no bra. Her firm, beautifully shaped breasts had no need of support. They stood out like ripe cantaloupe melons. Roger licked his lips . . .

Scandal in Paradise

Anonymous

First published in Great Britain in 1994
by HEADLINE BOOK PUBLISHING

A HEADLINE DELTA paperback

10 9 8 7 6 5 4 3 2 1

ISBN 0 7472 4398 0

Typeset by
CBS, Felixstowe, Suffolk

Printed and bound in Great Britain by
HarperCollins Manufacturing, Glasgow

HEADLINE BOOK PUBLISHING
A division of Hodder Headline PLC
338 Euston Road
London NW1 3BH

Scandal in Paradise

Chapter One

The bedside telephone rang.

Beneath the sheets, Amanda grunted a muffled curse at having forgotten to disconnect the extension. It was not the best time for a conversation. She was just trying to prime Giles for a spirited early morning fucking session.

Reluctantly, Amanda let his warm, soft cock slip out of her wet mouth with a faint and liquid plop.

The simple fact that it *was* soft gave her pause for afterthought. Giles, normally a superstud when it came to any form of sexual gymnastics, had proved a sad disappointment both this morning and the previous night – partly due no doubt to the fourteen pints of Old Thunderwind he had downed before retiring to bed. Perhaps a telephonic interruption at that precise moment might save them both any further frustration and embarrassment.

Crawling out from underneath the sheets, Amanda lifted the receiver off the hook.

'Amanda?' said a male voice. 'It's Roger . . . Roger Vennings. Remember me?'

A faintly dreamy smile curled Amanda's lush lips.

Even after five years, just the name and the purring tones of that beautifully modulated voice were enough to send a tingling wave of pleasure vibrating deep into her cunt and start the juices flowing.

'Well, Roger,' Amanda purred back. 'A smooth tongue and a rough cock. A perfect combination in a man. How could I possibly forget?'

Giles exploded out from the bedsheets, sitting upright with a hurt expression on his handsome face.

'I say, steady on, old girl,' he complained. 'You're supposed to be with me, remember?'

Amanda pressed the earpiece of the telephone against her bare stomach. With her free hand she groped for Giles's flaccid prick and gave it a meaningful squeeze.

'Supposed being the operative word,' she pointed out sarcastically. 'And don't start acting like a jealous husband. Roger is a very old and dear friend.'

Giles slumped back on the pillow sulkily as Amanda turned her attention back to the telephone.

'So, Roger . . . How lovely to hear from you.'

'Yes, well – thought I'd give you a buzz,' Roger went on. 'The thing is, I have a little proposition to put to you. Are you doing anything right now?'

Amanda removed her hand from Giles' cock. 'No, unfortunately not,' she said petulantly.

'Great!' Roger sounded relieved. 'So how about me coming over to discuss a little joint business venture with you?'

Amanda was immediately on her guard. A fun-loving companion and great screw he might be, but Roger Vennings had some serious shortcomings as a businessman.

'What's the pitch, Roger?'

Roger sounded aggrieved. 'No pitch, sweetheart. Solid business, all the way home to the bank. Trust me.'

Amanda tried hard to recall the last time she had trusted Roger. Was it the sex-orgy holidays for Kuwaiti oil sheiks scheme, or had that come before the guaranteed sure-fire penis-extension plan? Although times and dates were a little fuzzy, one fact was easy enough to remember. Both had been costly and total disasters.

However, she had little time to dwell on past failures. Roger was now well into his second phase of enthusiastic sales talk.

'The point is, I heard from a couple of the girls about this business you recently inherited – this Paradise Country Club. And, with new businesses being what they are at the moment, it occurred to me that you might well need some spare cash, which happens to be one thing that I have rather a lot of right now.'

That part, at least, sounded promising. 'Go on,' Amanda murmured warily. She was vaguely aware of Giles stirring in the bed beside her, his hand probing between her thighs and forcing them apart. She gave a little moan as two of his thick fingers

3

slipped between her fleshy labial lips and began to gently tease her clitoris.

'No, don't groan,' came Roger's voice over the telephone. 'I'm really serious. I started up this sex rejuvenation clinic about a year ago, and it's going like the clappers. I'm raking it in but I need to expand my theatre of operations. So what do you think?'

'I'd rather not think. The answer's no,' Amanda said flatly.

Giles had begun to tweak the sensitive little bud of her clit between his finger and thumb. Amanda felt the old familiar ripples of pleasure pulsing into the moist recesses of her hungry fanny. With his free hand, Giles lifted her wrist and moved it under the bedclothes, dropping her hand on to his rapidly stiffening prick. Amanda squeezed the thick shaft lovingly, rubbing the ball of her thumb over its blunt, hot head.

'Look, I can't really talk about this any more – something big has come up,' she told Roger.

But he was not to be put off. 'Listen, Amanda, I just bet you're really short of money right now. Am I right?'

'Yeah – really hard up,' Amanda agreed.

For some reason, Giles seemed to assume her last words were directed at him. He lunged over suddenly, throwing one leg across Amanda's thighs and heaving himself into the missionary position. Amanda felt the bulbous helmet of his handsome cock pause briefly at the moist portals of her cunt before he rammed his full nine inches deep inside her. She realised, thankfully, that she had underestimated Giles's powers of recovery from the negative effects of Old Thunderwind. She let out a little shriek of pleasure.

'Hey, that's better,' Roger said. 'It's nice to hear you sounding so enthusiastic. So, can I come round and discuss it with you in more detail?'

'You can't come now,' Amanda almost screamed into the receiver.

'I wasn't damn well planning to,' muttered Giles, who was just getting into his stroke. 'I've waited all night for this hard-on, and I'm not going to waste it now.'

Amanda began to grunt heavily as Giles plunged his throbbing rod in and out of her juice-filled honeypot.

'I recognise that sound,' came Roger's voice. 'I take it you're rather busy at the moment?'

'Hard at it,' Amanda agreed fervently. She began to gyrate her hips in time with Giles' thrusts, enabling him to ram even deeper into her hungry cunt with every stroke.

'I'll be round in an hour,' Roger said. 'If you're not finished by then I'll throw a bucket of water over you.'

He hung up.

Giles stopped his furious fucking for a moment, propping himself up on one elbow and looking Amanda squarely in the eye.

'Now, do I have your complete and undivided

attention?' he wanted to know.

Amanda hooked her legs over his back, pulling him down as she raised her hips and thrust upwards on to his impaling rod.

'You do now,' she said with enthusiasm, letting out a thin squeal of delight as Giles resumed his hot and powerful thrusts into her brimming love canal.

Dropping the telephone receiver over the edge of the bed, Amanda slid her hand under the rounded cheeks of her beautiful arse. Lifting her buttocks slightly, she gently inserted one finger into the tight little hole of her anus, wiggling it around to increase her pleasure.

So tell me about this very old and very dear friend of yours,' Giles said, as they both lay back in the bed enjoying a steam bath of their own perspiration.

Amanda regarded him carefully. She had never thought of Giles as being the jealous type, but then you never can tell with men, she reasoned to herself.

'I did have a life before I met you,' she said cautiously. 'And although we've had a lot of fun together, there's no commitment, you know that.'

Giles seemed to have recovered his natural equilibrium. He smiled disarmingly. 'Look, I don't want to own you, Amanda,' he said gently. 'And anyway, after the Hunt Ball is over and the sale of the house and land has gone through, I'll be disappearing anyway. I was just interested, that's all.'

'I knew Roger back in the days when I worked for a dating agency, before I started my own escort agency,' Amanda began. 'He was what we girls in the trade used to call a procurer.'

'A pimp, do you mean?' Giles asked.

Amanda shook her head. 'No, not exactly. Roger had a lot of good business contacts. He'd book girls to show visiting executives and foreign buyers a good time, organise parties . . . that sort of thing. Besides his weakness for getting involved in slightly shady deals, Roger was a damned good organiser.'

'And good in bed too, I take it?'

Amanda giggled. 'Yes, that too. But you're better,' she added, lying.

Giles preened visibly, to Amanda's inward amusement. Men were such egotists when it came to sexual prowess. Mind you, he did have something to be rather proud about. Amanda reached for it under the bedclothes.

'Shall we go for seconds?'

Without waiting for an answer, she dived under the sheets and wrapped her soft, full lips around his beautiful weapon. Giles groaned softly, spreading his legs so that she could nuzzle down into the hot valley between his thighs. He was stiff again in seconds, as Amanda's skill as a fellatrix sent the hot blood pumping up the thick shaft of his prick. He placed his fingertips gently under her chin, to lift her head away.

Amanda shook her head, her mouth still clamped

tightly around his pulsing tool. Her cunt had already been filled and satisfied. Now it was her mouth's turn to get some pleasure.

She sucked furiously, pausing occasionally to lick the underside of his swollen balls with a hot tongue.

Giles surrendered to the inevitable. He lay back and enjoyed the delicious agony of Amanda's mouth, lips and tongue fluting and teasing at his cock until finally he shot a gush of hot come into the back of her throat.

Chapter Two

Amanda was in the bar chatting to Andrew, the head barman, when Roger arrived. She looked up as he strode in, with that irrepressible bounce in his step that she remembered so well from the past.

Even after five years he seemed just as she remembered him: tall, blond, suntanned and forever grinning as though he alone shared a private joke with the rest of the world.

Amanda motioned him to join her at the bar and Roger parked himself on the next stool. He leaned over, gave Amanda a brief peck on the cheek and just sat quietly, smiling.

Andrew had just been bemoaning the amazing sexual prowess of Charles, the ex-chauffeur who had recently joined him and his wife, Sally, as bar and catering assistant. He saw no reason to interrupt his detailed confession merely because a complete stranger had arrived. Pausing only to serve Roger with a pint of lager, he carried on.

'Thing is, I hardly ever get to give Sally a good straight fucking anymore,' Andrew complained. 'I think we've only made it about ten times in the past week. Charles is at her all the time – he's like a bloody rabbit.'

'But I thought you both liked the swinging scene,' Amanda said, not quite understanding what Andrew was complaining about.

'Oh, don't get me wrong. The threesomes are terrific,' Andrew said with enthusiasm. 'It's just that I can't keep up with the randy sod. I think he stores come like a camel stores water.'

'So what about Sally? What does she think about it all?' Amanda wanted to know.

'Oh, Sally's as happy as a monkey with two pricks,' Andrew retorted. He broke off to flash Amanda a slightly rueful grin. 'Quite literally,' he added.

Roger fished in his jacket pocket, pulling out a small business card, which he handed to Andrew across the bar.

'Look, I think I might be able to help you,' he offered generously.

Amanda snatched the card from Andrew's fingers after he had read it.

'The Priapus Sex Rejuvenation Clinic,' she muttered, reading the lettering on the card. 'Awaken even the most jaded sexual appetite and rediscover the libido of your youth.' She turned to Roger. 'This is your latest scam, I take it.'

Roger looked quite hurt. 'No scam, dear girl, believe me. It really does work – that's why I'm making so much bloody money. I just can't cope with the demand at the moment. You wouldn't believe how many men

10

and women in their forties and fifties there are out there with hard cash to pay for a hard prick.'

'So when did you become an expert sex therapist?' Amanda asked, still highly sceptical.

Roger shrugged. 'No expertise needed, really. It's a complete programme I happened to come across when I was in Amsterdam a year or so ago. A bit of hormone and drug therapy, group encounter sessions, a few porno movies and a strict regime of diet and exercise – seems to do the trick every time.'

Andrew's face was alight with enthusiasm. 'When can I start?' he wanted to know.

Roger gave him a wink, glancing briefly aside at Amanda.

'That could be down to the boss,' he said, somewhat mysteriously. He took a couple of swigs of his beer and fell silent. It was obvious that he didn't want to say more until he had discussed things in more detail with Amanda.

Andrew took the hint. 'Well, I guess I've got things to do,' he said, somewhat reluctantly. 'I suppose I ought to go down into the cellars and clean out my pipes.'

After he had left, Roger turned to Amanda, his mischievous grin even more roguish than usual.

'Talking about cleaning out pipes, how about you helping me to clean out mine?' he suggested. 'It's been a long time, Amanda, my sweet.'

Amanda smiled. 'How long is it, exactly?'

'About the same length as it was before. What do

you want it in, inches or centimetres?'

Amanda punched him lightly on the arm. 'Roger, you're impossible.'

'No, I'm dead easy,' Roger countered, then stared Amanda fully in the eyes, switching on the charm like an electric light. 'Seriously, how about it? Let's you and me get it on together again. We used to have some pretty good sessions, didn't we?'

Amanda found the offer more than tempting. Roger's blue eyes had the uncanny knack of looking totally convincing even when he was lying through his teeth. Before she totally melted under the gaze of utter love and passion, she tried at least some token resistance.

'I thought you wanted to talk business?' she said.

Roger grinned faintly. 'I never discuss business on a full pair of balls,' he told her, swinging himself off the bar stool and taking her hand. 'So – where do we go?'

Amanda was lost. 'We'll use one of the private lounges,' she said, starting to lead the way. 'No-one is likely to disturb us at this time in the morning.'

Even as she spoke, and led Roger out of the bar into the hallway, Amanda was acutely aware of an odd, niggling sense of doubt in the back of her mind. Although she was already imagining his hot, rampant cock reaming into her yawning cunt with some relish, she was also wondering if she had done the right thing by allowing him back into her life again. For in all the rush to renew an old liaison, and the memories of great times shared, there was one little factor which she had conveniently chosen to forget until that precise moment. And that was the incredible sexual power that Roger Vennings had always managed to wield over her.

It was still there, as strong as ever. The pricking, liquid tingling in her cunt and the hot flush spreading around her nipples told Amanda that quite clearly. There were few men who had the power to turn her into a willing and submissive love slave. Even fewer who could make her do, willingly, what she might otherwise regard as depraved or distasteful. At the mere touch of his fingers on her bare flesh, Amanda knew that she would once again become a quivering useless lump of jelly which could be moulded and shaped into any sexual position that he chose to dream up. That her mind would become nothing more than a part of her hungry cunt, and no thoughts or feelings other than pure, unadulterated lust would be possible.

It was an awesome thought. More to the point, it made her feel vulnerable at the very time she should be feeling strong and in a position of dominance. Being a love slave didn't quite fit in with the new image of Amanda the property-owning business-woman.

But it was all a bit too late now, Amanda reflected. She could already feel the hot juices trickling out from the crevice of her golden cunt on to the soft and sensitive flesh of her inner thighs. There was an emptiness inside her which seemed to penetrate all the way to her womb and which could only be filled and satisfied by Roger's stiff, throbbing prick.

They reached the nearest of the small private lounges, normally reserved for the use of club members and their guests who were in too much of a hurry, or who had forgotten to book one of the upstairs bedrooms. Like just about everything else in the Paradise Country Club, the rooms were basic, sparsely furnished and designed purely for sexual use. Roger closed the door behind him as Amanda led the way to a long low-slung couch.

She started to sit down, but Roger grabbed her roughly by the shoulders, holding her upright.

'No – not yet,' he muttered, his eyes boring into hers. 'I want to see your naked body again, Amanda. All of it.'

His hands slipped over the back of her shoulders and down to her waist, his fingers hooking into the material of her thin sweater and bunching it up into soft folds. With one smooth, swift movement, he pulled the garment up over her head and down her arms, tossing it casually to the floor.

As usual, Amanda wore no bra. Her firm, beautifully shaped breasts had no need of support, standing out proudly and enticingly like a pair of young, slightly underripe cantaloupes, each decorated with a pert, pink nipple.

Roger licked his lips with appreciation at the sight, yet made no move to touch and fondle the soft and tempting flesh. He turned his attention to Amanda's skirt instead, deftly flicking open the three side buttons with his nimble fingers and allowing it to slip to the floor. Touching Amanda for the first time, he gently prodded her in the stomach, urging her to step backwards so that he could kick the skirt away. Then it was time to remove her tights, and finally her white silk panties so that her lush young body was fully exposed in all its shapely beauty.

Slowly, in an almost predatory fashion, Roger moved around her like a cat stalking its prey. He circled her, his eyes taking in her flat stomach, the flaring curve of her thighs, the golden triangle of pubic curls which hid the moist and slippery entrance to her soft cunt. Moving behind her, Roger completed his visual feast by noting the smoothly rounded perfection of her buttocks, the curve of her back, the smooth squareness of her shoulders.

Finally satisfied, Roger stood in front of his naked prize again and reached out to touch the firm softness of her breasts. Cupping each delicious orb in his palm, he lifted them as though testing for weight and ripeness, his thumbs flicking lightly over the pink buds of the nipples until they twitched and stiffened with anticipation.

'You're as beautiful as ever,' he murmured, the sight of the gorgeous body bringing a rush of sensual memories. He leaned forwards, bowing his head slightly so that he could run the tip of his tongue across the bulging top of each breast in turn and then

15

down the warm, soft valley between them.

Amanda purred contentedly at the feel of his hot tongue on her skin, a purr that turned quickly into a sort of throaty growl as he reached the stiffening bud of her left nipple and licked it. She reached out and began picking at the buttons of his shirt as he took to his pleasure more eagerly, drawing each delicious cherry in turn into his hot mouth and sucking greedily.

Roger took a step back as Amanda undid the last of his shirt buttons. Shrugging it off, he unclipped his belt, dropped his trousers to the floor and stepped out of them. Amanda's eyes fell to his white boxer shorts, bulging ominously from the pressure of his straining erection trapped inside them.

Unbidden, her fingers dropped to the tautly stretched material, tracing the gently throbbing contours of the stiff, imprisoned cock beneath it. Straightening it so that the stiff member lay upright against his belly, Amanda felt a little thrill of pleasure to note that the swollen, purplish head of the monstrous love weapon protruded above the waistband of the shorts. She stroked it with the tip of one long, painted fingernail and smiled as Roger quivered at the sensation. So, sexual power was a two-edged sword, she reminded herself. Even though she still slightly feared Roger's sexual dominance over her, Amanda took satisfaction from remembering that he, too, had always been like putty in her hands.

Or in her mouth! Amanda dropped to her knees and pressed her face into Roger's crotch. Opening her mouth, she seized the stiff outline of his cock between her teeth and began to chew at it like a dog with a bone.

Roger's whole body arched and stiffened with an involuntary spasm as he felt the hot moistness of her breath through the thin cotton material. He pulled back with a jerk, dropping his thumbs into the top of the shorts and yanking them down to his knees.

His stiff cock, freed from its cloth prison, sprang out, slapping Amanda softly on the forehead. Closing her eyes, she worked by sense of touch alone, gliding her wet tongue up the blood-engorged underside of Roger's formidable cock and kissing the swollen head gently with soft, pursed lips.

'Want to find out what you've been missing?' she teased, pulling her mouth away from the twitching tool. Amanda rose to her feet and pressed her body against his, her soft breasts crushed against his hard, manly chest. She reached down and took his hand, guiding it smoothly under her burning crotch, pressing his fingers against the hairy mound of her pubis. She gyrated her hips slowly and sensuously, so that the tips of his fingers caught against the soft folds of her labia, prising them apart for just long enough to smear them with the wet juices that were beginning to flow from the deep walls of her cunt.

'Remember this cunt?' she asked him. 'Remember

how good it could be to that big beautiful cock of yours?'

Roger warmed to Amanda's teasing game, as his own flood of memories were stirred. Now it was his turn to grasp her hand, forcing it down to his stiff prick and folding her fingers around the rigid shaft.

'How about you remembering this cock?' he countered, pumping her wrist up and down. 'I'll bet you haven't forgotten how good this feels, pumping and thrusting away inside you. Best cock you ever had, Amanda, before or since. Aren't I right?'

Despite her mounting excitement, Amanda actually thought of Phillipe, the French gardener, and his truly amazing love machine at that precise moment, but it seemed a pity to spoil the moment by being too candid. It was easier to tell a white lie. She squeezed Roger's more than adequate prick lovingly, moaning with passion.

'Oh yes. The biggest and best cock I ever had,' she assured him, reminding herself that any sensible girl makes the most of what she has to hand, be it cock, candle or hairbrush handle.

The reassurance seemed to inflame Roger with aggressive sexuality. Roughly, he pushed Amanda backwards. The back of her knees caught the edge of the couch and she sprawled into its welcoming softness.

In a second, Roger had jumped forwards, kneeling astride her thighs with his stiff prick pressed hard against her breasts.

'Well now you're going to get this cock again,' he promised. 'I'm going to fuck you all over, every delicious inch of you.'

Grasping her full breasts in both hands, he squeezed the pliant flesh, pressing them tightly together so that they totally encased his rampant prick.

'First I'm going to fuck your tits,' Roger told her, promptly making good his word by sliding his cock up and down in the warm, enclosing valley he had created.

'Dribble . . . spit,' he croaked out. 'Drool some saliva down on to my cock to make it nice and slippery.'

Amanda did as she was told, rolling her tongue around inside her mouth to stimulate the flow of oral juices and rolling them into a liquid ball before pushing it out over her soft red lips. It dribbled down on to the dry, burning head of the prick thrusting up between her breasts, making it glisten in the morning sunlight which streamed in through the half-open curtains.

'More,' Roger commanded, even though his cock was now slipping and sliding between her tits like a hot candle.

Amanda dredged up another mouthful of saliva, but as she started to drool it out over her lips again, Roger changed his mind.

'No, keep it in your mouth,' he snapped. 'Make it

hot and wet for my cock. I'm going to fuck your mouth now.'

He eased himself forwards, rising on his knees to bring the bulbous head of his prick into perfect line with Amanda's half-open and glistening soft lips. Her tongue darted out obediently to probe underneath it, lifting and guiding it towards her mouth. Positioning her lips around the swollen head, she sucked it in softly and wetly.

The first three or four inches of Roger's eight-inch weapon slid smoothly into her mouth. Amanda gulped greedily, trying to cram more of the delicious meat into her throat. Her cheeks bulged as Roger thrust forward, equally eager to plunge as deeply as possible into the wonderfully warm and wet tunnel that awaited him.

Amanda mouthed his thick cock gently, using her tongue and gums, until she was sure she could feel it stiffen and thicken even more.

She was not mistaken. Roger let out an animal-like roar of male dominance as he felt his cock rise to full, throbbing magnificence. He pulled out of Amanda's dripping mouth, his eyes flashing with the sheer intensity of his arousal.

'Now I'm really ready to fuck you stupid,' he announced triumphantly. 'Turn over, I want to take you from behind.'

He helped Amanda to sit up, urging her to lean forwards over the back of the couch so that her breasts hung down and her beautiful arse stuck up in the air at a most enticing angle. Jumping up on to the couch, he took one rounded cheek in each hand, prising them apart to reveal the golden cleft of her brimming cunt showing like the bull's eye of a target for his love arrow. One sharp push drove him deep into her well-oiled fanny until his bare belly slapped against the cheeks of her arse. Leaning over her back, he pumped his hips frantically, driving his weapon deeper and deeper into her yawning hole until Amanda felt filled with cock all the way up to her eyeballs. She let out a low, throbbing moan of pure pleasure, bucking her bottom against his savage thrusts as he plunged into her.

Above the grunts and the groans, and the wet smacking sounds as Roger's piston thrashed into Amanda's gushing love canal, neither of them heard the door behind them sigh gently open. Nor did they hear the sensuous purr of satisfaction from the lush and scarlet lips of the red-haired beauty who had entered the room.

Had either of them been in a position to view the newcomer, they would have seen a tall, voluptuous female encased from throat to toe in shiny black leather, fitted so skin tight that it accentuated every curving inch of her magnificent body. Set in a perfect oval and high-cheekboned face, a pair of emerald eyes glinted with plain and unvarnished lust at the sight of two people in the full throes of carnal passion.

The lecherous green eyes fell upon the white cheeks of Roger's heaving bottom, bobbing up and down as he humped furiously into Amanda's bubbling cunt. The woman reached down to the thick, metal-studded belt that she wore around her slim waist, her fingers closing over the knotted handle of a black leather bullwhip tucked into it.

Pulling the weapon out, she crept up silent and cat-like behind him and flexed the supple shaft of the whip in her hand. Turning slightly sideways, and judging her distance carefully, she flicked her wrist deftly, sending the business end of the whip cracking towards Roger's exposed and delicate buttocks.

Roger let out a thin squeal of pain and surprise as the whip stung his bare flesh, raising a thin red weal against the white skin. His head jerked round, his eyes suddenly taking in his unexpected tormentor, and the look of surprise and pain on his face changed to one of recognition and pleasure.

The woman in black flashed him a lascivious smile. 'I just couldn't resist it,' she purred, her eyes flashing wickedly. 'I'm sure you won't object if I join in.'

Amanda, with her head hanging down the back of the couch, had no way of knowing what was going on. She was only aware of Roger pausing briefly in his furious humping, of a strange female voice, and the repeated cracking sound of the whip as the leather-clad dominatrix sent the stinging end cracking against Roger's tender flesh time and time again.

Then Roger was pumping into her again, his thrusts more urgent and savage than ever. Amanda groaned as she felt her orgasm rising from deep inside her belly, rippling out in waves like a pebble thrown into a pond until they reached every muscle and fibre of her body. She began to grunt heavily in time with his pulsing thrusts, a torrent of minor obscenities escaping her slack lips between gasps for breath.

'Oh yes . . . pump it into me . . . slam your big beautiful cock up to my womb . . . ram your thick dick in as far as it will go . . . come on, spurt it into me . . . shoot your hot come into my gushing hole.'

The words seemed to excite the woman in black leather. She redoubled her efforts with the whip, her free hand dropping to her crotch where she rubbed the prominent black bulge of her own Mound of Venus furiously.

'Yes, come on Roger, pump your sauce into her,' she urged, her beautiful face contorted into a mask of pure lust. 'Empty your cock and balls into that hot slimy cunt.'

Roger's arse was a moving blur of white flesh and red lash marks as the combination of pain and pleasure drove him wild. He slammed wetly into the erupting geyser of Amanda's cunt as the first pumping spurts of her orgasm squirted out around the sides of his thick cock. Amanda's legs began to thrash wildly as the secondary wave of orgasm hit her, turning her whole body into a quivering, trembling, melting and flowing goo of sexual lava. With one last scream of delight, she let herself go and surrendered to the power of the volcano that was erupting inside her.

Roger felt the burning intensity of her orgasm permeate his own body and followed her lead, surrendering himself completely to the all-consuming sexual power of the moment. As the last lash-stroke burned into his flesh, he felt all pain miraculously disappear as his balls exploded and gushed jets of sperm along his pulsing cock and into Amanda's waiting cunt.

Chapter Three

'So, now that we've got to know each other again, let's catch up on the chat,' Roger suggested brightly.

Having dressed, they had returned to the bar, where they had poured themselves a well-deserved drink.

Amanda eyed up Madame Whiplash, flashing a prompting and inquisitorial look at Roger. 'Haven't you forgotten something? Like introducing me to your friend, for instance.'

'Ah, yes – silly me. Amanda, this is Letitia, my chief sex therapist. An invaluable member of my team,' Roger said.

Letitia's eyes sparkled with genuine friendliness. She held out one slim, black-gloved hand. 'Hi, Amanda. Hope you didn't mind me giving Roger a bit of a booster, just to perk up his performance.'

Amanda accepted the proffered hand and shook it warmly, accepting Letitia's obvious offer of friendship at face value. Despite a certain amount of plain old-fashioned jealousy at the girl's stunning good looks, she couldn't help but feel a strong sense of admiration for any woman who could exercise such obvious power over Roger. Whatever the true nature of their relationship, Amanda mused, it was definitely Letitia who held the whip hand – both figuratively and literally.

'Tell me – do you always go around looking like something out of the Spanish Inquisition?' Amanda asked.

Letitia grinned. 'I had a rather difficult client at the clinic just before we left,' she explained. 'There wasn't time to change, but I have some ordinary clothes in the car.'

'You can use one of the bedrooms if you want to freshen up,' Amanda offered. 'Help yourself to a key from the reception desk.'

Letitia stood up, taking the clear hint. 'Right, well I expect you and Roger have things to discuss. I'll go and change and see you later.'

Roger waited until Letitia had left the bar before he spoke again. 'Well, how about filling me in on the details behind this place?'

Amanda shrugged carelessly. 'Not much to tell, really. I guess you know the basics. An old client of mine died on the job, and left this place to me in his will. It's all pretty run down, as you can see, but the basic business is still here, and I think it could be a going proposition. It's down to me to turn it into a little gold mine.'

'And what have you done so far?' Roger wanted to know.

'Well, I have a few of my old escort girls from the

agency helping me out. Some of them bring clients down for overnight or weekend stays, others work here part-time providing a bit of glamour for the local trade. Next week we are holding the annual Hunt Ball for Giles, our local squire, and I'm hoping that it will start things moving in the way of other more up-market social functions.'

'I take it that the Paradise Country Club is basically just a bonking shop at the moment,' Roger put in bluntly.

There didn't seem much point in trying to disguise the truth. 'That's about it, in a nutshell,' Amanda admitted.

Roger rubbed his hands together in a gesture of enthusiasm. 'Well, Amanda my dear girl, I really think we can be of the greatest possible mutual benefit. Our two businesses are almost perfectly complementary to each other. Basically, you have the premises and the facilities, and I have the clients with the money.'

Amanda thought for a few moments. It all seemed to make perfectly good sense. Despite her earlier reservations about Roger's little schemes, she couldn't help feeling rather optimistic.

'So how do you see this collaboration actually working?' she asked, wanting to get down to some hard details.

'Simple,' Roger said. 'I move some of my clients and business down here, and you make money from accommodation, bar and food takings and any other little services they need provided. And believe me, after finishing the sex rejuvenation course, most of them are raring to use just about any sexual service there is going.'

Amanda thought about it all for several more moments before making up her mind. It was, she had to admit, a rather attractive proposition – assuming that everything went as smoothly as Roger saw it mapped out.

'Well, I guess you could use the old gymnasium,' she muttered eventually, thus sealing her fate and opening up the path of mayhem and madness that was to follow.

Roger grinned from ear to ear. He held out his hand. 'Then we have a deal?'

Amanda nodded. 'Deal,' she confirmed, sealing it with a formal handshake. 'Just as long as you're going to be straight with me, Roger Vennings.'

He assumed the look of a choirboy preparing to sing the Ave Maria. 'Amanda, I swear upon the three great lies of our time,' he vowed.

'Which are?' Amanda wanted to know.

Roger's look of innocence gave way to a wicked grin. 'Yes, I love you; of course I will still respect you afterwards; and I promise I won't come in your mouth,' he joked.

'Spoilsport,' Amanda joked back. She poured fresh drinks to toast the success of their joint venture.

Letitia tripped lightly down the stairs from the

bedroom. Having changed her leather gear for a simple white frilled blouse and a pair of tight blue jeans, she looked no less stunning. Freed of the restricting tightness of her 'Madame Whiplash' costume, her lush, full breasts seemed even more prominent, filling the blouse almost to bursting point and with her large, dark nipples showing clearly through the thin, stretched material. The skin-tight denims accentuated her incredibly slim waist, ballooning outwards as they barely managed to contain the swelling roundness of her generous buttocks. With her make-up skilfully retouched and her gorgeous red hair flowing over her shoulders almost to her waist, she presented the sort of picture that turned men's heads in the streets and raised almost instant erections in their trousers. Which was exactly the effect she had on Andrew, who had just come out of the kitchen and was heading towards the reception desk to pick up the spare key to the coldroom.

He stopped dead in his tracks as Letitia waltzed into his line of vision, his eyes nearly popping out of his head. His mouth dropped open like a fish out of water, flapping weakly as he desperately tried to force out some sort of introduction or chatty opening line.

Letitia did it for him. 'Hi there,' she said brightly, in the open, friendly way that was second nature to her.

Andrew remained silent – only the rapidly

increasing bulge in the front of his trousers spoke volumes on his behalf.

Letitia regarded Andrew's swelling cock like a cat confronted with a bowl of cream. Her green eyes sparkled.

'You're pleased to see me, I notice,' she murmured, grinning.

Andrew followed her line of vision down to his crotch and squirmed with embarrassment.

'It's all right. You don't have to be shy about it,' Letitia told him. 'I'm used to having that effect on men. That's why I'm so good at my job.'

'Your job?' Andrew managed to croak out, finally.

'I'm a sex therapist,' Letitia told him frankly. 'And if I couldn't get a man horny, I wouldn't be very much use, would I?'

Andrew was opening up to the girl's totally candid attitude. Finding his tongue at last, he responded. 'Are you anything to do with this sex rejuvenation clinic that Amanda's friend was talking about?' He fished in his pocket, producing the card that Roger had given him.

Letitia recognised it at once. 'Ah, I see you've met the boss.'

Andrew nodded. 'I was thinking of joining up for the course,' he said.

Letitia beamed. 'Great,' she said enthusiastically. 'How about taking your first treatment right now? No time like the present, as they say.'

Andrew could hardly contain himself. It was like

having all his birthdays and Christmases rolled into one. Despite his excitement, his brain was still managing to work more or less normally, and there was just one little problem, he reflected. It was obvious that Letitia had assumed him to be one of the clients of the Paradise Club. She might not be quite so generous if she realised he was merely a member of the staff. He saw no reason to set her straight.

'That would be terrific,' he agreed.

'Well, your room or mine?' Letitia asked.

Andrew thought quickly. If he took her down to his staff accommodation it would give the game away. Besides, he most certainly didn't want to share this vision of sexuality with the randy Charles.

'Probably best if we use yours. My room's in a bit of a mess,' he said finally.

'No problem.' Letitia turned back towards the stairs and headed back to her bedroom. Andrew followed her like a shadow, wincing with pain as every step made his tightly stretched trousers squeeze against his balls.

Letitia motioned to the king-size waterbed as she led the way into the bedroom. 'You just get your clothes off and make yourself comfortable while I get things ready,' she told Andrew, who was more than happy to comply at once.

Stripping off his clothes in double-quick time, he lay back on the gently rocking mattress as Letitia crossed the room to her overnight case and began to take things out and lay them on the top of the vanity

31

unit. She poured a glass of water from the sink tap and brought it over to him, tipping two small brown capsules into his hand.

'Take these,' Letitia commanded. 'Just swallow them straight down.'

'What are they?' Andrew wanted to know. He was a little dubious about the use of drugs in general.

Letitia smiled reassuringly. 'Nothing illegal or dangerous, I promise you. Just an essential part of the treatment. Believe me, if you think you've got a hard-on now, just wait until this stuff gets into your system.'

As Andrew grudgingly swallowed the pills, Letitia returned to the vanity unit and picket up a video-cassette, which she inserted into the bedside TV- and video-unit. Pausing only to peel off her blouse and wriggle out of her tight jeans, she moved back towards the bed as the small screen flickered into life.

'Now we watch a movie while the pills get to work,' she murmured, laying down on the bed beside Andrew and pressing her warm flesh against his.

Andrew lay back contentedly, feeling the reassuring glow of their skin contact. Even though his throbbing erection was causing him acute but delicious physical pain, he made no move to touch Letitia's voluptuous body, or initiate any sort of sexual advance. Somehow he sensed that the girl needed to be in total control, that she promised him delights such as he had only imagined in his wildest wet dreams, and that there was no hurry. Sex with Letitia would not be the hasty, furious business of a cock plunging blindly and hungrily into an anonymous and impersonal cunt – it would be a total experience, a close and highly personal intermingling of two intimate bodies.

Letitia wiggled slightly, snuggling her firm thighs closer against his as they both watched the flickering television screen.

There was no preamble. The film opened on a full-blown orgy scene, the camera at first taking in a wide-angle shot of dozens of naked bodies writhing in a sexual frenzy like mating frogs. Then the scene suddenly changed to a graphic close-up of the face of a young blonde girl, avidly sucking at a huge black cock that was being pumped furiously between her thick red lips.

A thin dribble of saliva oozed from the corner of the girl's mouth as the massive prick slipped in and out of her throat time and time again. The girl's face was impassive and unmoving, apart from tiny twitchings from the muscles in her throat and neck as she gulped at the intruding cock, trying to suck it deeper into her wet mouth.

Andrew felt the pain in his bursting cock become even more acute, spreading out into his heavy balls and making them dance and twitch as though stung with an electric cattle prod. He managed to tear his eyes away from the television screen for just long enough to glance down at his rigid prick, noting with a sense of pride that it looked bigger and stiffer than he could ever remember it.

Andrew had always been slightly ashamed of his cock, thinking that it was too short, and something of an odd, conical shape. But the rampant prick he now saw rearing up from between his legs was a prick to be proud of – a real man's cock, long and thick and angry, with swollen red veins and a purple, almost gleaming, helmet that could prise apart the labial lips of the most voluminous cunt.

He wondered, vaguely, if the drugs had actually affected the size of his prick, or were merely working on his mind, making him feel more virile and confident. In a way, he realised, it didn't really matter either way, the important thing was that he felt more manly and supremely aware of his sexuality than he had done for years. Strangely, at that very moment he would gladly have foregone sex with the beautiful Letitia to be with his own plump and less attractive wife. Sally would really appreciate his new superprick, Andrew reflected. And it would show that smug bastard Charles a thing or two, he registered as an afterthought.

Andrew's eyes returned to the movie, where the big black cock had been joined by a second stiff weapon probing at the blonde girl's slack lips. She opened her mouth wider to try and accommodate the two offerings together, her jaw dropping slackly open as she attempted to swallow all that hot and throbbing meat into her drooling mouth.

The camera panned down from her face to her full breasts, where two mouths sucked hungrily on the creamy flesh, and two sets of teeth nibbled at a pair of erect red nipples. Continuing down over the smooth flat stomach, the camera faithfully recorded the girl's own hand working intently at the blonde bush of her cunt, three fingers rammed deep into her wet hole while her thumb flicked back and forth against the glistening, swollen bud of her clitoris.

Andrew felt Letitia move against him, her hips gyrating slightly as she flexed her stomach muscles and began a slow, grinding motion of her pelvis. It was clear that the sexual action on the screen was beginning to get to her, stimulating the flow of juices inside her beautiful, flame-covered cunt. But still she made no obvious moves to start their own sexual play. Andrew waited patiently, trusting her implicitly to know exactly when the time was precisely right. He concentrated on the film, sensing that the slightly detached voyeurism of watching pornography was an essential part of the therapy.

The blonde girl's eyes rolled wildly. It was clear that she was rapidly approaching the point of orgasm. The two men fucking her hungry mouth alternately jabbing deeper into its sopping recesses, making the girl's cheeks bulge outwards as both thick cocks plunged in and out in perfect unison in a sort of sexual choreography.

The girl, now past the point of no return, wrenched her mouth away suddenly, letting the two wet and glistening cocks flounder in the air while she gave vent to a long, shuddering moan. Her whole body

went into convulsions as the full power of her orgasm
hit her, racking her body with a thousand rippling,
trembling spasms. Then the greedy lips were back
again, sucking voraciously at the bulging head of
each cock in turn, her wet tongue lapping the thick
sides of each rigid shaft.

The two men seemed to respect the girl's right to
pleasure, making no attempt to ram their cocks back
into her mouth. It was finally her choice alone, as she
lapped and nibbled at the black prick with renewed
vigour until it jerked and began to pump thick gobbets
of come on to her lips and chin. As the first cock
spurted, the girl turned her attention to its companion,
wrapping her mouth firmly around it and squeezing
it with her lips until it too discharged a full load into
her throat.

Finally, she fell backwards to sprawl full-length
on the floor, her face wreathed in a smile of satisfaction
as she gulped down the hot and creamy nectar.

The camera panned across the orgy scene, starting
to close in on another humping configuration of male
and female bodies – but it was enough. Letitia
discreetly thumbed the remote control she had placed
by the side of the bed and the television screen
suddenly went blank.

Andrew's heart thumped in his chest as he realised
that the time had come. He turned sideways to press
his chest against Letitia's ripe, soft breasts as she
cuddled into him.

Her hot lips brushed his neck, seeking the sensitive

areas just behind his ears. Finding them, Letitia kissed and tongued the erogenous zones with skilful precision and delicacy, making the hairs on Andrew's neck stand up and tingle.

Letitia slithered down in the bed, transferring her attentions to his hairy chest. Her mouth found his small nipples, and she began to tease them with delicate bites of her white, even teeth. Andrew shivered with pleasure, feeling a warm flush spreading down his chest and belly into his thighs.

Andrew lay quietly, totally absorbed in Letitia's selfless and agonisingly exquisite love-making. Minutes passed as her hot mouth and tongue sought out every inch of his body, lavishing kisses and soft, moist caresses wherever they descended.

Time seemed to stand still for Andrew. He had never known love-making remotely like this. For all his years of sexual experimentation and pursuit of new and more bizarre experiences, sex had always been primarily a frantic thing, an urgent and burning need to race towards climax and final gratification.

Again, he supposed that it was the drugs that were affecting his sense of time and reality. There seemed to be absolutely nothing of importance in the entire universe except the throbbing splendour of his still cock and the feel of Letitia's soft lips and flesh as she caressed and cosseted him.

As always, Letitia threw her heart, soul and body into her job. It was her way, to become so totally involved with her subject that he would no longer be just a patient, a client. Such was her dedication that, for as long as it lasted, Andrew really was her lover, the man who commanded her total adoration and sexual commitment.

She began to coo soft words and phrases of endearment as she continued to stimulate and excite him. Her kisses carried the feel of genuine passion, her caresses the tenderness of real love. Andrew basked in it all, feeling more emotionally charged than he had since he was a teenager, and more sexually potent than he had been in his late twenties.

It was time to enter the second act of their love play. Letitia pressed her soft lips close to his ear once again, whispering softly and sensually.

'Now it's your turn, Andrew. Discover my body – explore it, experiment with it – find out where it is most sensitive, most responsive.'

Andrew did as he was bid, kissing the corners of her luscious mouth, her eyelids, her hair. His lips and tongue ran down the firm young flesh of her neck to her throat, pausing to lick and explore the little hollow just above her collarbone and feel the response stirring within her.

As slowly and carefully as she had progressed with him, Andrew continued his voyage of discovery. His mouth found the swelling softness of her breast and his tongue traced out the smooth and rounded contours of each delicious creamy orb in turn.

'My nipples, Andrew, suck my nipples,' Letitia pleaded with him.

It was an invitation he was more than happy to accept gratefully. Andrew fastened his hot lips over the nearest stiff little bud and savoured it like some delicate and exotic fruit. Then to its equally delicious twin, playing it with the tip of his tongue, pulling at it with pursed lips, appreciating the faintly sweet, womanly taste of it.

Letitia lay silently now, her eyes closed and her body humming with the faint and delicate vibrations of rising passion. She knew that she had primed Andrew perfectly. She had aroused him, set him on course and now it was time to become receptive, passive, his for the taking.

Andrew also seemed to sense instinctively that it was time for the gentle love play to end and for the third and more aggressive phase of passion to begin. His hand strayed to the hot valley between her thighs, probing to seek out the molten oasis of the deep and bubbling well that was hidden there. Andrew's fingers brushed across the silken curls of her pubis, traced the faint bulge of her Mount of Venus and finally discovered the moist and slippery entrance to that secret cave of carnal pleasure.

Slipping smoothly in to its slithery and inviting recesses, Andrew marvelled at the sheer boiling heat of Letitia's silky cunt against his sensitive fingertips. It was as though he were feeling the insides of a woman for the first time, gaining privileged access to a wonderful, secret world that he had only every before seen on some dry and dusty map. His knuckles brushed the stiff, swollen bud of her clitoris, making it twitch under his touch and evoking a low moan of pleasure from Letitia's ripe lips.

'Fuck me now, Andrew. Fill my hungry cunt with your lovely cock,' she muttered thickly.

Andrew withdrew his fingers from the tunnel of love. Heaving himself up, he threw himself over her and between her long and shapely legs. Placing his hands under her knees, he lifted them up, spreading her thighs apart and raising her delicious bottom from the mattress so that her delectable cunt and pert little arsehole were both fully exposed to his admiring gaze.

The pain-pleasure in his bursting cock was now too terrible and delicious to bear any longer. Andrew wriggled, adjusting his position until its swollen head was poised against her soft and inviting cunt lips. Just one gentle push and his cock was sliding into the slippery but firm grip of her sucking fanny, whose hot walls clamped around his rigid shaft like a well-fitting and liquid glove.

Andrew began to fuck as he had never fucked before. Slowly and gently at first, and then with rising pace and passion until he was finally plunging in and out of the spewing, slopping hole like some mad machine pushed way beyond its normal operating limits.

After the build-up, it could not last indefinitely for either of them. They climaxed together, in a gushing torrent of sperm and vaginal fluid which left them both drained yet surprisingly invigorated.

It was some time before either of them moved again or spoke. It was finally Letitia who broke the silence.

'For your next lesson,' she promised, 'I'll teach you how to hold back your orgasm for as long as you like.'

Chapter Four

The midday post had arrived, and with it the batch of handbills announcing the Hunt Ball which Amanda had ordered from the local printer. As Roger and Letitia were busy sizing up the gymnasium for their new clinic, and there wasn't much else to do, she decided to go into the nearby village to display a few notices. As it was a pleasant day, and as she didn't quite trust Andrew's rather battered old pick-up truck, she decided to walk the four miles into Amesford.

Half an hour after setting out, she was beginning to think that she had been a trifle over-optimistic. The country lane was pitted and rough, and for some reason she didn't seem quite as fit as she had thought she was. The fact that her lack of energy might have something to do with two rather heavy sex sessions in one morning didn't quite occur to her.

So it was with a sense of relief that she heard the sound of a car engine coming up the lane behind her. Turning, she saw a smart new Range Rover heading in her direction. Stepping to the side of the lane, Amanda stuck out her thumb in the traditional manner of the hitchhiker and hoped that the Range Rover was being driven by a man. For some reason she had great faith in the kindness and generosity of country people, and the assumption that the local yokels would be more or less harmless.

The car was indeed being driven by a man, although he didn't really fit the part of a country yokel – no smock, no chewing straw and no frayed hat. The driver was undoubtably one of the rural yuppie set, clad in the standard uniform of green wellies, waxed green jacket and sturdy, sensible cavalry-twill trousers.

The Range Rover cruised to a halt and the driver leaned out of the wound-down window.

'Got yourself lost, young lady?'

The enquiry was friendly enough, the smile genuine.

Amanda smiled back. 'Not lost – just less fit than I thought I was. Going to the village?'

The driver nodded. 'Hop in.' He reached across and opened the passenger door as Amanda skirted round the front of the car.

Climbing into the Range Rover, Amanda settled back in the plush upholstery and reached for the seat belt.

'Here, let me help you,' said the driver, just a shade too helpfully. He reached across, his hand just happening to brush across her breasts as he pulled the seat belt over towards the clip. Fixing it in position, he adjusted the straps – and Amanda was again conscious that, as he did so he managed to make more contact with her thighs than was strictly necessary.

The faintest of warning bells sounded in her head. This was certainly no harmless country bumpkin, she was sure. Most important, at that moment, he didn't look like the type who was likely to whisk a strange female off to a deserted spot and force unwanted attentions on her.

Amanda's initial considered judgement was that he probably had little trouble getting all the women he needed. Obviously the type who liked to try it on, he would probably take a straight no for an answer, providing it was said forcefully enough. She relaxed in the seat as he slipped the car into gear and moved off.

He took one hand off the steering wheel, extending it sideways. 'Name's Clive Brannart, pleased to meet you.'

Amanda accepted the proffered handshake, feeling a slight and unexpected pleasure at the warmth of his skin. Hot-blooded, that was for sure, she reflected.

'Amanda,' she said, completing the introductions. They drove in silence for half a mile or so.

Finally Clive glanced sideways again, noticing the sheaf of handbills that Amanda was clutching. 'Making some deliveries?' he asked, conversationally.

Amanda peeled off one of the bills and showed it to him. 'Just thought I'd advertise the Hunt Ball next weekend,' she explained. 'We're holding it up at the

Country Club for the first time.'

Clive smiled knowingly. 'Ah, so you're the new owner of that place,' he muttered. 'I'd heard you were quite a good-looker. I can see that I wasn't misinformed.'

A slight frown creased his smiling face for a moment. 'I should watch out who you show those handbills to, though. There's quite a strong League Against Bloodsports operating around the village. Some of them could get a bit nasty.'

Amanda was instantly on the defensive – perhaps a little too obviously so. If she was totally truthful with herself, she had to admit that she wasn't too keen on the idea of packs of hounds ripping foxes to pieces, but she had tried to disassociate holding the Hunt Ball from the actual mechanics of the hunting process.

'We're not talking about mass murder of the local wildlife,' she said forcefully. 'Just a banquet and a bit of a piss-up. Where's the harm in that?'

Clive shrugged. 'Just thought I'd mention it, that's all. If it makes you feel any better, I always attend the Hunt Ball, so you have one customer at least.'

'And hunting? What are your views on that?' Amanda asked.

Clive grinned. 'Oh, I like the thrill of the chase all right,' he said. 'But not foxes, if you get my meaning.' In case there was any doubt at all, he ran his hand lightly over Amanda's thigh.

'I get your meaning most clearly,' Amanda

muttered, hoping that Clive could hear the annoyance under the sarcasm. She was becoming more than slightly pissed off with the groping-hands routine.

They were just coming in to the outskirts of the village. Out of the window, Amanda spotted the swinging sign of an old thatched pub.

'Oh, this will be just great,' she said quickly. 'If you could just drop me off here.'

Clive looked a trifle disappointed as he brought the Range Rover to a halt outside the pub. 'Perhaps we'll bump into each other again soon,' he said hopefully as she got out.

Amanda smiled sweetly, praying under her breath that he bumped into a very large steamroller first. She had no way of knowing at that moment that she would very shortly be more than glad to hop back into the comparative safety of his car – roving hands or no roving hands!

Meanwhile, the pub seemed as good a place as any to start putting up her posters. Amanda sauntered inside, noting that it was the real McCoy, an archetypal country pub, complete with low beams, rows of horse brasses and a motley collection of ruddy-faced, farmer-type locals seated at the rustic tables.

Somehow, the decor gave her a false sense of security. Expecting a warm country welcome, Amanda smiled sweetly at several of the customers as she made her way to the bar. Abruptly, the buzz of conversation faded to a sullen silence, and her smile

47

was met by a sea of frowning, distrustful faces.

Undeterred, Amanda stood at the bar and waited patiently. Some two minutes later, she was still standing there while the barman studiously ignored her and served other customers.

'Excuse me,' Amanda piped up eventually. The barman slid over at an insultingly slow pace, glaring at her with undisguised hostility.

'What do you want?'

'I'd like a drink, please,' Amanda said brightly, hoping that a positive attitude would help to break down the obvious sense of resentment.

The barman eyed her suspiciously. 'It wouldn't be one of them fancy concoctions you'll be wanting, with bits of fruit and little umbrellas and suchlike? Us don't cater for them strange city tastes down here.'

Amanda fell in. So that was the reason for the guarded hostility. The locals obviously resented what they regarded as 'townies'. She racked her brains for a suitably rustic drink.

'Oh, I'm just a simple country girl at heart,' she said finally, in desperation. 'What do the locals drink?'

The barman grunted, unconvinced. 'Cider, mostly,' he muttered. 'Good old farmhouse brew.'

'Great. I'll have that then,' Amanda said.

'In a liqueur glass, I suppose?' said the barman sarcastically.

Amanda glanced nervously around the pub. Most of the locals appeared to be supping pints. 'No, give me a pint,' she said, trying to sound as enthusiastic as possible.

The barman jerked a pint of murky yellowish-brown fluid into a tankard and slid it across the bar. 'One pound twenty pence,' he grunted.

Paying for the drink, Amanda lifted the glass to her lips, anticipating the sweet, appley aroma of most commercially brewed ciders. She was sadly disappointed. The sour, acidic smell of the stuff in her glass crawled up her nostrils, making her want to retch.

However, she was committed now. Her credibility was at stake. Bracing herself, she tipped the glass and gulped down the first two inches of the foul brew. As the sour, acid taste of the stuff burned in her mouth and throat, Amanda felt tears prickling in her eyes and the bile rising in her stomach. For a moment, she feared that the devil's brew would eat its way straight down through her stomach-lining and start leaking through her panties. However, the stuff actually managed to go down and stay there. Emboldened by this early success, Amanda took an-other good long swallow and slammed the glass back on the counter, noting with some satisfaction that she had managed to consume nearly half of its contents.

She managed to smack her lips with pretended enthusiasm. 'Lovely drop of stuff,' she lied, hoping to gain a little time before finishing it. The barman merely scowled and continued to look at her suspiciously.

The second half of the pint went down surprisingly easily. Equally surprising was the fact that Amanda thought it tasted better. She jiggled the empty pint pot on the counter.

'Give me another.'

The barman's look of hostility was tinged with the merest hint of respect.

'Don't see many women who can down a pint of farmhouse like that,' he said grudgingly. 'So what you doing in these parts, then?'

Amanda waved the sheaf of handbills under his nose. 'Just promoting next week's Hunt Ball. Perhaps you'd like one to put up on your notice board.'

Amanda slurped at her second pint, failing to notice the way the barman slipped the leaflet very quickly under the counter or the brief and excited buzz of conversation which broke out at one of the nearby tables.

There was no doubt about it, cider definitely tasted better the second time around, Amanda reflected. She continued to pour the stuff down her throat, assuming that the odd blurring of her vision was something to do with the smoky atmosphere in the bar. It wasn't until the glass was empty and her legs started to wobble slightly that Amanda even considered the possibility that she was getting pissed.

She was about to order a third pint when she was joined at the bar by one of the other customers.

'That's no drink for a lady,' said a deep baritone voice with just a hint of a country burr. 'Perhaps you'd like to join me in a nice drop of scotch.'

Amanda looked up at her new companion, thinking that if his face would only stop moving around and going in and out of focus, he might be quite handsome.

'Thanks,' she said simply.

'Make 'em both doubles,' the stranger said to the barman. He turned his attention back to Amanda. 'Name's Jack – Jack Morton. I own the garage at the other end of the village.'

'Pleased to meet you, Jack,' Amanda said with a slight slur to her voice. 'Call me Amanda.' She picked up the glass of whisky as soon as it hit the counter and raised it to her lips.

Jack ran his eyes over the handbills. 'Hunt Ball, eh?' he mused. 'So you must be from that place up the road.'

Amanda nodded. It was a mistake, since for some reason she found it extremely difficult to stop her head moving again. To steady herself, she drained the glass of scotch.

'Let me get you another,' Jack offered, with a surreptitious wink at the barman. Another suspiciously large double appeared on the counter in seconds. Time slipped away rather quickly, with Amanda getting drunker and drunker with every passing minute.

'Well, a few of the lads are coming over to my place to try out a new batch of home-made elderberry wine,' Jack announced finally. 'How would you like to come with me?'

Warning bells rang in Amanda's head, but they were drowned out by the roaring of alcohol. With the taste for the demon drink in her, Amanda wasn't thinking straight. 'Great idea,' she said drunkenly, struggling to scramble up from her bar stool.

With Jack supporting her, she managed to lurch across the bar towards the door. Seconds later, she was in the back of his station-wagon and heading for the garage, which actually turned out to be some distance outside the village.

Jack ushered her out of the car and into the workshop. Behind them, half a dozen other cars pulled up, discharging their strictly male passengers.

As promised, Jack quickly produced four bottles of home-made plonk and handed them round. Amanda seated herself on a pile of empty cartons and old rags and uncorked her private bottle and started to drink.

As if some secret and unspoken message had gone out, several other men arrived and drifted into the workshop. They stood around, occasionally passing a bottle of wine amongst each other and regarded Amanda silently.

In her alcoholic stupor, Amanda thought it slightly off that Jack had not bothered to introduce her to anyone else, but the faint sense of unease faded as the strong wine hit her system. Several minutes passed in complete silence, which was eventually broken by the noise of one of the men pulling down the metal shutters of the workshop door.

This time the warning bells clanged so loudly that

Amanda could not fail to hear them. With a sudden premonition, she forced her eyes to focus and looked around nervously. In a sudden moment of panic, she realised that she was the only female in the place and that everyone, including Jack, was staring at her in a very strange manner. There was a malevolent, brooding atmosphere all of a sudden, which made Amanda shiver with fear. The men had started to move towards her, and although they weren't speaking, Amanda could sense some sort of communication between them all, as if by some kind of telepathy.

Amanda's fear began to show in her eyes. She was sobering up very rapidly.

Jack advanced towards her, a cruel, cold smile playing thinly on his lips. 'Feeling trapped, are you?' he asked. 'Feeling scared, and helpless, and vulnerable? Not sure what is going to happen to you, not even sure why it's happening, but sensing real fear, real terror?'

Amanda opened her mouth to say something, but only a frightened little croak came out.

Jack continued to move towards her. 'So now you might understand a little of how a fox cub feels when it is held at bay by a pack of howling, bloodthirsty hounds who just want to tear it to pieces,' he went on. 'So how does it feel to be the prey, and not the hunter?'

Amanda suddenly understood what it was all about. Inadvertently, she had stumbled into the meeting place of the local League Against Bloodsports – flashing about a whole bundle of posters advertising the forthcoming Hunt Ball! It was a bit like storming into the Holy Mosque in Mecca reading aloud from Salman Rushdie's *Satanic Verses*.

There was nothing Amanda could do but wait, breathless and frightened, for the next development. Somehow, she sensed that any attempt at smart talking wasn't going to do her any good at all.

Jack had started to fiddle with the thick leather belt around his waist. 'Well I reckon we'd best teach you a little lesson,' he said thickly.

Amanda felt a renewed sense of panic. The belt looked rather nasty, and she was a total coward when it came to physical pain. It was Jack's next words, however, that really brought her fear to a head.

'So what might be a fitting and proper punishment for a girl like you?' he muttered, talking to himself rather than anyone else. 'Seems to me that someone from a place like that Country Club up the road will have had all the experiences there are to be had with men. Only seems to me that there might just be one she hasn't come across before. Ain't that right, lads?'

Jack's words were greeted with a chorus of assenting grunts from the other men in the workshop – a sound quickly followed by the clicks of a dozen other belt buckles being unfastened.

Only then did it fully sink in to Amanda's head. Jack wasn't taking off his belt to whip her – he was taking it off to let his trousers down. Following him as the natural leader, all the others quickly followed suit. Calmly and methodically every man in the place carefully took off his trousers.

Stepping out of his pants, Jack moved forwards and grabbed Amanda roughly by the shoulder. With his other hand, he reached for the neckline of her blouse, ripping it away in a shower of buttons. There were several breathless grunts of approval as her ripe, full breasts were exposed to full public gaze.

As Amanda started to struggle, two men stepped forwards and held her fast, as Jack turned his attention to the fastening of her skirt. When that was off, he tore her panties away with a rip of silk and threw them carelessly into a far corner of the workshop.

Naked, shivering with a mixture of fear and disgust, Amanda regarded her tormentors, her now clear brain racing into overdrive as a rush of adrenalin neutralised the effects of the alcohol.

Punishment – that was the key, Amanda figured. Rape had very little to do with sex. It was mostly about humiliation, the need to degrade and punish the woman for some imagined transgression. As long as the men thought they were achieving that, they would go ahead with their nasty little plan. But if she could convince them that they might be doing her a favour, it might tip the balance in her direction.

Amanda forced a lascivious leer on to her face, panning the room and gazing at each exposed and throbbing erection in turn.

'Hey, boys – now we're really talking my kind of business,' she said, trying to sound like the greatest nymphomaniac in history. 'You've got some really great cock there between you – reckon this could be quite a party.'

In truth, some of the massive and angry-looking cocks that she could see might well seem quite attractive under different circumstances, Amanda thought, briefly. She had to remind herself rather forcefully that she was only acting.

She straddled her legs, stoking the insides of her soft thighs in a suggestive manner. 'So who's going to be first for the honeypot?' she asked. 'Which one of you bunch of sheep-shaggers knows how to do it to a real woman?'

Jack's face was a study of mixed emotions. Amazement, disappointment and sheer disbelief contorted his features into a passable imitation of the village idiot of the year.

'The bitch is actually going to enjoy it,' he managed to croak.

'Oh, arr – that makes a few of us,' put in one of the men enthusiastically.

Amanda could sense that the atmosphere was at flash-point. It was possible that Jack might not be able to retain his position as ringleader for much longer. It was time for her to make the most of her temporary advantage. Her eyes roved around the workshop, desperately seeking out something that could be used as a weapon.

A large jerrycan of petrol against the far wall grabbed her attention. Continuing to scan the workshop, her eyes fell upon a pile of welding gear, and nearby, a handy box of matches. The germ of a daring plan began to hatch in Amanda's head.

As Jack and his cronies began to move into a circle around her, Amanda made a dash for the petrol can. Gathering it up in her arms and unclipping the spout cover, she swung the can around in a wide arc. Petrol spewed out – at exactly groin level. Three of the men nearest to her caught a couple of pints at just below the waist and squealed out in pain as the fluid stung their most sensitive parts. Jack was right behind them. Amanda shook the can again, making sure that he received a double dose of her special genital douche. Then she made another run for the box of matches and snatched them up, drawing a single match out and holding it poised against the striking patch.

There was a sudden and stunned silence. Everybody froze.

Amanda broke it at last. 'Well, lads, it would seem that cooked cock and baked balls are on the menu,' she said, with a malicious leer. 'Who wants to turn this little party into a barbecue?'

Jack stood there with petrol dripping off the end of his rapidly dwindling prick. 'You wouldn't dare,' he hissed, but his voice didn't carry much conviction.

Amanda regarded him with a sneer. 'You really

think so?' She made a threatening gesture with the match against the side of the box, noting with satisfaction the way the men all cringed back in terror.

'You've all got about twenty seconds to open that bloody workshop door,' Amanda muttered forcefully. 'After that, we start frying tonight.'

There was a mad scramble to get to the door first. As the heavy rollers started to move, there was a second dash to duck underneath it and make a break for the open air.

Amanda backed towards the door, still holding the match in strike position. The spilled petrol was evaporating fast, and there wasn't time to rescue her clothes. She ducked out under the door and made a run for it.

Amanda didn't stop running until the outskirts of the village were in sight. It was only then that she paused to consider her new problem – being stark naked in broad daylight! She wondered, briefly, if she could brazen it out by appearing nonchalant – perhaps posing as an avid naturist out for an afternoon stroll. Thinking about it seriously, it didn't seem like a good bet. Chances were six to four on she would end up in the local nick on a public indecency charge.

Salvation turned up in the unexpected form of Clive the groper. With a sense of relief, Amanda recognised the Range Rover that suddenly came to a screaming stop beside her. Clive leaned out of the window, his face registering an odd mixture of delight and bewilderment.

'Amanda! What on earth has happened to you?'

Amanda didn't wait to explain before running to the car and wrenching open the passenger door. Climbing in, she wrapped her arms rather half-heartedly over her naked breasts. Somehow, it didn't seem quite so bad being in the buff with someone she had at least been introduced to.

Clive suddenly became the perfect gentleman. Quickly stripping off his jacket, he wrapped it around her shoulders. Amanda was particularly grateful that he made no attempt this time to clip in her seat belt for her.

'We'd better get you home as soon as possible,' Clive said, slipping the car into gear. He drove for some distance before speaking again. 'You can tell me about it if you want to, you know.'

Amanda's earlier fear and tension had started to evaporate, and she felt merely foolish.

'I nearly got graped,' she said.

Clive's mouth fell open. 'Raped, do you mean?'

'No – graped. There was a whole bunch of 'em.' It was an extremely old, and somewhat infantile joke, but it served to finally wash away the unpleasantness of the afternoon. She began to giggle.

Chapter Five

Roger and Letitia had spent the day preparing for the transfer of the Sex Rejuvenation Clinic with great enthusiasm. The Paradise Country Club was, as Letitia had pointed out at least a dozen times, the best possible find for untold riches since Tutankhamen's tomb.

Roger still could not quite believe his luck, firstly for finding a place that was so superbly suited to his purposes and secondly for persuading Amanda to fit in with his plans quite so easily.

'We're going to make a bloody fortune,' he told Letitia gleefully, for at least the tenth time.

'And Amanda?' Letitia murmured.

Roger shrugged carelessly. 'She'll do all right out of the deal. Don't worry, I'm not going to rip her off. Well, not too much, anyway.'

Letitia shrugged. What happened to Amanda was not her concern. 'How soon can we be up and running?'

'Two days – three at the most,' Roger said confidently. 'I've already arranged for the equipment to be brought down, now that we know it will all fit into the gymnasium. Bernard is coming down

61

tomorrow morning to start reorganising the kitchens, and I've asked Karen to contact some of our most regular clients and inform them of the new venue.'

Letitia pouted. 'Do we have to bring Bernard down here?' she complained. 'That slimy shirt-lifter gives me the creeps.'

Roger grinned. 'Listen, my old darling, Bernard might be as bent as an antique corkscrew, but what he doesn't know about cooking and serving aphrodisiac foods could be written on the back of a gnat's condom packet.'

'Well I don't like him,' Letitia said, a trifle petulantly.

Roger laughed again. 'You don't like anyone who won't fuck you – male or female,' he pointed out, not unkindly.

Despite her misgivings, Letitia smiled. 'You could be right there,' she agreed readily. 'Anyway, back to business. What now?'

Roger considered for a moment. 'Well, we've checked out the gym, approved the guest rooms, and the equipment is on its way. Perhaps we ought to go and take a look at the sauna and massage parlour, I'm told the Paradise boasts a Swedish masseuse who can put even your magnificent tits to shame, my dear Letitia.'

The redhead's emerald eyes twinkled with renewed interest. 'That I've got to see,' she purred. 'And touch, if I get a chance.'

Roger gave a slightly dirty laugh. 'Great minds

think alike, it seems. Right, then, the massage room it is.'

Arms around each other's shoulders, they sauntered out in search of Freda, smiling happily.

As the attractive couple strolled into her private domain, it was Freda's turn to smile. Not just one, but two delicious treats to fill her life with sunshine. Hastily discarding the large electric vibrator which she had been considering, she rose to greet them appraising each young, firm body in turn.

'Hi,' Roger started. 'Don't know whether Amanda has mentioned it or not, but we are starting up a new business here in the next few days.'

Roger broke off suddenly, seeing the slightly puzzled frown that had wiped the smile from the Swedish girl's face.

'Sorry, not much English speak,' Freda managed to get out.

Letitia took over. 'We're going to be running a sex clinic here. You know sex?'

The smile was back on Freda's face, even broader than before. She nodded her blonde head enthusiastically. 'Yah, sex is word I know good. You want sex now?'

Without waiting for an answer, Freda began to open the buttons on the blouse of her crisp, white uniform, allowing her huge and magnificently shaped breasts to swing free. It was a truly spectacular sight.

Roger and Letitia tore their eyes away from the

two soft and creamy delights for just long enough to exchange a knowing, grinning glance. 'Looks like we've come to the right place,' Letitia murmured, licking her full red lips with the tip of her agile tongue.

Roger said nothing. His full attention was once again taken up in admiring the masterpieces of mammary perfection which were Freda's pride and joy. He continued to gape with undisguised admiration as the girl turned her attention to her skirt, unclipping and dropping it to the floor to expose the whole of her muscular but shapely body in all its glory.

It seemed a lead that it would be ungracious not to follow. Letitia quickly followed suit, stripping down to her own glorious nakedness. Roger took his time, carefully removing his shirt and trousers and folding them up before peeling off his underpants.

Freda reviewed the feast of youthful flesh on display with enthusiastic anticipation. She concentrated on Letitia first, noting the stark contrast made by the girl's spectacular red hair against the whiteness of her firm young skin, making the V of her pubic hair look like the triangular beard of the very Devil himself. She appraised the firm, full breasts with their large brown aureoles and prominent red nipples, the slim curvature of the girl's waist and hips and the lithe sensuousness of her long legs.

Turning to Roger, Freda was not the first woman

to feel a buzz of excitement at the sight of his broad, hairy chest or the flat, well-muscled plane of his stomach. Dropping her admiring eyes a little, she took in the wild fuzz of his pubic hair, and the handsome, generous cock which sprouted from the hairy bush like some luscious tropical fruit. Although still only semi-erect, Roger's prick was a sight to make most women's throats go a little dry, and start the juices trickling deep inside the recesses of their love tunnels.

Beneath her excitement, Freda was troubled with the problem of indecision. Which fleshy treat to savour first? Which ripe young body to satisfy the hunger of her growing sexual appetite?

It was a question that was also bothering Letitia slightly. She glanced aside at Roger somewhat uncertainly. 'Well, who goes first?'

Roger was feeling in a generous mood. Besides, he wanted to indulge himself a little, watching the two women explore each other's gorgeous bodies.

'Maybe I'll just watch for a while,' he suggested. 'Let you two warm things up a bit while I get the old love pump primed.'

Letitia accepted the offer gratefully, taking a few tentative steps towards the expectant Freda. Roger's hand flew to his prick, pumping it up and down as the two big-breasted lovelies moved together.

'Have a tit-fight,' he urged excitedly. 'Let's see you both have a battle of the boobs.'

Letitia got the picture. She clasped her full breasts

65

in both hands, squeezing them together so that her two red nipples jutted forwards like fleshy spikes. Watching her advance, Freda caught on to the game quickly. She pinched her own huge nipples between her fingers and thumbs, stretching them out from her massive soft breasts like a pair of hand-held weapons. The two girls inched closer and closer together, until they stood challenging each other less than a few centimetres apart.

Letitia bent forwards at the waist slightly, so that her own pink buds closed the gap and made fleeting contact with Freda's large brown nipples. Even Roger felt the tingle of excitement that rippled through the two women at this most sensitive and intimate contact.

'Go on,' he urged throatily, 'rub your tits together, grind them into each other.' He slowed his masturbation to gentle strokes as his cock jerked and stiffened into a full and throbbing erection.

Letitia took a step forward, bringing her body into full frontal contact with Freda's succulent, soft flesh. The Swedish girl groaned deep in her throat as she felt Letitia's firm but pliant breasts mashed against hers, and sensed the warmth of the beautiful redhead's belly and crotch pressed against her own. She began to rock, slowly and sensuously from the hips, the movement of her body absorbed by the cushioning of her balloon-like breasts. Nipple clashed with nipple, one delicious creamy mound seemed to melt and flow into the other.

Emboldened to take the game one step further, Letitia threw her arms over the Swedish girl's shoulders and around her neck. Pressing her hips forwards provocatively, she ground her pelvis in a sideways and circular movement, mixing the two bushes of blonde and red pubic hair into an impressionist depiction of sexual fire.

Freda responded enthusiastically. Grunting loudly, she thrust forward to grind her pelvic bone deep into the comforting softness of Letitia's fleshy and swollen cunt lips. The two women began to writhe against each other, as if trying to press every square inch of their bodies together, melt and fuse their separate flesh into one amorphous mass of tit and belly, cunt and thigh.

Roger looked on with rising excitement, his prick jumping and dancing in his hand like a live thing. Glancing aside briefly, his eyes fell on the wheeled massage table lying against the nearby wall, and a new idea came to him.

He dashed across the room, quickly wheeling the massage table back and rolling it into position behind Letitia's heaving buttocks. Freda, who had seen what he was doing, took up the initiative, using her greater weight to force the redhead back slightly so that the low table made contact with the back of her knees. With Freda pressing upon her, Letitia sank back and wriggled into position on the table with Freda clambering on top of her.

Now the sexual wrestling match began in real

earnest, as both women used the solid base of the table to lend more power to their frenzied gropings. Freda pressed her entire body weight down, crushing Letitia against the thin mattress. Letitia herself used the table as a fulcrum, bucking her hips and buttocks up in an aggressive retaliation against the Swedish girl's frantic thrusts.

Roger's excitement passed critical point. He could no longer just stand and watch. Still grasping his stiff prick, he moved into position at the foot of the table and stood poised behind Freda's pumping, rounded arse. Pulling the two sets of legs apart, he tugged insistently at Letitia, urging her to slide further down the table to accommodate his desires. With some difficulty, she did so, wriggling down inch by inch until her gaping wet cunt protruded over the end of the mattress and Freda's smooth buttocks were poised enticingly above.

Roger wriggled forwards into position, his belly pressed up against Freda's delicious rear. Carefully, he guided his long prick between the two girls until it was enclosed in a warm and moist cunt sandwich. Moving his hips, he slid his cock in and out slowly, coating it with a liberal and lubricating film of glistening love juice from two frothing cunts.

Withdrawing his primed weapon, Roger looked down at the alternative delights that confronted him. It was really no choice at all. His cock had slipped into Letitia's welcoming cunt a hundred times, and, although the thrill and the pleasure never waned, there was always the extra excitement of a new experience.

Gasping his throbbing tool firmly, he lifted it up so that the shiny, juice smeared head was poised between Freda's heaving buttocks. Prising them apart with his other hand, he aimed his love arrow at her tight little arsehole and stabbed forwards.

Freda let out a thin squeal of surprise and excitement as she felt Roger's large cock penetrate what had previously been virgin territory. Thoughtfully, she stopped writhing against Letitia's lush body for a few seconds, giving him time to ease his beautiful cock even deeper into her hot hole.

With a last savage lunge, Roger buried his cock up to the hilt in the tightest and hottest hole he had ever encountered. Freda's internal muscles clamped around his rigid shaft, squeezing and massaging it with an almost painful pleasure.

With the delicious softness of Letitia's gorgeous body beneath her, and the throbbing hardness of Roger's cock buried in her rear, Freda was experiencing a heady mixture of sensations which made her mind reel. She began to moan – a low, melodic rhapsody of passion which gradually rose in both pitch and volume until she was howling like a crazed dog in the moonlight. Roger found the sheer intensity of her arousal quite unnerving, but oddly stimulating. His thrusts became more forceful, more urgent, as the strange sexual power that the three of them had released sucked his mind as well as his body into a turbulent maelstrom of pure lust.

Letitia, who always gave and received all in any kind of sexual activity, was not immune. She too responded with increased urgency, pumping her buttocks up from the massage table in her frenzied attempts to mash every square inch of her flesh against the writhing, burning heat of Freda's muscular body.

Breast to breast, stomach to stomach and cunt to cunt, the two women rapidly climbed the heights of sexual passion towards the ultimate plateau of orgasm as Roger's bursting balls began to register their own desperate need for release.

A sudden, high pitched shriek from Freda was the signal to trigger all three of them off in a spectacular mutual orgasm. Letitia's body suddenly jerked, shuddered and went into a series of convulsive spasms. Freda felt a hot and liquid eruption from deep inside her, and a veritable tidal wave of love juice gushed from the tunnel of her cunt to spray against Letitia's crotch and thighs. Roger's final deep thrust and the hot spurt of his lust into the burning back passage was almost like a second climactic bonus.

The power and intensity of the encounter and its triumphant outcome had exhausted them all. Roger staggered backwards, his still twitching tool popping out of Freda's tight arse like a champagne cork. He sank to the floor, gasping for breath as the two girls collapsed across each other, the sweat glistening on their bare skin, their succulent breasts rising and falling as they fought for breath.

Nobody spoke. It was one of those moments in life when there just aren't any words, in any language, which seem to have any particular relevance.

Chapter Six

It was going to be a busy night, Amanda realised, glancing round the already crowded bar. There were several of the faces – and bodies – of those she had come to accept as regulars. Angie and Carol, the two small-time hookers from the village, were well in evidence, attracting a small crowd of interested males who were bidding for them with double gin and tonics in something between a slave auction and a game of three-card brag.

Amanda smiled to herself. The stakes would get a lot higher as the evening progressed and the two girls got tanked up. As usual, they had booked a bedroom between them for the night, and would, during the course of the evening, take a succession of clients upstairs for anything from single ten-minute quickies to full-scale orgies lasting an hour or more. Although the rent on the room probably didn't even cover the cost of wear and tear on the waterbed, the two girls still made reasonably good business, thanks to their prodigious thirst for alcohol and Amanda's foresight in installing a modified condom machine in their room which dispensed French ticklers at five pounds a time. On one of their most productive nights, the two girls were quite capable of swelling the Paradise Club turnover by £200 or so.

Amanda noticed that Batman was also putting in one of his sporadic appearances. As usual, he was drinking alone, but with one eye on his glass and the other open for the best possible female pick-up of the night.

The name Batman had been given to him by Andrew, who had once found a Polaroid photo under his bed which showed him dressed up in a shiny plastic cape and rubber face mask, standing up against the bed headboard as a naked woman slapped his protruding prick with the business end of a kitchen spatula.

Whether he had any other peculiar sexual fetishes, nobody had ever bothered to find out. The black cape and face mask had been enough to earn him his nickname, and it had stuck.

Amanda also recognised several of the female faces in the crowd from her days in the escort agency business. As she had suspected when she first took over the club, many of her old friends and colleagues had rallied round her, glad to have a new place to bring their clients and happy to pay Amanda a small percentage out of the take.

But there were also quite a few new people that she didn't recognise, and most of those did not look like locals. Amanda could only assume that Roger was already making good his promise to attract clients from his sex clinic for a sample of the Paradise Club's peculiar sexual delights.

Satisfied with the healthy business in the bar, Amanda sauntered out to the reception area, where Sally was busy behind the desk.

'Hi. How are things looking with room bookings for tonight?'

Sally smiled broadly. 'We're almost full. Isn't it great? We haven't been this busy on a Tuesday night for over a year.'

Amanda regarded the woman's beaming face. 'I'm glad to see that increased business makes you so happy.'

Sally made a low chuckle deep in her throat. 'Oh, it's not that, it's Andrew,' she volunteered. 'I don't know what has happened to him, but he's taken on a whole new lease of life. He's been like a young stud again all day, getting a new erection every ten minutes or so.'

Amanda sounded impressed. 'Can't be bad. What have you been feeding him?'

Sally grinned wickedly. 'Cunt, mostly. I don't know about his cock, but I've certainly managed to wear his tongue out today.'

The two women shared a dirty laugh together before Amanda moved on to check over the other paying facilities of the club. A quick check into the massage room confirmed that Freda was booked up with appointments for the evening, and there was a well attended, big-stake poker game underway in the games room. With Gloria, the big-busted blonde Amanda had brought down from London as the resident croupier, many of the players were paying more attention to her tits than the cards in their hands, with the result that the house percentage was substantially up on average.

More than satisfied, Amanda returned to the bar, where she propped herself up on a bar stool and ordered a large vodka martini.

Like his wife, Andrew was in an ebullient mood as he served drinks. Further down the busy bar, Charles appeared to be sulking.

'What's up with him?' Amanda asked, with a discreet nod at Charles.

Andrew smiled happily. 'He hasn't had a chance to get at Sally once today,' he confided. 'Every time he's felt like a quick one, he's found me already on the job. Sally even turned him down for a threesome in the cellar, which is really something.'

Amanda grinned. 'Does this mean you're going back to thoughts of a monogamous marriage?'

Andrew looked shock. 'Good Lord, no. I wouldn't want to take all the fun out of life. It's just nice to take the cocky sod down a peg or two for a day or so.'

'So what's the big secret?' Amanda asked.

Andrew gave her a conspiratorial wink. 'Your friend Roger's young colleague, she's quite a special kind of woman.'

'Ah.' Amanda fell in. 'So the lovely Letitia has been giving you her special services.'

'Not half,' Andrew agreed enthusiastically, and promptly launched into a full and no secrets barred account of his morning session.

At the end of it, Amanda was feeling quite horny herself. She pondered for a few minutes, not quite sure what to do about it. Finally she decided. It was time she had a serious chat with Giles about the guest list for the Hunt Ball. Tonight would be as good a time as any to mix business with pleasure.

'Can I borrow your station-wagon?' she asked Andrew, draining her glass.

'Going somewhere nice?'

Amanda smiled secretively. 'Just thought I'd pop down to the Manor House.'

Andrew fished in his pocket, bringing out a small white pill. 'Here, take one of these,' he suggested. 'Letitia gave them to me, and they certainly seem to do the trick.'

Amanda stared at the pill for a few seconds, finally shaking her head. 'I don't think I need any aphrodisiacs to get me going,' she said, not unkindly.

Andrew waggled the pill in his palm. 'I didn't say it was for you, did I?' he pointed out. 'I'm sure that Giles is more than capable, but with one of these slipped into his drink, I can virtually guarantee he will have an extra bit of poke in his pecker.'

Amanda leaned over the bar to kiss Andrew on the forehead. 'You might have a point there,' she conceded, taking the pill out of his hand and slipping it into her handbag.

'The car's out the back behind the kitchen,' Andrew called after her as she started to walk out of the bar.

The corridors of the club were a hive of activity, with couples creating an almost constant two-way stream of traffic between the bar and the bedrooms. Amanda glanced at her watch. It was still only half past eight, and the night's sexual frolics were already well under way. The knowledge served to heighten her own carnal appetite, and she found herself thinking of Giles's massive stiff cock plunging in and out of her hungry pussy. It was a delicious thought. Amanda decided to take a short cut through the pantry to save time.

Walking through, she was instantly alerted by two unusual things. Firstly the kitchen light was on, and secondly she could hear sounds of movement from inside. Amanda stopped in her tracks, concerned by these two unusual factors. As she had just seen Sally, Andrew and Charles, the nocturnal visitor could not be one of them, and there was no reason for any one of the guests to have strayed into this part of the building.

Fearing that the interloper might be a burglar, Amanda wondered what to do. She was just passing the cold-meat locker. Slipping the catch as quietly as she could, Amanda armed herself with a large frozen leg of lamb. Brandishing it like a club, she stormed into the kitchen, half expecting to see some burly ruffian there.

There was indeed a man in the kitchen, but burly he certainly was not. Nor could ruffian be applied to someone wearing eye shadow, lipstick and dressed in a floral pinafore.

Amanda gaped at him for several seconds, struck speechless. It was the stranger who first broke the silence.

'And just who do you think *you* are?' he demanded in a high-pitched, rather indignant voice. 'I don't like women in my kitchen.'

Amanda bristled with anger. It wasn't just the thing about "*my*" kitchen, it was the way he had managed to make the word "women" sound like a cross between a toad and a dog turd.

'I just happen to own this place, kitchen and all,' she said angrily. 'So who the hell are you, which is more to the point.'

The creature became a little less petulant. Drawing himself up to his full five feet three inches, he squared his puny shoulders and announced proudly: 'I am Bernard, the chef.'

'I don't care if you're Zorba the Greek,' Amanda shot back. 'What the hell are you doing here and who said you could start messing about in my kitchen?'

That really blew Bernard's cool. Wrinkling up his exquisite little nose and fluttering his mascara'd eyelashes like a pair of demented butterflies, he exploded into righteous indignation.

'Mess about . . . mess about?' he screamed shrilly. 'Bernard the chef does not mess about. Bernard the chef creates the finest erotic and aphrodisiac food in Europe, for the discerning palates of the rich and famous.'

Amanda was still unconvinced. 'Bernard the chef also creeps around other people's kitchens in the middle of the night,' she pointed out. 'So what's it all about?'

Seeing that his bluster and high-handed attitude was having little or no effect on the phlegmatic Amanda, Bernard resorted to a tone of somewhat patronising explanation.

'I work for Mr Roger and Miss Letitia. I was given to understand that I will henceforth be expected to perform my culinary miracle in these rather primitive kitchens. Therefore, I was trying to see what could be done to convert this roadhouse cafe into a genuine gourmet establishment.'

Amanda suddenly understood, but was in no mood to be apologetic. Although she had nothing personal against homosexuals of Bernard's type, the little man had rubbed her up the wrong way and she didn't care for his insulting tone.

'Well, henceforth you can call me Miss Amanda,' she said, mimicking his rather affected speech. 'And henceforth you can ask my bloody permission to do any sneaking around these premises.'

She turned on her heel, heading towards the door. Reaching it, Amanda found that she just couldn't resist one last little twist of the knife.

'Oh, Bernard, sweetie,' she cooed in a deceptively

friendly voice. 'I'll bet I know what your speciality of the house is.'

'Oh yes?' Bernard said sarcastically.

'Yes, it's pouf pastry,' Amanda said sweetly, wafting out of the kitchen with a picture of Bernard's anguished little face forever imprinted on her mind. She was aware that she had made an enemy, but somehow doubted that he would be much of a threat to her.

It proved to be a miscalculation.

Amanda parked the car in the driveway of Giles's crumbling manor house and walked up to the door. Having heard the sound of the car tyres on the gravel, Giles was already opening it. He bent down to plant a light kiss on her lips, a warm and welcoming smile on his handsome face.

'Hi, Amanda. So what is it? Business or pleasure?'

Amanda smiled. 'I thought perhaps we might get in a bit of both.'

Giles's eyes twinkled at the thought. He ushered her into the hallway, pointing the way to the lounge out of politeness, even though Amanda was only too well aware of the way.

'Well, let's have a drink, for a start,' Giles said as Amanda seated herself on his antique chesterfield. 'Scotch all right? I haven't much else in the house at the moment, I'm afraid.'

Amanda nodded. 'Scotch will be fine.'

Giles poured two large tumblers of whisky and

carried them over, sitting down beside her. Amanda could feel the heat of his thighs pressed against hers. She shifted slightly, putting a few inches of space between them. 'Let's get the business part sorted out first, shall we?'

'Which is?' Giles asked.

'The guest list for the Hunt Ball. I thought it was time we got it sorted out,' Amanda said.

Giles chuckled, delving into his trouser pocket. 'I've already written it out.' He produced a slip of paper and handed it over. 'So, that takes care of business. Now, shall we get down to the pleasure?'

Without waiting for an answer, he moved up close again and slipped his hand under Amanda's skirt, his fingers hooking into the elastic top of her panties without any preamble. In a matter of seconds, the flimsy garment was lying on the floor at her feet and Giles's nimble fingers were once more entwining themselves in the springy bush of her cunt hairs.

'You do seem rather over-eager tonight, I have to say,' Amanda murmured, slightly hurt that Giles seemed to have little time for romancing or love play.

He gave a deep sigh, withdrawing his hand. Turning his head, he gazed directly into her eyes, an apologetic look on his face.

'You're right – I'm sorry,' he mumbled, rather sheepishly.

There was something wrong, Amanda could sense it. 'What is it, Giles?' she asked gently.

There were a few seconds of embarrassed silence

as he tried to get the words right in his head.

'Look, Amanda – you and I have had some pretty good times over the past few weeks, haven't we?' he started, hesitantly.

Amanda nodded. 'Sure we have. So?'

Giles fidgeted awkwardly on the chesterfield. 'I had a telephone call from Clive earlier this evening,' he announced.

The name took a few moments to register in Amanda's head. Then she remembered her rescue earlier in the day. 'Oh yes, Clive. Nice chap. So, what about him?'

'He told me the circumstances of your meeting,' Giles went on. 'He also more or less hinted that he was rather smitten with you and that you had agreed to a date.'

Amanda felt her guard going up. 'Look, Giles, he did me a great favour and I said I might see him again some time,' she said in a cool tone. 'So what's the big deal here? I've already told you, I don't allow myself to become the sole property of any man – not even you.'

She patted his knee in a vaguely comforting manner. 'Come on, Giles, don't get all heavy on me . . . please.'

Giles let out another deep sigh. 'The truth is, Amanda, that's getting rather difficult for me,' he admitted, finally. 'The point is, I accept you for what you are, I accept your – shall we say – rather colourful past, and the way you choose to live your life now.

But basically, I think it is time for me to back out.'

Amanda wasn't quite sure what Giles was actually trying to say.

'So in other words, you're worried that I'm a bit of a scarlet lady?'

Giles managed a faint smile. 'No, it's not really that at all. You're just a bit out of my league, that's all. I'm a pretty conventional guy, if you really must know. I've enjoyed our little fling, but I can't afford to get any further involved. Dammit, Amanda, I've started to think that I might be falling in love with you, and I know that's not what you want or even what I could cope with. So I figured it was time to call it a day, let this little affair draw to its logical conclusion.'

Amanda looked at his strained, sorrowful face and suddenly felt rather tender and motherly towards him. She threw her arms around his shoulder, hugging him against her.

'Oh Giles, you are sweet,' she said, a faint catch in her voice. 'I'm sorry I can't be the nice little woman you want, and probably deserve. But you're right, I've grown quite fond of you, too, but I know things couldn't last indefinitely between us.'

Amanda fell silent for several minutes, trying to analyse her own feelings. It was true, she did feel a sort of sisterly affection for Giles, but the real sharp end was that she enjoyed the good sex that they had shared together much more than any sense of commitment. Basically, Giles was a bloody good lay, and that was really about it.

'So this was going to be one for the road, as it were?' she said eventually.

Giles gave her a sheepish smile. 'That was the general idea.'

'Well I think it's a perfectly splendid idea,' Amanda said, hugging him again. 'So, if this is to be our last time, I think we ought to make it special, take our time about things. Don't you agree?'

Giles looked almost relieved. 'You mean you won't feel that I'm just using you?' he queried, not quite sure of his ground any more.

'How can you use someone who is more than willing to give?' Amanda countered. 'Sex is a two-way street Giles. Both partners get back as much as they are willing to put in. And in your case, you put in quite a lot.'

The double entendre was quite intentional. Amanda smiled inwardly as Giles saw the joke and visibly brightened. He leaned over to kiss her, the gentle pressure of his lips belying the pent-up passion behind it.

Amanda traced the tip of her hot, wet tongue around the outline of his fleshy lips, probing gently for entrance. More than willingly, Giles opened his mouth slightly, allowing her in. Amanda licked the soft underside of his upper and lower lips before exploring further into his hot mouth.

Giles began to respond, crushing his mouth against hers as Amanda's snaking tongue darted into his throat, teasing and tantalising. His hand dropped to her breasts, gliding gently over each swelling curve in turn, picking out the tiny bulge of her nipples through the material of her blouse.

Amanda pulled back slightly, pushing him gently away. 'How about putting some nice music on,' she suggested. 'A bit of Vivaldi might be nice.'

'Of course.' Giles rose and crossed the room to the stereo system. Bending over his collection of albums and CDs, he began to select something suitable.

Amanda took advantage of his turned back to fish out the pill that Andrew had given her. She dropped it into Giles's whisky glass, noting with relief that it started to dissolve almost immediately. If this was to be their last fuck, she rationalised to herself, then it might as well be a really good one. Better to go out with a bang than with a whimper, she thought.

By the time Giles returned, there was no sign that the drink had been tampered with. Amanda urged him to finish it before she once again snuggled close and took up their lovemaking where they had left off. She moaned softly in her throat as he began to kiss her again, while his fingers started picking open the buttons of her blouse.

She turned her own attention to his shirt, soon exposing his hairy chest to the touch of her fingers. She stroked the manly chest gently, feeling the regular pounding of his heart and the slow rise and fall of his breathing. The rhythm picked up noticeably as Amanda's blouse fell away and his hands began to move against the soft, warm flesh of her naked breasts.

Amanda unbuckled the belt of Giles's trousers, zipping open his flies and helping him to shrug them off. He was already rock hard, his prick throbbing and angry in stark contrast to the relaxed pace of his lovemaking. It was, Amanda supposed, somehow symbolic of his inner confused passions. While part of him wanted a woman to love and trust and respect, the basic animal part of his male sexuality wanted dominance, lust, the sheer aggressive power of cock throbbing into soft and yielding cunt.

Amanda slipped off her skirt. Now totally naked, their two bodies fell together on the comfortable expanse of the chesterfield as the love play moved into a secondary and more urgent phase.

Giles's fingers once again found the blonde hairs of her pubic bush and strayed through it on their way to the soft and slippery button of her clitoris. Amanda stiffened involuntarily as the sensitive little bud twitched at the contact, sending a little shiver of sexual electricity rippling up through her belly. She fell back as Giles lifted himself over her, spreading her thighs apart with his knees and lowering his stomach towards hers. As he let down his weight, Amanda could feel the stiff hardness of his prick against her pelvic bone, the warm softness of his swollen balls dangling between her thighs.

Still proceeding at an unhurried rate, Giles shifted his position so that the twitching tip of his generous tool touched lightly against the soft walls of her labia. She could feel the bulbous head just barely penetrating her hot and rapidly moistening slit, promising satisfaction but not delivering it. Amanda squirmed, now it was she who urgently needed the sexual act to move into its final phase.

But Giles had other ideas. He jerked his pelvis carefully, making sure that the tip of his cock just brushed against her clitoris, making the hot little button tingle anew. Amanda felt small tremors of anticipation shudder along her thighs, making her legs jerk like those of a puppet, and sending waves of shivering pleasure all the way down to her toes.

Giles slipped his hands under the firm cheeks of her bottom, lifting her pelvis towards him. He began to jab at her cunt with short, slow strokes which again excited her clit while denying the hungry mouth of her cunt any sense of satisfaction.

With something of a shock, Amanda realised that she was well on the way to a primary orgasm before he had even thrust into her. Her body spasmed as the first waves coursed through all her most sensitive and erogenous areas, finally converging at some spot deep inside her belly. The orgasm broke gently, like spring waves over weather-beaten and rounded rocks. Giles felt the trembling of her lower body and the gushing wetness of her love juice against the sensitive head of his cock. Even though he was far from ready, he did not wish to deny her the pleasure of full penetration. He thrust deep inside her, jabbing his prick with a rolling, rocking motion which touched every inner recess of her flowing cunt.

Amanda moaned as the full orgasm broke, shuddering through her like a series of convulsive shocks. Finally, with a dreamy smile on her face, she let her body go slack and relaxed into the comforting softness of the chesterfield.

Giles did not intend to let her off that easily. Amanda had wanted a final fuck to remember, and he was going to give it to her. Besides, he could not remember feeling so totally charged up with sexual vigour for many years. Some inner sense told him that tonight he would be able to fuck for hours and still be ready for more.

He began to move inside her again, thrusting deep and hard until he could feel the head of his prick reach the end of the hot and slimy tunnel and slam against the constricting mouth of her cervix. He kept this pace up for several minutes, until he could feel Amanda's body coming to life again beneath him, as his sheer abundance of sexual energy seemed to flow into her, recharging her.

Amanda arched her back, heaving her buttocks up to match his thrusts and drive his full and satisfying length even deeper inside her. The hors d'oeuvres had now been consumed, it was time for the main course – something substantial and meaty, and satisfying enough to appease a real sexual hunger.

He was rock-hard inside her now, and ready to appease his own lust. Digging his fingernails into the soft flesh of her bottom, Giles began to stab into her in earnest, driving his mighty weapon along the slippery walls of her cunt like a pile-driver.

'Oh yes . . . yes.' Amanda started to grunt and groan, spitting out a few isolated words along the way. 'That's it . . . fuck me . . . yes, yes . . . deeper.'

It was time to let himself go completely. Giles abandoned himself to the pursuit of his own animal release, bucking up and down on the chesterfield as he slammed his hard meat in and out of Amanda's all-consuming cunt with furious abandon. Their two bellies smacked together wetly, by now coated with a liberal smearing of perspiration and Amanda's love-juice, which had spattered off the sides of the plunging cock within her.

Eager to intensify his pleasure as he had hers, Amanda delved deep inside herself for extra reserves of energy and thrust her body up against his, wriggling her pelvis and contracting her inner abdominal muscles so that the walls of her slippery cunt squeezed and massaged the stiff cock inside. Giles let out a throbbing moan of pure pleasure as the delicious sensations flowed down his stiff shaft and into his balls. His buttocks were a moving blur of flesh as he vibrated inside her in the final stages of male passion.

With consummate timing, Amanda sensed the critical moment and threw her legs up and around his back at the very second his balls jerked and triggered off the spurt of hot semen to their master.

Tightly enclosed in her vice-like grip, Giles could only buck his hips frantically as the pulsating wave of pleasure along his stiff shaft heralded the release of his hot and sticky stream.

'My God, that was fantastic,' Amanda breathed, when the throbbing of Giles's body had finally ceased, and he had pulled out of her. She looked down at his cock with an admiring and grateful smile. Stroking it like one would reward a faithful pet, she blew it a kiss.

'Who's a clever boy, then?'

The sated and semi-flaccid tool twitched gently under her touch, as though responding.

Giles let out a little cry of surprise. 'My God, the little bugger's coming back for more, I'd swear it.'

Sure enough, his tool was again distending, swelling in thickness as yet another rush of inflamed blood rose to pump it up to full erection again.

He turned to face Amanda, his face betraying his own amazement. 'I think this could go on all night,' he muttered.

Amanda smiled secretly, knowing something he didn't.

'That's fine with me,' she murmured, reaching down to wrap her fingers around the rapidly stiffening part.

Chapter Seven

Behind the bar, Charles was consuming as many drinks as he served. Not usually a till-dipper by nature, he balanced out his growing alcohol bill by overcharging Angie and Carol's constant stream of gin-and-tonic buyers, or simply added an extra drink for himself on every large round. It was a routine that had worked wonders during the evening, since Charles had personally accounted for the best part of a whole bottle of Glenlivet malt, and at least seven double brandies.

He glanced at his watch, barely able to discern the hands on its oddly blurred face. It was nearly a quarter to twelve. Fifteen minutes before his shift ended, and still no apparent chance of getting his end away before he went to sleep.

It was all too frustrating – hence his recourse to the soothing powers of booze.

Basically, the past few weeks had spoiled him. Coming, as he had done, from a boring and unexciting job as a chauffeur into the heady and hedonistic world of the Paradise Club, his previous sexual experiences had been confined to the odd pick-up or a quick tumble in the back of the Rolls with his previous employer's housemaid. His wealth of weird and wonderful experiences with the swinging and sexually inventive Andrew and Sally had given him a taste for more exotic things, and a sexual frequency to which his previously under-used cock had responded with increasing enthusiasm. Now, suddenly, it seemed that Sally had gone off the boil and Andrew was deliberately freezing him out of the little sex games the three of them had enjoyed at least five times daily.

Charles helped himself to another large brandy and tried to remember how much he now needed to add to the next round to balance the books. Hopefully, he cast a bleary eye around the room, just in case there were any spare and unattached females in evidence. It did not look promising.

He looked at his watch again. Five to twelve. Charles sighed with resignation. It looked like being a long and lonely night. Finishing off his drink, he palmed a couple of miniatures under the pretence of wiping the bar shelves and surreptitiously slipped them into his trouser pocket.

Andrew was busy serving a large round of drinks. Charles took the opportunity to make an early departure from the bar, via the cellar. His shift was almost over anyway, and there was always the vague chance that he could catch Sally on her own and at least get in a quick knee-trembler or a blow job before going to bed.

The cellar was empty. Charles cut across past the wine racks and let himself into Andrew and Sally's private sanctum with his pass key. With a bit of luck, Sally might have retired to bed early, or even better, be taking a shower. He particularly liked fucking Sally in the shower. It gave him an extra kick to see the way her plump white tits squashed up against the steamy glass panels as he rumped her from behind.

Both bed and shower were unoccupied. With mounting frustration, Charles took one of the small bottles out of his pocket and drained the contents. As an afterthought, he made his way somewhat unsteadily back to the wine racks and selected a bottle of Chateau Margaux. An evening of drinking on an empty stomach had made him hungry as well as steaming drunk. Charles decided to raid the kitchen for a midnight snack before retiring to his room.

Bernard was also feeling rather frustrated. Back in London, he would by now have been tucked up comfortably in bed with one of his many boy-friends, or cruising the gay clubs looking for a bit of rough trade. Here in the uncivilised wilds of rural England, neither option was available to him. So he had thrown himself into his work instead, spending the night setting out his equipment and knocking up a few of his more exotic erotic dishes to pop in the freezer. Although he would never have dared to admit it, Bernard was not past cheating with the old microwave from time to time.

He reviewed his creations with pride – the large tit-shaped blancmanges with glacé cherry nipples, the stuffed oyster shells in a bed of crispy fried seaweed which looked exactly like a gaping fanny, and the special 'Dirty Dessert' achieved with two blanched peach halves and a painstakingly carved banana shaped into a large prick with a spurt of freshly whipped cream issuing from its tip.

This last delicacy proved too hard to resist. Taking two large cock-shaped candles from his private cupboard, Bernard set them on the kitchen table, lit them and settled down to an intimate candlelit dinner for one.

Bending over his creations, Bernard slavishly ran his tongue up and down the moist surface of the banana, scooping up a tiny gobbet of cream as he did so.

It was in this position that Charles found him as he blundered drunkenly into the kitchen to make a quick sandwich.

Bernard looked up from his private feast in surprise, his initial shock quickly turning to delight. A man! More to the point, a thoroughly drunken man, who looked far enough gone not to know the difference between an ant and an elephant. Bernard's mind raced, reviewing the possibilities. At the most optimistic level, it was possible that he would get to stuff more than a banana in his mouth before the night was out, if he played his cards right.

Charles was equally surprised to find the kitchen occupied. He tried to focus his eyes to appraise the stranger, finding it rather difficult. However, he could dimly make out the permed and bleached hair, the facial make-up and a slim, flat-chested body. Charles hadn't actually had much direct contact with homosexuals, and they unnerved him a little, but he could recognise a fairy when he saw one, even in his present inebriated condition.

Suddenly feeling awkward, Charles started to back out of the kitchen, but the sudden change of direction was more than his befuddled brain could cope with. His legs suddenly turned to jelly and things began spinning round in front of his eyes. Reeling and tottering, he staggered sideways and crashed into the fridge, which luckily provided enough support to keep him upright.

Bernard flounced across the room to the rescue. 'Oh, you poor dear,' he shrilled. 'Let me help you to a chair.' Slipping his arm around Charles's back, he helped him stagger across the kitchen to the table and lowered him into a chair.

Bernard fussed around him like a mother hen. 'Can I get you anything, dear? A glass of water perhaps? Would you like an aspirin?'

Charles's grip on reality was fast slipping away. That last miniature of brandy had been the straw to break the camel's back. As he struggled to sit upright and hold his head up, he was only dimly aware that he was sitting at a table, with food in front of him, a bottle of wine in his hand, and someone dressed in a chef's hat and a pinafore buzzing around him like an excited fly and trying to serve him in some way. Through the blurring haze of alcohol, all these factors could really only fit into one scenario: he had somehow blundered into a restaurant, and the waiter/waitress (for Charles was no longer quite sure of that, either) was trying to take his order. The fact that he had only popped in to make a cheese sandwich was now completely forgotten.

'Wasson the menu?' Charles managed to slur drunkenly.

Bernard gave a little yelp of pure delight. 'Oh, you darling man,' he trilled. 'You're going to have dinner with me.' Rushing to the nearest cupboard, he pulled out another setting of plates and cutlery and laid the table for two.

Sitting down, he served out two portions of the vaginal oyster dish and sat gazing across the table at his unexpected dinner companion with rapturous admiration. 'Eat up, dear. I'm sure you'll enjoy this.'

Charles lowered his eyes to the table and the plate in front of him, not at all sure how to start eating what appeared to be a large, hairy green cunt with creamy goo oozing out of it. Something told him that this wasn't quite a standard knife and fork job. Experimentally, Charles inserted one finger into the creamy slit and wiggled it around. Then, pulling his sticky finger up to his mouth, he sucked it clean.

Bernard watched him with adoring eyes, shivering

a little with pleasure as Charles's finger popped out of his mouth again.

'Good, isn't it?' he squealed excitedly.

Charles's shrug was noncommittal. Having never eaten cooked fanny before, he wasn't sure what it was supposed to taste like. However, the faintly fishy flavour was not unpleasant. He stuck his finger in again and scooped up another large dollop.

'Actually, most people use a spoon,' Bernard pointed out, delicately scooping up a portion of the fried seaweed and nibbling at it delicately.

Thankful for this piece of useful information, Charles took up his own spoon and began to shovel the minced oyster concoction into his mouth. It was surprisingly good, he eventually realised. Not only did it leave a most pleasant aftertaste on his palate, Charles had to admit that it was the first food he had ever tasted that actually seemed to make his cock twitch as he swallowed it. The two sensations together made for a highly individual and interesting eating experience. In silence, he finished eating the dish and pushed it aside with a loud belch.

Bernard visibly shuddered with pleasure at this butch and manly gesture. He did like his man friends on the rough side.

'Dessert, darling?' he cooed, proffering the prick-shaped banana. Just to show how it was done, he stabbed his own phallic fruit a with a dessert fork, lifted it to his mouth and began sucking the end of it in a deliberately sexual and provocative way, rolling his eyes with delirious pleasure as he did so.

Even in his drunken state, this was not a gesture that Charles was prepared to emulate. Seizing the nearest knife, he slashed his banana into pieces and transferred them to his mouth with a spoon. The action caused Bernard to shiver with horror, and a look of pain crossed his painted face.

'Oh, you're so *aggressive*,' he murmured coyly, with a little flutter of his eyelashes.

Producing a corkscrew from his pinny pocket, Bernard deftly uncorked the bottle of wine that Charles had left on the table. He poured two large measures into glasses, pushing one across to Charles. It was in his best interests, Bernard had realised, to keep Charles's alcohol level well topped-up.

Charles lifted the glass to his lips and drained it in two large gulps. Bernard reached across the table with the bottle to refill it. It was time to make his move. Filling the glass to its brim, Bernard reached down on his side of the table with his left hand and gave the tablecloth a swift tug. Just as planned, the full wine glass toppled over, spilling its contents over the tabletop and into Charles's lap.

Bernard was up like a flash, darting around to the other side of the table with a solicitous look on his face. He gazed down into Charles's crotch area with feigned horror.

'Oh you poor dear. Red wine is absolutely terrible for stains. Here, let me mop it up before it ruins your nice trousers.'

Suiting his actions to his words, Bernard snatched up a clean table napkin and began to dab delicately at the spreading dark stain in Charles's lap – paying particular and gentle attention to the area around the flies.

Charles stared down in drunken bemusement at the manicured and nail-varnished hand fussing around his crotch. Despite himself, he was dimly aware that his cock was twitching perceptibly under the gentle but insistent touch of Bernard's fingers.

Bernard also felt this extremely promising development with rising excitement. His mopping action became more of an open caress, stroking the slowly stiffening organ beneath the material with undisguised delight. He watched the growing bulge in Charles's trousers with eager anticipation.

'No, it's no good, dear,' he trilled, when he thought the time was absolutely right. 'That stain isn't going to budge. We'll have to get those trousers off and into a cold soak before they are absolutely ruined. Here, let me help you.'

Without waiting for permission or encouragement, Bernard's nimble fingers began to loosen Charles's belt-buckle and flick open the fly-catch. He slid the zipper down, exposing a now throbbing full erection in Charles's Y-fronts.

'Oh dear, it's gone right through to your underpants,' Bernard cooed. 'I'm afraid we'll have to get those off as well.'

Stone cold sober, Charles would probably have

objected as Bernard hurriedly divested him of his trousers and underpants. However, with his normal inhibitions cancelled out by the effects of alcohol, and Bernard's aphrodisiac food coursing through his system, he just sat back and let it happen. In a matter of seconds, he was sitting bare-bottomed in the chair, with his huge throbbing prick pointing to the kitchen ceiling.

Bernard positively drooled at the sight of the magnificent weapon. Saliva bubbled in his mouth, making him gulp frequently to swallow it again. He ran a dripping pink tongue over his lips, making his subtle pink lip gloss shine in the light of the table lamp.

There was no obvious objection from Charles. Bernard seized his opportunity without further ado, dropping to his knees beside Charles's chair and burying his face between his legs. His tongue lapped out, licking at Charles's swollen balls and underside of the stiff shaft, making little grunts of pleasure in his throat as he worked at the delicious treat.

Tracing the full length of Charles's impressive cock with his tongue, Bernard realised that he had scored better than he had dared to expect. Although, at the end of the day, a cock was just a cock, Charles was the proud possessor of quite a remarkable piece of equipment. Well over eight inches long, and impressively thick, it certainly put one of his phallic bananas to shame.

Pausing only to wet this lips again, Bernard placed

his mouth over the bulbous purple head of the beautiful prick and slid down its full length, sucking its stiff and throbbing delights deep into his mouth and throat. He gobbled at it slavishly, using his tongue to lash wetly around its thick circumference and sucking in the sides of his cheeks to apply a gentle massage to the sides.

Charles felt an electric thrill of pleasure ripple through his loins. Even through the dimming effects of the booze, he could sense that Bernard was giving him the best blow job of his life. Although Sally was no mean fellatrix, she lacked the total dedication and delicately skilled technique that Bernard was now applying to his cock. Charles began to squirm in his chair with sensual pleasure as Bernard's oral manipulations made his erection throb and stiffen to bursting point.

Bernard continued to satisfy his hungry mouth for several minutes, using all his acquired skill, knowledge and experience to control Charles's natural bodily functions. Each time he could feel the hot cock pulse in his mouth, Bernard skilfully eased off his sucking, letting his lips merely slide up and down the glistening shaft with the minimum of friction. His skill, and the orgasm-slowing effects of alcohol enabled him to keep the beautiful prick good and stiff, making sure that Charles never quite got past the point of peak excitement.

Eventually, however, Bernard realised that the aching hunger in his hot little arsehole also needed to be appeased. Withdrawing his mouth from Charles's glistening wet cock, he jumped to his feet and ran across to the nearest food cupboard, looking for some suitable lubricant with which to anoint the stiff weapon.

In quick succession, Bernard rejected sunflower oil, butter and cooking fat. His eyes fell upon a bottle of virgin olive oil, and lit up. Quite convinced that Charles had never fucked another man before, it seemed a totally appropriate choice.

Grasping the bottle, Bernard ran back to Charles, still sitting expectantly in his chair. Quickly divesting himself of his white chef's trousers, Bernard slapped a healthy coating of oil on to his dry arsehole and turned his attention to Charles's dancing cock, smearing it liberally with a shining film of lubricant.

Then, straddling Charles's legs, Bernard wriggled into position and reached down to grasp the stiff and slippery prick, manoeuvring it into position against the tight little ring of his arsehole.

With a faint sigh of pure bliss, Bernard allowed himself to sink down upon the full and glorious length of the shining sword, quivering with pleasure at the feel of its thickness against the enclosing walls of his rectum.

This new experience was also a highly pleasant revelation to Charles, who marvelled at the highly agreeable tightness of the hot, enveloping sheath which seemed to suck in and massage his throbbing tool at the same time. He responded with a thrust of his buttocks, driving his cock even deeper into Bernard's receptive arse until he could feel his balls slap against the little chef's smooth bottom.

Bernard gave out a little squeal of delight as Charles's great cock filled him to overflowing. He bounced up and down feverishly, contracting his sphincter muscles in a milking action which quickly had Charles panting with unexploded passion.

Glancing down, Charles noticed that Bernard's own long, thin and dog-like cock was also at full erection, sliding warmly against his belly as the little chef jumped eagerly up and down upon the object of his greatest delight.

Having come this far, Charles pondered drunkenly, there seemed no reason why he should not explore and enjoy the homosexual experience to its full. Bending his neck as far as he could, Charles dropped his open mouth towards Bernard's bobbing tool and seized it between his lips.

Bernard shrieked as his prick plunged into Charles's hot mouth. Quickly wrapping his hands around the back of Charles's head, his fingers entwined themselves in the barman's luxuriant hair. Pulling down with gentle but insistent pressure, Bernard forced his prick deeper into Charles's mouth as he sank back upon the man's impaling prick and allowed him to control the action.

Charles took to the bizarre configuration with remarkable adroitness. Digging his hands into Bernard's soft bottom, be began to bounce the little man on his cock while avidly licking and sucking at his rising and falling prick.

Bernard, his sexual clock already primed by having had Charles's cock in his mouth and arse, came first, spurting a thin jet of come on to Charles's tongue. Not quite sure what to do with it, Charles scraped it against his teeth and spat the hot emission out as discreetly as he could. Straightening his head again, he concentrated his attention on satisfying his own needs, plunging Bernard up and down on his pumping shaft until he too shot a gush of semen into the man's burning arse.

Squealing with satisfaction, Bernard wriggled his buttocks furiously, spreading the cooling and comforting slime around the inside of his tight little passage. Finally, he slipped off Charles's lap and sank to the floor, whimpering contentedly and lapping the insides of his thighs like a devoted dog.

Basking in the warm afterglow of his own spectacular orgasm, Charles failed to notice that his trousers remained lying crumpled on the floor – unsoaked and now irrevocably ruined with wine stains.

Later, he would write them off as a small price to pay for one of the most unusual and stimulating sexual experiences of his life.

Chapter Eight

It was nearly two o'clock when Amanda finally got back to the club. Most of the activity seemed to have died down – the majority of overnight guests had already retired to their rooms and were engaged upon their own individual sexual pleasures. However, there were still a few couples and single males in the bar, and Andrew was still happily serving drinks. Amanda seated herself on a stool and attracted his attention with a wave.

'The usual?'

Amanda nodded, and Andrew poured her a large vodka martini, serving himself a small scotch at the same time. He leaned across the bar, dropping his voice to a whisper.

'We've got a slight problem,' he announced. 'The Batman couldn't find his own woman tonight. He wants us to provide one for him.'

Amanda shrugged carelessly. 'So where's the problem? There are at least six of my girls here tonight.'

'All booked on all-nighters,' Andrew informed her.

'So how about Angie or Carol?'

Andrew shook his head, gesturing discreetly to a group of about five men at the far end of the bar. 'Angie and Carol are both busy at the moment – and those guys are already in the queue.'

Amanda frowned for a moment. Then, remembering the Batman's peculiar sexual fetish, a smile returned to her face. 'What about Letitia? That's exactly her speciality.'

Again, Andrew shook his head regretfully. 'She and Roger are holding a sex clinic session in the gym. So – any other suggestions?'

Amanda racked her brains. 'Freda?' she suggested eventually.

Andrew grinned cynically. 'Freda would beat the poor bastard to death,' he pointed out. 'You know how over-enthusiastic she gets. Anyway, she's with Sally at the moment. Girls night off together, if you know what I mean. I think Sally was feeling a bit pressurised from all my attentions lately and wanted a bit of female company, so to speak.'

Amanda sipped at her drink, dismissing the problem once and for all. 'Well, so it's tough luck on the Batman. He'll have to go without for tonight.'

'He wanted to pay two hundred and fifty pounds,' Andrew murmured. He raised his own glass to his lips, giving Amanda a strange look over the rim.

'You've got to be joking, Andrew,' Amanda blurted out, catching his drift.

The barman grinned. 'Why not? You'll be getting out of practice if you keep on fucking just for fun.'

Amanda shook her head vehemently, not even wanting to consider the matter seriously.

'Could be a laugh,' Andrew put in, goading her. 'And we can't really afford to lose such a regular and well-paying customer.'

Amanda reconsidered. Two hundred and fifty quid was a lot of money to throw away, after all. And Andrew was right – approached in the right frame of mind, it could be treated as just a good laugh. However, there were other considerations and problems.

'I haven't got the right gear, for a start,' she pointed out, identifying the first and major complication.

'You could always borrow Letitia's,' Andrew said, a little too glibly.

Amanda flashed him a slightly reproving glance. 'You've already planned this one all out, haven't you?' she accused.

'Let's just say that I have considered the problem carefully,' Andrew admitted with a broad grin. 'So, what do you think?'

Amanda drained her glass at a gulp. 'I think I'll need another couple of large drinks,' she said firmly.

Fortified by Andrew's encouragement and three more vodka martinis, Amanda helped herself to the pass key from the reception desk and made her way up to the room that Roger and Letitia were sharing. Assured that they were both heavily involved elsewhere, she let herself in and flicked on the bedroom light.

Feeling slightly guilty about sneaking round someone else's room, Amanda had to remind herself that Roger probably wouldn't mind, and that her intrusion was all in the cause of furthering their mutual business interests anyway. Half-convinced of this, Amanda set about rummaging through drawers and cupboards for Letitia's black leather dominatrix gear.

She found it quickly, folded neatly inside one of the drawers complete with a small selection of whips, belts and other minor instruments of flagellation. Pulling the leather suit from the drawer, Amanda shook it out, checking it for size.

A small red book fell to the floor, opening at its centre pages. Amanda bent down to retrieve it, fully intending to replace it in the drawer without looking at its contents. However, she was unable to prevent her eyes falling on a list of names – and some of those names immediately gave her a bit of a jolt.

Her curiosity aroused, Amanda quickly flipped through the rest of the book. It was dynamite! Even at a quick glance, Amanda could see that there were at least half a dozen prominent members of parliament amongst the names, with at least one cabinet minister and a leading light in the opposition. There were also four life peers, a prominent television personality and an internationally famous pop star. Against each name was a list of dates and sums of money – many of them running into four figures and occurring at regular monthly intervals.

To Amanda, it was immediately obvious that the sheer amounts involved could not possibly be for simple sex rejuvenation classes. Equally obvious was the fact that Roger and Letitia were running a highly profitable little sideline in blackmail.

Several things fell into place in Amanda's mind. The book explained how Roger had so suddenly become a man of means, and probably provided the reason for his need to move his centre of operations. With so many important and influential people on the list, things could have been getting a little tight in London. Moving out to the sticks was probably Roger's answer to taking the heat off for a while.

The sound of voices outside in the corridor made Amanda jump. Panicking, she tossed the book back in the drawer and closed it. The voices stopped, right outside the door. With a sinking feeling, Amanda heard the sound of a key being inserted in the lock.

Reacting out of fear, Amanda bolted for the interconnecting door to the next room, hastily inserting her pass key and throwing it open. Hardly aware that she still had Letitia's kinky clothing bundled in her arms, Amanda threw herself through the door and closed it behind her. She leaned back against it, her heart pounding.

'Well, it's about bloody time someone showed up,' a muffled male voice announced in a rather peeved tone.

Amanda jumped again, her eyes darting around

the room for the occupant. The room appeared to be empty.

'Thirty-five minutes I've been waiting,' complained the mystery voice again. 'I thought I'd get better service for two hundred and fifty quid.'

The mention of the money clued Amanda in as to the identity of the hidden occupant. More by luck than by judgement, she had chosen the Batman's room into which to make her escape.

'Well, can we get started, please?' came the voice again.

Amanda reviewed the room again, bending down to look under the bed, just in case. There was absolutely no sign of life. Puzzled, she moved into the centre of the room and called out in a low voice. 'Where are you?'

'I'm in the bloody wardrobe, of course,' came the reply. 'Where else do you think I'd be?'

It was a good question, Amanda mused. Where indeed? She walked across the room to the wardrobe and threw open the double doors.

Securely bound with ropes and chains, the Batman had managed to wrap himself up and suspend himself a few inches in the air from the metal clothes rail. He was wearing his rubber face mask, his plastic cape and a pair of high-heeled boots. Other than that, he was naked. His large, stiff prick protruded through the open front of the cape, backing up his claim that he had been waiting in a state of total frustration for some time.

Through the narrow eye-slits of his hood, Batman regarded Amanda moodily.

'You're not even dressed up,' he moaned. 'This really isn't very good at all.'

Amanda smiled apologetically. 'Sorry, things have been a bit of a rush tonight.'

Batman grunted, having noticed the dominatrix gear in Amanda's hands. 'Well, you can get changed now,' he muttered, his angry tone softening. 'Close the wardrobe doors while you get undressed. I hate seeing naked women.'

Amanda obliged, closing the wardrobe doors and moving over to the bed, where she threw down Letitia's black leather gear and started to peel off her own, conventional clothes.

The leather suit wasn't a bad fit, considering Letitia was considerably bigger in the tit department and enviably slimmer around the waist and hips. Amanda finished zipping up the suit and took time to make a quick appraisal of the general effect in the mirror.

Strangely enough, she quite liked herself in the outfit, which showed off her own more than reasonable figure and blonde hair to stunning advantage. Fetching a selection of pain implements from Letitia's room, she returned to the wardrobe and opened it again.

This time, Batman was considerably more subdued. 'That's more like it,' he murmured in a satisfied voice. His cock twitched a couple of times in sweet anticipation.

'I've been a bad, bad boy,' he intoned in a deep and sorrowful voice. 'I expect you'll have to punish me rather severely.'

Amanda wasn't quite sure what was expected of her. She decided to play it by ear.

'Yes, you certainly have been a very naughty boy,' she scolded harshly. 'And what sort of punishment do you think your awful behaviour deserves?'

Batman's eyes glinted dully beneath the mask. 'Something excruciatingly painful, I should think,' he suggested helpfully.

Amanda flicked the end of a whip experimentally at his dangling balls. The knotted end of the thin leather thong made a sharp cracking sound on contact. Batman let out a thin squeal of agony.

'Oh yes . . . that's it,' he said eventually, when the pain had subsided. 'But I think you're being very lenient with me. I really have been very, very bad indeed.'

Amanda cracked the whip again, this time sending the lash to the inside of his bare thighs. A bright red weal immediately sprang into evidence against the white flesh.

Batman jerked convulsively in his chains like a mad marionette. His cock twitched up and down for several seconds as the waves of pain racked through his body. 'Again, again,' he pleaded.

Amanda looked through Letitia's other implements, eventually choosing a flat leather strap heavily studded with small metal inserts. Moving closer, she slapped his dancing prick from side to side a couple of times, then stood back to observe the reaction.

It was minimal. Batman grunted briefly, then hung motionless.

Obviously the blows had not been hard enough, Amanda told herself. Stepping forward again, she took a really good swing and smacked at his cock as though she was sending a cross-court return in a Wimbledon final. It seemed to do the trick. Its recipient let out a wail of agony and danced up and down for a good ten seconds. Encouraged, Amanda tried a backhand smash and a couple of high lobs for good measure. When Batman's battered prick finally swung to a standstill again, Amanda noticed that it was starting to turn a bright pink colour.

She picked up the whip again, adding a few red stripes to his thighs and stomach for overall colour effect. A last couple of strokes curled around to his bare buttocks seemed to finish Batman off completely. With a sobbing, shuddering moan, he began to shake violently from side to side like someone throwing a fit. His stiff cock flapped up and down like a wounded bird for a few moments, then shot out a thick gobbet of come.

Amanda raised the whip one last time.

'No – that's enough,' Batman called out anxiously. 'You've punished me more than enough for tonight, thank you. I'll settle the check in the morning.'

Amanda was amazed. 'You mean that's it? That's two hundred and fifty quid's worth?' She waggled the whip. 'I don't suppose you'd like to go for an even five hundred?'

Having released himself, Batman's peevish tone was returning. 'That will be quite sufficient, thank you,' he snapped. 'Now if you would be so good as to close the wardrobe door again, perhaps you would leave me in peace.'

Amanda shrugged. 'Anything you say, old sport. You're the customer.' She seized the two wardrobe doors, slammed them closed and turned towards the door.

A horrible, blood-curdling scream of agony assaulted her ears as she reached for the door handle. Amanda wrongly assumed that it was the last stage of the game and didn't bother to look back.

Had she done so, she might have caught a glimpse of the end of Batman's cock wedged between the two doors of the wardrobe. A series of anguished cries echoed down the corridor behind her as she made her way back to her own room.

Chapter Nine

Amanda woke late. Bright light streamed in through the bedroom window and across her face. She blinked painfully, finally able to identify the source of illumination as the sun, now nearly at its highest point in the sky.

There was a stale, dry taste in her mouth, and a spirited band of tribal drummers were playing a discordant but insistent tattoo inside her skull. She attempted to prop herself up in the bed, noting that for some reason her head seemed less willing to leave the pillow than other parts of her body. Amanda groaned softly, recognising all the symptoms of the classic hangover.

Finally, she was able to open her eyes enough to look around the room. Letitia's black leather outfit and flagellation gear was laying in a crumpled heap at the foot of the bed, instantly reminding her of her most urgent problem. Somehow, she had to sneak it back to the room before it was missed, and Roger or Letitia had any reason to suspect that she might have seen their incriminating little book.

But first, she needed at least three cups of coffee

inside her. With some difficulty, Amanda dressed herself and staggered downstairs to the morning room.

Sally looked disgustingly chirpy and bright. 'Hi, have a good night?' she inquired.

Amanda shot her a scathing look. 'Are you taking the piss, or what?'

Sally looked apologetic. 'Sorry. Did all that commotion keep you awake, then?'

Amanda regarded her blankly. 'Commotion? What commotion?'

'Don't tell me you slept through all that noise and blue flashing lights all over the place,' Sally responded, looking surprised.

'It would seem so,' Amanda retorted, sarcastically. 'So, what the hell went on last night?'

'A whole fleet of ambulances at three o'clock in the morning,' Sally told her. 'It really surprised Andrew and I, I can tell you. All these years he's been coming here and we never even suspected he was the chief of the Flying Squad. They certainly gave him the VIP treatment last night, that's for sure.'

Amanda took a deep breath. 'Sally, do you mind telling me what the hell you are blathering about? Who is the chief of the Flying Squad, why were all the ambulances here, and what exactly happened?'

'Why, the Batman, of course,' Sally explained at last. 'Poor bastard somehow managed to get his prick jammed between the wardrobe doors in his room. But don't worry too much, I had Charles clean

118

most of the blood out of the carpet.'

'Oh.' Amanda assimilated this information for a few moments. 'I suppose he didn't leave a cheque before they carted him off, by any chance?'

Sally shook her head. 'Didn't even pay his bar bill, I'm afraid. He did manage to mutter something to me as they carried him by on the stretcher, though.'

'Which was?' Amanda asked.

'Something about asking for punishment, not mutilation,' Sally said. 'It didn't make much sense to me, but then I expect he was in a great deal of pain.'

Sally scurried off to fetch the coffee. Amanda sat, fidgeting nervously and not really capable of worrying too much about Batman's unfortunate accident or her lost £250. All she could really think about was that little red book and its possible consequences. Being roped in as an accessory to a major blackmailing racket was not on her list of life's planned objectives.

Sally returned with a full pot of coffee, poured two cups and sat down to join her.

'Oh, by the way, we had a rather mysterious character check in this morning,' she announced suddenly.

'Oh really?' Amanda still wasn't really listening.

Sally nodded. 'Yes, very odd indeed, if you ask me.'

Amanda realised that some sort of response was expected from her. 'So what's so mysterious about our new guest?' she asked. 'What name did he check in under?'

'John Smith,' Sally said, as though this had some special significance.

Amanda didn't understand. John Smiths made up nearly eighty per cent of the Paradise Club's visitors' book. 'So what's new?' she asked Sally, with a faint shrug.

'He checked in for a whole month,' Sally announced. 'And he brought enough luggage with him to withstand a major siege.'

This information finally made Amanda sit up and take notice. It was highly unusual for any visitor to stay for more than two nights. To book in for a whole month was unheard of. It was, as Sally had hinted, highly suspicious.

'What's he been doing since he got here?' Amanda wanted to know. 'Where is he now, for instance?'

'Last time I saw him, he was lurking about in the shrubbery with a camera and a large telephoto lens,' Sally volunteered. 'Like I said, there's something very suspicious about our Mr Smith.'

Amanda drained the coffee in her cup and sighed wearily. 'Well I suppose I ought to go and check up on him,' she muttered, without much enthusiasm. She suddenly remembered the problem with Letitia's clothes. 'Oh, by the way, do you know where Roger and Letitia are this morning?'

Sally nodded. 'They went up to London for the day. Roger said something about picking up some more equipment.'

More likely picking up a few more blackmail

payments, Amanda thought to herself. However, it was good news. As long as Letitia had not already checked her drawers, it meant that she could hide any signs that she had seen the incriminating list.

With a little more time to play with, Amanda helped herself to another cup of coffee to help clear her hangover. As she sipped at it, Charles bounded into the room, humming happily to himself. He seemed in particularly high spirits.

Sally called him over. 'Oh, Charles, I noticed that you knocked off early from the bar last night. Were you feeling a little queer?'

The happy smile faded from Charles's face immediately. To both Sally and Amanda's amazement, he suddenly turned a bright shade of red and began to stammer furiously.

'Of course not . . . whatever made you think that? I haven't the faintest idea what you're suggesting.'

Without another word, he turned on his heel and stormed out again. Sally and Amanda exchanged puzzled glances.

'What on earth did I say?' Sally asked, not really expecting an answer.

The red notebook was still lying just as Amanda had hurriedly tossed it. It appeared to be a good omen, since Amanda figured that it would have been removed to a place of safety had any suspicion been aroused. She was sorely tempted to look around for other evidence, but eventually decided against it. It could well be that the less she knew, the better. So, carefully, Amanda replaced Letitia's clothes and instruments of torture and left the room as quickly as possible.

She sauntered into the grounds in pursuit of the mysterious Mr Smith, eventually finding him half way up a yew tree near the potting sheds. It seemed an odd pastime for a man who was obviously in his early fifties, but Amanda decided not to make a song and dance about it. Instead, she merely smiled disarmingly and called out a friendly good morning.

A large and extremely expensive looking camera fell out of the tree. For one terrible moment, Amanda feared that it would be followed by the large and expansive Mr Smith, but despite his shock, he clung to his branch resolutely. He looked down, a rather sheepish expression on his face.

'Get a better view from up there?' Amanda asked sweetly. She waited as Mr Smith clambered back down the tree with as much dignity as he could muster.

'Who are you?' he demanded suspiciously.

'Amanda Redfern. I own this place,' Amanda told him bluntly. 'And I'm not sure that we are insured for dangerous sports like tree climbing.'

Mr Smith ignored the jibe, picking up his camera and shaking it experimentally. Nothing rattled. Satisfied that it was unbroken, he slung the strap over his shoulder and started to walk away. Amanda fell into step beside him.

'I hear you're going to be with us for a whole month,' she said, conversationally. 'Planning a nice little rest in the countryside, are you?'

Smith gave a noncommittal grunt, speeding up his walk. It was obvious to Amanda that he was not going to be very forthcoming. She had already decided that Sally was right. There *was* something very odd about their new guest.

Amanda glanced back at the yew tree they had just walked away from. It didn't take much figuring out that someone would have a particularly good view of the club's upstairs bedroom windows from its branches. The telephoto lens on Smith's camera tended to support the theory that he had, in fact, been doing a bit of photographic peeping tom business – although what he really expected to see at midday was another little mystery in itself.

She turned her attention to Smith himself. Somehow, he didn't look like the normal voyeur type. He was too confident, too professional in his attitude and bearing.

A faint bell rang in her head. Perhaps that was the clue. Could it be that Smith was a private eye, perhaps here to gather evidence on one of the customer's marital infidelities? It seemed a plausible answer.

'Photography your little hobby then, is it?' Amanda asked, probing.

Smith realised that she wasn't going to give up. He ceased trying to race away from her, slowing his pace to a normal walk. 'As a matter of fact, it is,' he said. 'I'm a twitcher.'

Amanda wasn't quite sure what that was. She recognised 'flasher' or 'wanker' but 'twitcher' was a little sexual deviation she had never come across. She smiled at Smith understandingly. 'Hey, look, you don't have to worry about your personal preferences around here, you know. Everyone has one little weakness or another. Anything goes at the Paradise Club.'

Smith flashed her a scathing look, deciding not to bother explaining that twitcher was the popular term for a bird-watcher. 'So it would appear,' he muttered. 'I understand that a senior police officer was sexually attacked and mutilated here last night.'

Amanda reacted defensively. 'I think "attacked" is rather strong,' she protested. 'The unfortunate man merely had a little accident.'

'Roped up, chained, beaten black and blue and his pecker half-severed. That's quite an accident,' Smith observed sarcastically. 'I'd hate to be around here when anything serious happens.'

It wasn't a line Amanda could really follow, so she let it go. 'So where do you come from, Mr—'

'Smith. John Smith.'

Amanda nodded. 'Ah, yes. What an unusual name.' Sarcasm wasn't a purely male prerogative. 'Down from London, are you?'

'As it happens, yes,' Smith snapped rather testily.

'I must say, Miss Redfern, you ask a lot of questions for a club proprietor.'

'Just like to get to know my guests,' Amanda replied sweetly. 'Especially those who are going to be with us for a while.'

Smith was fast losing his patience. 'Yes, well – I'm afraid I have a lot of work to do,' he said firmly. 'So if you'd excuse me, I'll be about my business.'

It was his first real slip, and Amanda seized on it. 'Work, Mr Smith? I thought you were here on holiday?'

The look of annoyance which crossed the man's face was plain to see, and confirmed Amanda's suspicions that Mr Smith was not what he appeared, or pretended, to be. It would definitely be worth keeping a further eye on his activities, she decided. However, it was probably best to leave things for now.

'Right, well – I'll let you get on then,' she said. 'No doubt I'll be seeing you again during your stay.' Amanda started to walk away.

Smith looked after her, a slightly worried frown on his face. Miss Amanda Redfern was far too nosey for his liking. He would have to be far more careful than he had first thought. His mission at the Paradise Club was too important and too delicate to risk exposure at such an early stage.

He would have to tread very carefully indeed, for absolute discretion was of the utmost importance, and there was more at stake than anyone realised.

Chapter Ten

The encounter with the strange Mr Smith had unnerved Amanda. She didn't care for mysteries, or too many complexities in life. She was also feeling more than a little guilty about Batman's unfortunate accident, knowing that she had basically been responsible by getting involved in something that she did not fully understand.

She strolled aimlessly, her mind in a bit of a turmoil as she tried to figure out some way to clear away all the negative and uncertain worries from her head.

In a strange way, she regretted the final and glorious fuck with Giles, and the way that they had both mutually agreed that it was over. Part of her needed him now, needed the comfort of lying in his arms and feeling the dominance of his male strength taking all control and responsibility away from her. To be just a woman, taking a woman's pure and simple pleasure from being reamed by a huge and urgent male cock.

In the midst of these reveries, Amanda realised that she was walking vaguely in the direction of the potting sheds. An image of Phillipe, the simple-minded but essentially innocent young French gardener, swam into her mind's eye.

Perhaps her subconscious was trying to tell her something, Amanda thought. Perhaps the simple and uncomplicated pleasure of sex with someone as undemanding as Phillipe was exactly what she needed right now.

Amanda brightened. He was, after all, her personal protégée in a way. She had been the first to coax him away from his unhealthy obsession with masturbation and introduce him to the pleasures of a woman's body for the first time. Even ignoring the potentially soothing therapeutic qualities of a rematch with the young man and his truly remarkable prick, it would be nice to see him again, find out how he was getting on now that Desiree Waites had taken him under her matronly wing.

The more Amanda thought about it, the more attractive the prospect seemed. She headed directly for the potting sheds with more purpose in her step, and a much easier mind.

Phillipe's simple face lit up with undisguised pleasure as Amanda approached. Amanda felt a strange little lump in her throat as she saw him, and realised just how much he had changed. He was no longer locked and imprisoned in the lonely little world of his own traumatized mind. Gone was the frightened, nervous look of a trapped animal. He had been freed to live in the world of real people, and had decided that he liked it. It was a world in which he could take part, have a proper role to play. While he might never compete on an equal intellectual level with many of his peers, Phillipe had discovered warmth, and emotion, and the simple joy of physical and mental communication with others. This basic, but fundamental discovery had transformed him.

Phillipe jumped up, dropping the child's reading book that he had been studying so avidly. He ran towards Amanda eagerly, his handsome young face beaming with happiness and innocent adoration.

'Hello, Phillipe,' Amanda said simply.

Phillipe positively radiated joy and love at the sound of his own name falling from the beautiful lips of his beloved beautiful blonde lady. But he had learned a name, he had learned how to communicate.

'Hello Miss Amanda,' he said proudly, his heart bursting with the sheer exultation of shared existence. He threw his strong arms around her neck and hugged her.

Amanda kissed him lightly on the lips, smiling happily. She was glad she had come, already feeling infected with his joyous new enthusiasm for life, which washed her own negative thoughts away in a soothing, cleansing wave.

Releasing her, Phillipe spread out the blanket that he had been sitting on and motioned for Amanda to share it with him. They sat down together, hugging like a couple of long-lost friends.

They sat in silence for several minutes, taking

pleasure from the warmth of each other's bodies and the quiet peace of the moment. Finally, Phillipe cuddled down and laid his head on Amanda's soft breasts. He looked up at her, his eyes wide and innocent.

'We make love now?' he asked.

Amanda smiled down at him. 'If you want to, Phillipe,' she murmured. 'If you want to.' She kissed him lightly on the forehead.

Phillipe raised his head, reaching up for Amanda's succulent mouth with his. His hot lips closed over hers, pressing tightly without crushing, moving gently against the soft and yielding flesh as he rolled his head almost imperceptibly.

Amanda felt a tingle of unexpected pleasure. Phillipe had learned more than simple English and social graces from Desiree Waites, it was obvious. She had clearly been instructing him in the gentle art of kissing – and making rather a splendid job of it at that.

Phillipe's tongue snaked gently but insistently between Amanda's half open lips, probing lazily past her teeth and deep into her throat. Slowly, as his own passion mounted, the pressure of his lips increased, and Amanda could feel his hot breath filling her mouth in panting little gasps.

She tore her lips away, kissing the side of his handsome face, the sensitive spot behind his ears, the side of his firm neck. Phillipe responded by pressing his body more tightly against hers, his hands coming up to press softly against her swelling breasts, tracing the fleshy contours of each delicious, yielding mound with his fingertips.

Cupping each breast in the palm of his hands, he lifted them as though testing for weight and ripeness, running his thumbs sensuously down into the deep valley of her cleavage.

Amanda began to pick at the buttons of his shirt, soon exposing his broad, manly but almost hairless chest. She lowered her mouth, kissing each little nipple in turn, teasing them with her tongue, savouring the masculine scent and taste of his body.

Phillipe took his own cue from Amanda's actions. Lifting her blouse, he pulled it up and over her arms and shoulders, allowing her full and bra-less breasts to swing freely into his field of vision. He bent his head, covering one soft but firm breast with his hot lips, savouring the delicate womanly scent of her in his nostrils and the pliant warmness of her juicy flesh against his stiff tongue.

The proud and jutting tip of Amanda's breast slipped easily into his open mouth, the stiffening sweet bud of her nipple a tasty titbit to be nibbled and sucked at gently. Amanda placed her hands behind his head and pulled him more urgently against her, forcing more of her lush breast into his hungry mouth.

'Oh, Phillipe – you're so sweet and gentle,' she murmured, shivering with pleasure as he transferred his attention to her other breast, covering it with warm kisses and licking the jutting nipple like a ripe fruit.

Her hands dropped to her skirt fastening, unloosening it and sliding it to her ankles. Amanda wriggled slightly, kicking the garment away so that she sat there clad only in her flimsy silk panties.

Phillipe again followed her lead, shrugging off his trousers and pants until he was naked beside her. He leaned over her, pressing her slowly backwards until she lay full-length upon the blanket.

Amanda peeled off her panties and threw them carelessly aside. She shivered slightly as she felt Phillipe's body pressing upon hers, the exciting hardness of his massive prick against her soft belly.

It was time to slow things down, enjoy the pleasures of sight and touch before plunging headlong into the frenzied lust of copulation. Amanda rolled Phillipe away gently, sliding down beside him until his beautiful cock was laying along the deep valley between her breasts. She moved herself against it, marvelling at the throbbing hardness of the tumescent flesh against the swelling softness of her own, female organs. Bending her head slightly, she lightly licked its smooth and circumcised head with the tip of her tongue, tasting the faint salty flavour of his pre-coital secretions.

Phillipe slipped his hand between her soft thighs, bunching it against the hairy bush of her hot cunt, squeezing it gently as though it were a much-loved cuddly toy. Amanda squirmed, making a little grunting noise in her throat as she felt her stiff little clitoris jump and twitch in anticipation.

As if sensing her need, Phillipe slipped first one and then two fingers into her creamy slit, sliding them in and out with slow, deep strokes which started the juices flowing from deep inside her.

They lay like that for ages, feeling and touching and appreciating the most intimate parts of each other's bodies, until Amanda finally realised that her hungry cunt was desperate for the feel of his proud cock inside her.

Rolling Phillipe on to his back, she climbed over and straddled him, taking the throbbing shaft in her hand and guiding it to the lips of her flowing fanny. Gently, bracing herself on her knees, Amanda lowered herself on to its hard thickness, feeling as though she were impaling herself upon some sacrificial stake.

Phillipe groaned as his cock slid into the burning volcano of her cunt, and her hot juices boiled against his flesh. He lay back contentedly as Amanda rose and fell upon her knees, sliding her body up and down the stiff column of flesh with little cries of delight.

Amanda rejoiced in Phillipe's hardness inside her, each wonderful inch of it seeming to reach and touch and excite a different part of her. Her cunt was like something with a life of its own, sucking and massaging at the throbbing flesh with every stroke.

Like this, they fucked unhurriedly for what seemed like hours. There seemed no reason to become frantic, no incentive to abandon this gentle and delicious pleasure for the animal-like frenzy of orgasm-chasing lust. When Phillipe did finally come, it was almost a surprise to them both. No last pounding strokes before ejaculation, no violent slamming of cock into cunt, belly against belly.

Phillipe merely sighed deeply, as if with some overpowering inner satisfaction, and released his hot sperm into her with a warm and liquid gush.

To Amanda, it felt as though he were bathing her inside with tenderness and loving care, washing away the worries and frustrations of the morning.

Afterwards, they lay in each other's arms for nearly an hour, neither moving nor speaking. Their bodies had already said all that there was to be said between a man and a woman.

Chapter Eleven

'Well – did you see our mysterious Mr Smith?' Sally asked, when Amanda finally returned to the house.

Amanda nodded. 'I think you're right. There's something very strange about that man. We shall have to keep a very close eye on him.'

Sally looked triumphant. 'I've already been doing just that,' she confided. 'I sneaked a look around his room while you were both safely out in the grounds. You wouldn't believe the sort of stuff he has up there.'

Amanda was instantly curious. 'What sort of stuff?'

'Cameras, electronic gear – even what appears to be a radio transmitter or something,' Sally said. 'And a complete disguise and stage make-up kit, with false moustaches, beards, wigs and a couple of dozen pairs of glasses, all with plain lenses.'

'Perhaps our Mr Smith is something of a thespian,' Amanda mused.

Sally shook her head. 'No, that's only women, isn't it?'

Amanda flashed an exasperated glance. 'Thespian, idiot. Maybe Smith is an actor. Perhaps he wanted somewhere away from it all to rehearse a new part, or something like that.'

Sally was unconvinced. 'That wouldn't explain why I caught him taking photographs of our visitors' book with a miniature camera,' she said. 'Just after he came back to the house – I walked into the reception area to find him sneaking about behind the desk.'

'What did he do?' Amanda wanted to know.

'He just looked very startled and shot upstairs to his room,' Sally told her. 'He hasn't been down since.'

Amanda was reminded of the episode out in the gardens, when she had found him up the tree taking shots of the upstairs bedroom windows. It all pointed to the fact that Smith was definitely a snooper of some kind. But why? That was the unanswered question.

However, there were other things more important than worrying about Mr Smith and his strange ways. Amanda tried to push the whole business out of her mind and concentrate upon more pressing problems. The club needed some new supplies, for a start.

'I need to get into town,' she announced. 'Will you tell Andrew I'm borrowing his car?'

'Right.' Sally appeared to have an afterthought, 'Oh, if you're going into Amesford, you could pick up some fresh eggs from Flatfield Farm – it's only a mile or so outside the village.'

'Sure,' Amanda agreed readily. 'I'll call in on the

way back.' It seemed an innocent and simple enough errand.

Roger and Letitia, meanwhile, were on an errand that was far from innocent. Roger brought his car to a stop outside an expensive-looking house in a fashionable Chelsea mews.

'This is the place,' he announced to his companion. 'Let's go and collect what's coming to us, shall we?'

Letitia grinned. 'Otherwise we'll give the bastard what's coming to him, eh?' She unclipped her seat belt and slid sensuously out of the car. Together, they walked up the three stone steps to the front door and rang the bell.

The door was opened by an extremely attractive young girl in a maid's uniform.

'Can I help you?' she inquired.

Roger's eyes ran over her trim figure appreciatively. 'You could certainly help me,' he muttered. 'But right now we'd both rather see Sir Reginald, if you don't mind.'

The maid stood protectively across the threshold as Roger tried to push his way past her.

'I'm sorry, but Sir Reginald doesn't see any visitors without an appointment.'

Letitia laughed dismissively. 'Oh, he'll see us,' she said firmly, rudely knocking the maid aside as she marched into the house.

The maid went to race into the house to warn her employer, but Roger grabbed her arm firmly. 'I'd stay out of it if I were you,' he muttered, not unpleasantly. 'Letitia is an old friend. A very intimate friend, shall we say.'

The maid's dark eyes flashed briefly with resistance before the raw force of Roger's uncanny male dominance hit her. She trembled slightly at the feel of his strong and masterful grip on her arm, finally relaxing. 'Oh, it's like that, is it?' she said, the faint beginning of a knowing smile tugging at the corners of her generous mouth.

Roger smiled and let her go. 'Very much like that,' he assured her. 'Now, what say you and I go somewhere nice and private and let them get on with it? Sir Reginald isn't going to be needing your services for quite a while.'

The maid was smiling openly now, her eyes lit up with a sense of intrigue and excitement. She looked up at Roger with a flirty, coquettish look.

'But *you* might – is that it?' she murmured in a low, sexy voice.

'No might about it. I always was a bit partial to a maid's uniform,' Roger told her with a big grin. He reached out for the girl again, pulling her body against his and crushing his lips to hers. Casually, he kicked the front door shut and pressed the girl against the hallway wall, letting his full weight fall against her as he kissed her deeply.

The maid's hot tongue darted into Roger's mouth as she felt his belly press against hers, and his hard, manly chest squash into the soft fullness of her breasts. After several seconds, she managed to tear her mouth away, her breath coming in little warm gasps.

'Not here . . . we'll go upstairs to my room.' Sliding out from beneath him, she grabbed Roger's hand eagerly and led him towards the stairs.

Sir Reginald was sitting at his large, antique desk as Letitia burst, unannounced, into his library. He looked up in surprise.

'You,' he muttered thickly. 'I thought I told you that I didn't want to see you again.'

Letitia smiled disarmingly. 'But you didn't really mean it, did you, Reggie darling? Any more than you meant to cancel that last cheque for three hundred pounds. Roger and I were most hurt and offended by that. It was almost as though you thought you didn't need us any more. Didn't need *me* any more.'

As she spoke, Letitia had crept around the huge desk to stand directly behind Sir Reginald's chair. Moving forwards, she pressed her soft warm breasts against the back of his neck and ran her hands sensuously over his shoulders and down his chest. Bending slightly, she pressed her lush lips to the side of his ear.

'You didn't really want to hurt me – did you, Reggie?' she whispered in a deliberately provocative voice, breaking off to insert the hot wet tip of her tongue into his ear and wiggle it about.

Sir Reginald quivered in his chair. 'You don't

understand,' he quavered, his voice breaking with uncertainty. 'Things were getting too dangerous . . . my wife, my reputation . . . a man in my position . . .'

His voice tailed off as Letitia ran her hands down to his lap, stroking the soft bulge in his trousers.

'There's only one position for you, Reggie,' she whispered firmly. 'Down on your knees like a dog, licking at my juicy cunt.'

'No, please . . . just leave me alone.' Sir Reginald's tone was now one of abject pleading. 'I promise that I'll keep on sending the money. Only just stay away from me, stop tempting me.'

Letitia chuckled deep in her throat. 'Oh, Reggie, you really disappoint me. Did you really think it was just the money?' Her voice hardened. 'No, Reggie, I like to see you grovel, beg for it like the pathetic little creature you really are.'

She stroked his crotch again, feeling the swelling of his stiffening cock and smiling with inner satisfaction. She had him now, Letitia was sure. It was time to give Sir Reginald a little reminder of what she alone could make him do, completely overpower him with her sexuality. A love slave needed a little reminder from time to time, otherwise they got ideas above their station. Dangerous and costly ideas about breaking free.

'Come on, Reggie, down on your knees,' Letitia commanded imperiously. 'Show me how deeply and truly sorry you are.'

Broken, Sir Reginald rose from the chair and sank

to his knees on the floor, assuming a dog-like crouch. Letitia took his place in his chair, pulling up her skirt and tearing off her black silk knickers. She spread her thighs, exposing the red bush of her cunt to his view.

'Eat cunt, Reggie,' she bade him. 'Suck my beautiful pussy dry. Lick it until your tongue aches.'

Sir Reginald crawled up to her, burying his head deep into the hot crevice of thighs. Pressing his mouth over her springy mound, he spread his lips, stretching her soft slit apart like some split and over-ripe fruit. Letitia writhed against his face, grinding her cunt against his month, and nose, and teeth. She bucked her arse up and down, feeling the stimulation against her hot little clitoris and stimulating a flow of tangy juices to feed the sucking mouth.

'Feel me coming on your tongue, Reggie?' she asked him. 'Can you taste my slime on your lips and in your throat? Use your tongue – lap it all up, like the dog that you are.'

Sir Reginald pressed forward with renewed vigour, sending his firm tongue snaking deeply into the dripping crack, sweeping from one side to the other of the slippery, crinkly walls, probing into the hot, moist depths of the seemingly endless hole. He gulped as he worked, swallowing back the bubbling juices as they ran on to his tongue, slavering for more.

'Yes, suck it dry,' Letitia encouraged him, by now beginning to enjoy the physical sensation as much as the sense of humiliation and dominance. 'Drink every little drop of my love juice.'

Sir Reginald shook his head from side to side wildly, sucking the smell and the taste of her into his nose, his mouth and his throat, while his darting tongue continued to ream her hot tunnel like a little cock. He sank back on his haunches, and his right hand dropped to his zipper. Tugging his trousers open, he pulled out his stiff cock and began to jack himself off frantically, his fingers moving up and down the throbbing shaft in a blur.

Letitia groaned with pleasure as her little spurts of fluid became a steady stream, and the thrilling tingle of pre-orgasm started up deep in her belly. She reached out to grasp the back of Sir Reginald's head, pulling his face deeper into her burning thighs. His thrusting tongue jabbed away inside her with deep, regular strokes as his quivering lips slapped wetly against her slippery, pulsing little clit.

Letitia felt the first minor wave of orgasm and bucked her hips more frantically, rubbing her own labial lips against the hardness of Reggie's nose and chin. She gushed against his sucking mouth, looking down with pleasure as her own hot juices sprayed his face and neck.

Suddenly satisfied, Letitia kicked Sir Reginald in the stomach with her booted foot, sending him sprawling. Contorted into a near-foetal position on the carpeted floor, he continued to wank furiously until he finally came with a convulsive shudder, spurting his seed out on to the carpet.

A look of savage glee stole over Letitia's pouting red lips. She looked down at the pathetic figure in total disdain. 'Look what you've done, you disgusting little man,' she said. 'You've made a mess on the carpet. Now get down there and lick it up at once.'

Meekly, Sir Reginald lowered his face to the floor and began to lick up his own come from the thick pile of the carpet. Letitia watched him without pity, her normally beautiful face twisted into an ugly leer.

'Just one last little thing, Reggie darling,' she murmured coldly. 'Your little donation just went up in price. From now on, we'll be needing five hundred every month instead of three.'

Upstairs, Roger was finding Patricia, the young maid, more than willing to throw herself wholeheartedly into sex games. Life in Sir Reginald's household was rather formal and boring – a far cry from her previous position, where the master of the house had made frequent trips to her room for a good fucking session. Had Patricia even suspected Sir Reginald's secret desires, she would have accommodated him eagerly, for she liked nothing more than having a hot tongue thrust up her delectable little cunt. But alas, her new employer had seemed outwardly rather cold and aloof, and for the last three months or so she had been resigned to more limited sexual experience just at the weekends. So Roger was a very welcome break in her dull routine, and Patricia had made the most of her chance.

143

Having kissed and sucked his impressive cock into full, throbbing erection, Patricia was enjoying just playing with the stiff column of flesh. While Roger amused himself by tweaking her hot little clit between his finger and thumb, Patricia lovingly fondled his swollen balls, cupping them in the palm of her hand and gently squeezing them together until their upright attendant twitched and jerked in reflex.

Idly, she slid one long, painted fingernail under his scrotum, gently scratching the sensitive puckered flesh around his arsehole. Roger's balls danced in her hand, his firm young cock seeming to stiffen even further.

The time for play was over. Patricia seized the pulsing prick in a vice-like grip and began to rub it up and down with slow, deep strokes. Roger responded by jabbing three bunched fingers past her throbbing little clitoris and deep into her hot and juicy hole, thrusting in and out while rotating his wrist at the same time. The combined movement produced a thrilling tingle in the maid's belly, triggering off a fresh flow of slimy secretion to top up the already overflowing hole.

They came together by unspoken mutual assent, both realising that the optimum time had come. Patricia knew, instinctively, that the throbbing prick in her hand was at its peak – as thick and stiff and pumped full with raging blood as it ever could be. Roger's soaking fingers told him that the girl's beautiful cunt was hot and hungry, aching for the entry of a good hard cock.

They rolled together on the maid's single bed. Patricia reached up to grab a thick, soft pillow and stuff it under her buttocks, thrusting her hips upwards in a provocative and enticing manner. Roger pulled himself over her, straddling her slim and shapely legs. Peeling the pink folds of her labia apart with his two thumbs, he pressed the tip of his cock against the stiff little bud of her clit and plunged forwards.

His thick cock slid into her inviting sheath like a hot knife into butter. Roger reached under the pillow beneath her arse, bunching it up and pulling her hips up to meet his deep and rhythmic thrusts and squeezing her thighs tightly together with his knees.

Patricia sighed deeply as the meaty rod filled her aching pussy. She contracted her stomach muscles, increasing her already tight grip on Roger's imprisoned cock. Flexing and unflexing, she massaged the sliding shaft as it plunged into her depths, heightening both her and Roger's sensual pleasure at the same time.

For Roger, the feeling was indescribably erotic. Normally a slower and more sensitive lover, the exquisite sensations vibrating through his cock to his balls drove him into a frenzy of lust. His buttocks pumping furiously, he began to fuck Patricia with fast, deep strokes which seemed to take the blunt head of his cock all the way to her womb.

Quivering with excitement, Patricia thrust her

pelvis up to meet every downward stroke, raising herself on to her elbows to give her supple body greater leverage. Using them as a fulcrum, she swung her body to and fro in a vaguely circular motion, so that Roger's thick cock sloshed and waggled about inside her like a wild thing trying to escape from its captivity.

This triple assault on his senses was too much for Roger. His hips crashed against her soft flesh a few more times and then a convulsive shudder in his stomach announced his pumping orgasm. He shot his wad inside Patricia's steamy cunt in three short but violent spasms.

His passion satisfied, Roger would have rolled off the girl's hot and sweat-covered belly, but Patricia had other ideas.

'No, not now. You can't stop now,' she screamed, pulling her legs out from underneath him and wrapping them up around his back. She began to buck her hips and pelvis with renewed energy, raising her head to nibble his throat and ears and lick the side of his face.

Roger's cock, already starting to soften, soon felt the tinglings of fresh desire. Patricia, now sensing the beginnings of her own orgasm, worked her body up and down and from side to side, massaging and coaxing the imprisoned prick back to erect readiness. Her tight pussy was opening and closing like a soft and fleshy fist as the stimulating hardness grew inside her once again.

Fully stiff again, Roger pressed himself deeply into her and let the girl continue to do all the work. He contributed a few gentle thrusts of his buttocks as he sensed Patricia's breathing rate becoming more and more erratic, but other than that let the girl choose her own timing.

Suddenly Patricia's lovely body went rigid, her stomach became a tight knot of muscle and her legs wrapped around his back like the jaws of a vice. She began to moan softly in the back of her throat, her chest heaved in powerful, rhythmic spasms and her lips fell slackly open.

Roger took up the pace again, pulling himself up until his prick had nearly popped out of her gushing cunt and then slamming back in as hard and as far he could go.

Patricia's moan became a groan, and then a scream as Roger repeated the manoeuvre three or four times in quick succession. Her cunt tightened around his prick again, fluttering with internal movement as the shuddering waves of orgasm pulsated out from deep inside her belly.

Shaking her head wildly from side to side, her tongue lolling out of her open mouth, Patricia came like an exploding firecracker. Her sharp fingernails raked Roger's back for a few moments, and then her entire body seemed to melt into an enveloping warm bath of the most soothing and buoyant liquid.

As Roger too prepared to relax, Letitia's voice came from downstairs.

'Roger, you about through up there?'

Smiling at the young maid somewhat regretfully, Roger rose and dressed hurriedly. 'Duty calls,' he apologised, looking down at her tasty body spreadeagled naked upon the bed. As an afterthought, he fished in his pocket and dug out one of Amanda's visiting cards for the Paradise Club. He dropped it on to the bed beside her.

'Look, I'd really like to do this again sometime, perhaps you could come and visit me when you get a free weekend,' he murmured.

After he had left, Patricia raised herself on the bed and picked up the card, reading it carefully.

'Mister, you just got yourself a date,' she muttered to herself.

She dropped the card again and moved her hand to her dripping cunt, beginning to massage it gently and think of Roger's beautiful prick again.

Chapter Twelve

Amanda looked at the deeply rutted and muddy track that led up to the main buildings of Flatfield Farm. Somehow, she didn't think that the battered suspension of Andrew's old car was quite up to negotiating it. Switching off the engine, she resigned herself to walking up the 400-yard track.

Opening the door, she stepped out of the car, and immediately regretted not having invested in that essential of country *haute couture*, a stout pair of wellies. Ankle deep in thick brown mud, Amanda was in half a mind to forget all about eggs and beat a hasty retreat before things got any worse.

However, having made the detour out to the farm, and with her nice black patent shoes probably already ruined beyond salvation, it seemed rather foolish not to finish the job she had started. With a sigh of resignation, Amanda began to trudge up the muddy lane towards the farmhouse.

The farm seemed deserted, with no signs of life – human or animal. Amanda assumed that they kept the chickens out round the back of the buildings somewhere, and began to stroll in that general direction. She was just passing what appeared to be an empty barn when a hoarse shout behind her made her whirl round.

Her heart sank as she recognised Jack Morton, the would-be rapist garage owner from her unpleasant encounter a few days previously. At first, she only registered puzzlement, wondering what he was doing out here on what seemed to be a deserted farm. The fear only started when half a dozen other local lads poured from the barn, pointed excitedly towards her and began to fan out into a semicircle.

'It's that bloody slag from the country club,' Jack yelled out triumphantly. 'Get her, lads.'

Amanda froze in her tracks as Jack started to run towards her. Instinct told her to make a break for it, but common sense told her that there was no way she could outrun a bunch of country bumpkins through thick mud wearing a pair of high-heeled shoes.

Resigned to her fate, Amanda could only stand there with mounting panic as the mob closed around her.

Fixing a philosophical smile on her face to hide her fear, Amanda started to pick at the buttons of her blouse as Jack and his cronies closed in.

'Oh well, here we go again,' she said with pretended humour. 'What is it this time? A gang-bang in the barley? Or a hump in the hay?'

Jack came up behind her and grabbed her arm roughly. He appeared to be going through a long and laborious process of thought.

'Oh no, I've got a much better idea for you this time,' he said after a while. 'Come on lads, let's take her over to the milking shed.'

Amanda shuddered. That didn't sound too pleasant at all. All those cold and calloused hands!

'I hope you've got an electric milking machine,' she put in, affecting far more bravado than she really felt.

There was no reply. Amanda let herself be pulled in the direction of the shed. There didn't seem much point in putting up any attempt at physical resistance. Instead, she applied her mind to other things – like getting out of her present predicament, for a start.

Perhaps she could taunt Jack into having a go at her himself again, play him off against the others. After all, Amanda figured, a girl should be able to run faster than a man with his trousers flapping around his ankles. It might be worth a try, anyway.

Jack dragged her into the milking shed. Amanda looked round at the half a dozen cows in their stalls.

'Nice bunch of girls,' she observed. 'Which one's your fiancée, Jack?'

His only reply was to twist her arm painfully up behind her back. Amanda winced, but steeled herself not to show any obvious signs of pain.

Remembering her escape plan in the garage, Amanda glanced around hopefully, looking for anything which could be of help. In an untidy pile on the floor lay a few pots of paint, wooden poles, pieces of cardboard and a few finished protest banners proclaiming the existence of the League Against Bloodsports (foxhunting division). Amanda realised that she had blundered into the home base of Jack and his mates' hunt sabotage activities.

'Well, tough little lady, aren't you?' Jack sneered at her. 'Thought you could frighten us with that little petrol trick of yours, did you? Well I'm going to show you what fear is, you bitch.'

Amanda let her mind wander on to similar little tricks she would like to be showing them all right at that moment. Like connecting them all up to an electric fence by their foreskins, for instance, pumping horse liniment up their arseholes with an enema tube, or burying them all up to their necks in a field and then drag racing with a couple of combine harvesters.

Unfortunately, she didn't have much time to dwell upon such delicious thoughts. Jack dragged her across to the shed and pushed her down on to the stinking floor. Bending down, he fished among the pile of half-finished banners and finally produced a large clear bottle full of murky yellowish fluid. Stepping towards her again, he pulled the cork out of the bottle.

'If that's your piss, it's about time you got a good dose of penicillin,' Amanda managed to quip bravely, glaring at Jack defiantly. He was not amused.

Holding the opened bottle at arm's length, he upended it and began to pour the contents over her hair and shoulders.

Amanda shuddered as a truly foul smell assaulted her nostrils. Whatever it was in the bottle, it had a heavy, musky and cloying odour which made her think, for some odd reason, of an animal with extremely bad breath. As the liquid gushed over her face, Amanda screwed her eyes tightly shut and tried to stop breathing.

Only when he had completely emptied the bottle over her body and clothes did Jack throw it carelessly away. He stood back, joining his cronies and staring down at her with an evil grin on his face.

Amanda sat up, opening her eyes and wrinkling her nose in disgust at the foul stench which engulfed her. Strangely enough, although the experience was bad enough, she now felt an overpowering sense of relief. The sheer power and unpleasantness of the stench told Amanda that a gang-rape was now completely out of the question. Even the most dedicated country sheep-shagger would not want to be too close to such a super-pong. And if that threat was removed, Amanda felt sure that there wasn't much else Jack and his cohorts could really do to her, short of physical violence, and somehow she doubted that they would resort to that.

Amanda brightened up. It could be that this alone was their dull-witted idea of a fitting punishment. Bad as the odour was, Amanda could not imagine it resisting two hours' soak in a perfumed bath and the combined power of the world's deodorants. With a bit of luck, she could be her own sweet-smelling self before the day was over.

Feeling newly brave, Amanda could not resist throwing a few more taunts at her tormentors.

'What was that – you bastards' bath water?' she wanted to know. 'Or maybe some of your elderberry wine, Jack.'

Jack merely glowered at her.

'All right, get up,' he ordered.

Amanda scrambled to her feet, facing the men uncertainly. She still wasn't quite sure if her ordeal was drawing to a close.

'Now what happens?' she asked.

Jack laughed unpleasantly.

'Now you start running for your life,' he said in a hard, cold voice which made Amanda suddenly shiver with a new sense of fear.

She stared into his eyes, seeing real hate there. Her sense of terror returned. When she spoke again, there was little bravado – only a slight quaver of uncertainty in her voice.

'What is this bloody foul stuff you've poured all over me?' she demanded.

Jack nodded towards the pile of banners on the floor. 'Doesn't any of this stuff give you a clue?' he asked.

A sick, cold feeling started up deep in Amanda's belly as the first seeds of comprehension began to sprout in her mind.

'Fox scent,' she blurted out at last, in a shocked tone.

Jack nodded. 'You're getting brighter all the time,' he muttered. 'That stuff is what we use to lay a false trail for the hounds – send them on a wild goose chase to spoil the hunt. Only today, you're going to lay that false trail for us. And perhaps you can imagine what a hunt-crazy pack of hounds might do to you if they catch up with you. No doubt you've seen what they do to a real fox.'

Amanda shuddered again. Jack didn't need to draw any detailed pictures for her. She had seen plenty of photographic evidence of a fox's fate when the pack caught up with it. In blood-red techni-colour! Suddenly, she felt very, very cold and very afraid.

'If I were you, I'd start running,' Jack said almost carelessly. 'The hunt was due to start about half an hour ago. My guess is that the hounds will already be up and running by now, and we already made sure that they will head in this direction.'

That did it. Amanda suddenly felt new life come back into her jelly-like legs. She made a dash for the door of the milking shed, stopping in her tracks as another member of Jack's little gang suddenly entered, dangling a bundle of black plastic-coated wiring in his hand, which he waved about with something of a grand gesture. Amanda wasn't much of a mechanic, but she recognised a set of spark-plug leads when she saw them.

'As you might have gathered, there's not much point running for your car,' Jack called out from behind her. 'I'd say your best bet would be out over the fields.'

Amanda needed no second bidding. Pushing past the yokel who had sabotaged the car, she dived through the milking-shed door and set off at a brisk trot. Taking Jack's advice, she did not attempt to go back down the muddy track towards the car, but cut through the farmyard and into the back field, spurred on by a chorus of evil laughter behind her.

Once into the grassy field, and well into her stride, it all didn't seem quite so bad. As she ran, Amanda realised that the foul smell in her nostrils decreased, as the fumes from the stinking liquid wafted out and away behind her like a vapour trail. She was reasonably fit, Amanda reminded herself. A brisk jogging pace should keep her going for long enough to reach safety, or some place she could find temporary shelter. Feeling calmer now, she made it to the end of the field and paused for a couple of seconds to get her breath back. Above the sound of her own heavy breathing, and the pounding of blood in her head, she heard another faint sound in the distance. The single, clear note of a hunting horn.

It was time to get moving again. Praying for second wind, Amanda scrambled through the hedge which bordered the field, trying to ignore the thorny branches which tore at the thin cotton of her blouse and the bare flesh beneath.

Once through the hedge, Amanda found herself in another, smaller field, and two sights greeted her almost simultaneously. It was like one of those 'good news, bad news' jokes. Like waking up in hospital and the nurse saying: 'The bad news is that we had to amputate both your legs, and the good news is that Sister wants to buy your tights.'

Amanda's good news was the sight of another farmhouse across the field.

The bad news was the extremely large bovine creature inhabiting the field.

Amanda regarded the black monster warily. It was about twenty yards away, and although it was not quite possible to pick out things like rings through noses, Amanda was sure that the beast was of the male gender.

Amanda thought, suddenly, of a piece of advice once offered her by her father many years previously during a picnic trip to the countryside.

'If it doesn't have udders, avoid it,' he had said. At the time, Amanda had assumed he was imparting snippets of the country code and referring solely to cattle, although the experiences of her later life had tended to support the advice on a much more general level.

The creature in question most definitely did not have udders. It was, as they say, as titless as a ton of Twiggies, and many times more threatening. As Amanda stared at it, the bull noticed her for the first time and began to amble in her direction, snorting noisily.

Amanda backed up to the hedge she had just come

through, her heart pounding. The bull trotted up to within five yards of her and stopped, regarding her through large, menacing eyes.

Amanda considered her options. Basically, she had only two – either to retreat or to find a way past the four-footed obstruction. It was a choice that needed to be made quickly, time being of the essence, as they say.

As it had so many times before in her life, the thought of offering sex as a survival tactic occurred to her. Amanda raised her arm slowly, pointing to the next field and speaking to the bull in a soft, reassuring voice.

'Cows,' Amanda said. 'Lots of lovely, randy, sexy cows.'

The bull remained singularly unimpressed. It lowered its head, snorted again and tapped the ground with one of its front hooves. Something told Amanda that the beast was about to charge. Panicking, she broke into a sudden run, skirting sideways around the bull and making for the top end of the field. Glancing nervously back over her shoulder, she noticed that the bull had set out in pursuit, but at a slow and shambling trot rather than a full-blooded charge.

Suddenly, her foot caught on a small grassy knoll and Amanda was falling face-first towards a particularly nasty species of cow pie. It turned out to be a crusty one with a soft and well-filled centre. Very nasty indeed!

Even with this cushioned landing, Amanda had fallen heavily, the impact with the ground knocking the breath from her body. She tried to scramble to her feet quickly, but movement just wouldn't come. Amanda could only lie there in helpless horror as the bull ambled slowly over towards her, its head down and a nasty gleam in its eyes.

It was going to gore her, Amanda felt sure. Either that, or it was going to stomp her to death slowly, out of pure sadism. Thinking, oddly enough of all the episodes of *Eastenders* that she would be spared, Amanda closed her eyes in resignation and waited for the end to come.

The end certainly took its time. After several moments had passed, Amanda opened her eyes again. She was looking at the underside of a huge, black creature which stood, motionless, right across her prostrate body. Amanda's focus moved, quite naturally, to the area where the species packed its sexual equipment.

One thing was immediately apparent. There was something not quite right about the creature's offensive weaponry. The guided muscle was there all right, but the back-up system was missing. The surgeon's scalpel had done its dreadful work. This was a hapless hunk of beef which would never hump a heifer.

A bull without balls equals a bullock. Bullocks, Amanda's fund of useless information told her, tended to be completely docile and harmless creatures.

Deprived of their gonads, and any possible fun in life, they usually seemed content to wander aimlessly around empty fields, munching grass and waiting to be turned into Big Boy burgers and ladies' handbags while reflecting miserably upon the inscrutable ways of man.

However, it seemed that they were not above making a last gesture of defiance. As Amanda stared at the mutilated muscle, it twitched a couple of times, announcing the imminent issue of urinary discharge upon her helpless body.

It might be slightly preferable to the combined stench of fox scent and bullshit – but then again it might not, Amanda figured rather quickly. Finding sudden new reserves of strength, she rolled out of the firing line and scrambled to her feet, breaking into a slow and painful hobble towards the farmhouse as the bullock took a leisurely piss.

She headed directly to the front door of the farmhouse, past a small row of stalls in which a trio of horses regarded her moodily. Pounding upon the door, Amanda breathed a sigh of relief, fully expecting a friendly welcome to sanctuary at any moment.

It didn't come. Amanda knocked on the door again, calling out, 'Anybody home?'

There was still no answer. Tentatively, Amanda turned the door handle. To her surprise, the door opened. Amanda called out again, still receiving no reply.

It was obvious that the house was empty. Amanda again had to rethink her immediate options.

She could, of course, merely take shelter in the farmhouse. It was rather convenient that country folk appeared to be so trusting. Then, when the pack of hounds arrived, she could sit it out until the Hunt arrived upon the scene and explain her position to the Master of Hounds. The problem there was that he might not take too kindly to having his nice day out in the countryside completely spoiled for him. It could have serious repercussions upon the success or total failure of the forthcoming Hunt Ball – and subsequently upon the success or failure of the Paradise Country Club.

There were also the horses. Amanda reflected upon the possibility of mounting one and riding to the safety of her own grounds. This option also presented problems – namely Amanda's particular and peculiar troubles with the equine species.

In fact, she was an excellent rider, having taken regular lessons as a young child. It was only after she had reached puberty that the problem manifested itself. It had something to do with clitoral friction, Amanda had supposed, but whatever the cause, the fact remained that she only had to sit on a horse's back for a few moments before she began having multiple orgasms. Before she was sixteen, Amanda had come to the inevitable conclusion that it was well-nigh impossible to control a horse adequately when your legs are turning to jelly and your pelvic muscles are contracting twenty to thirty times a minute.

Undecided about what to do for the best, Amanda cast her eyes around the interior of the farmhouse, finally identifying a very welcome telephone.

Help was, after all, at hand. Amanda walked into the farmhouse kitchen and picked up the phone, dialling the club.

Sally's welcome voice greeted her. 'Hello, Paradise Country Club.'

'Sally, it's me, Amanda. I'm in a bit of a jam,' she said, not bothering with polite niceties. She explained the situation in brief, but graphic terms.

There was a strange crackling sound over the telephone line, followed by a couple of shrill electronic bleeps and then a low hum. Sally's voice suddenly changed to a deep baritone.

'Miss Redfern, you are in great danger. Now listen to me carefully.'

'Who is this?' Amanda wanted to know immediately.

'It's John Smith, as a matter of fact,' came the response. 'Now just don't ask any more questions and listen. The hounds were set loose some time ago and they will have picked up your scent by now. If they get to you before anyone can call them off, they could rip you to shreds.'

Amanda thanked him under her breath for those few comforting words. Sally's voice came back, sounding puzzled. 'Who's that? We seem to have some sort of a crossed line here.'

'Please put down the telephone and let me talk to Miss Redfern,' Smith's voice returned testily.

There was a dull click as Sally replaced the receiver, but the line stayed open. It suddenly occurred to Amanda that Mr Smith had been bugging her telephone line for some reason. However, this was not the time to worry about minor details.

'What should I do?' she asked, in a worried voice.

'First of all, lock yourself securely in wherever you are,' Smith told her. 'Make sure all doors and windows are shut. With that scent all over you, those dogs would cross burning coals to get at you. Leave the line open by keeping the receiver off the hook and I'll put a trace on this number. As soon as I get a fix on you, I'll try to call in a rescue helicopter. Now, is that understood?'

'I get the message, but I don't understand,' Amanda told him flatly. Bugged lines, telephone traces and rescue helicopters were all a bit outside her normal range of experience. Nevertheless, she did as she was told, putting the receiver down on the kitchen table and going around the house to check all the doors and windows. Finally satisfied that she was securely locked in, she sat down at the kitchen table and relaxed, at last able to review the strange goings-on rationally.

However, the harder she tried to think, the more confusing things became. The whole mystery of Mr Smith flatly refused to make any sort of sense. Finally,

Amanda found herself musing over some of his last words to her.

So the hounds would follow her anywhere? No doubt leaving a trail of bedlam and destruction in their wake. And where they went, the entire posse of the hunt would follow.

A sudden desire for revenge against Jack and his nasty little bunch flared into being – along with the faint stirrings of a wicked little plan to achieve it. Amanda realised for the first time that she could in fact turn the tables on her tormentors. She had a small private army of hounds and horsemen at her disposal. Led in the right direction, they could easily become a demolition squad.

As the plan gelled, Amanda began to smile to herself. Decided at last, she unbolted the farmhouse door again and ran out into the courtyard, heading for the horseboxes.

To hell with the problem of multiple orgasms! Amanda could only pray that her Bartholine glands packed up before the rest of her body did.

She opened the first stall and led out a fine-looking chestnut mare. There was no saddle, but it did have a nice bushy mane to cling on to. And perhaps her problem would not be quite so acute riding bareback.

Using the bottom of the stall gate as a step-up, Amanda threw herself into position on the mare's broad back.

Jack and his cronies had expected her to lay a false trail for them – and Amanda intended to do exactly that. A trail of havoc and destruction which would make them all regret the day they had tried to cross Amanda Redfern.

Chapter Thirteen

Roger and Letitia had reached the next address on their debt collection rota. Through the curtained windows, Cynthia Smyth-Ffinch watched their progress up the long gravel drive with an expectant smile on her face. She had deliberately not sent off her regular monthly hush-money knowing that they would call for personal collection. Which meant that she would get an extra helping of young Roger's very special talents. Her hungry cunt twitched and tingled at the delicious prospect. Her love juices were already starting to flow as she headed for the front door to let in her most welcome visitors.

'Ah, Roger,' she cooed with delight. 'How lovely to see you and your charming partner. I expect you've come to tick me off for not sending off my donation to your little charity on time.'

Roger gage her a chiding, but faintly amused look. He had already cottoned on to the little game Cynthia intended playing.

'Yes, you've been a very naughty girl, Cynthia,' he said, with mock severity, noting how the middle-aged woman positively shivered with pleasure at the term 'girl'. Actually, for forty-six, Cynthia Smyth-Ffinch was in extremely good condition, physically. Although running towards the plump side, her well-developed breasts were still shapely and firm to the touch, and her large, thick-lipped cunt could still exert a powerful contracting grip on his cock. With Cynthia, there was still an appreciable degree of pleasure in his business.

Cynthia continued her little ploy. 'Well, as you've taken the trouble to call personally, it's only right that I should make it a little extra this month,' she said. 'Perhaps you'd like to come upstairs with me for a moment, I seem to have left my cheque book in the bedroom.'

Roger cast a sly smile aside to Letitia, whose eyes flashed with amusement.

'I'll just make myself comfortable here,' she said, heading for the nearest comfortable armchair and sitting down.

Roger followed Cynthia out of the room towards the stairs, his cock already starting to harden inside his trousers at the sight of the woman's plump arse wobbling in front of him.

Once in the privacy of the bedroom, all pretence ceased. Cynthia quickly unbuckled the waist fastening of her skirt and dropped it to the floor, stepping clear and reaching up behind her back to undo the buttons of her blouse.

Discarding that, she unclasped her brassiere and let her large breasts swing free, standing there clad only in a pair of skimpy black panties. Roger regarded her with mounting enthusiasm, noting the soft whiteness of her belly with the large V of springy brown curls below it showing clearly through the thin material of the panties. Dropping to his knees on the floor, he inserted his fingers into the elasticated top of the panties and began to roll the garment down slowly towards Cynthia's knees. Bending forward, he kissed the inside of her fleshy thighs, causing the older woman to shudder with pleasure.

Rising to his feet, he bounced the two dangling and enticing breasts in his palms, lifting them upwards and outwards so that the jutting brown nipples stuck out like two tempting ripe fruits. Kissing each in turn, Roger concentrated his attention on just one firm bud, sucking it gently between his lips and wiggling his tongue over it until he could feel it stiffen and extend inside his mouth.

Cynthia was easily aroused. It took only a couple of seconds of this treatment before she was breathing deeply, and a pink flush had started to spread over her face and neck. She backed away towards the big double bed, sinking down on to it and lying there expectantly, her thighs slightly parted.

Roger undressed himself in double-quick time. There was no point to any extended love play or coy game playing. They were both fully aware of exactly what was required, and time was money, after all. Naked, Roger moved to the side of the bed and knelt down, his eyes now on a level with Cynthia's lush and willing body. He reached over to lay his hand flat upon her belly, beginning a slow stroking motion with his fingertips.

Cynthia sighed deeply with satisfaction.

'Oh, I do like that,' she murmured appreciatively.

Roger moved his hand slowly down towards her chubby thighs, his fingers curling over their roundness into the warm and slightly moist valley between.

Cynthia shuddered with pleasure and spread her thighs, making contented little sounds in her throat. Roger played with the thick lips of her cunt for a few moments, stroking and tickling the pulsing bud of her clitoris without making any attempt to venture into the hot and oozing cunt behind it. The violent trembling of Cynthia's body told Roger that she was already hovering on the edge of a climax. He would only have to slip one finger into her slippery slit and she would come at once, gushing over his hand. Roger decided to give her a bit of a run for her money. Withdrawing his hand, he jumped to his feet and ran across the bedroom to her clothes drawer, pulling it open and rummaging about until he had found what he needed.

'What are you doing?' Cynthia wanted to know as Roger returned to the bedside with two pairs of tights in his hands.

Roger did not answer. Throwing himself on to the bed on top of her so that she was pressed down with his body weight, he seized her hands and lifted them

170

above her head, quickly binding them tightly together with one of the pairs of tights. Then, sliding off her, he moved to the bottom of the bed and began to tie the second pair of tights to her ankle, finally looping them round the leg of the bed and lashing them tight.

Cynthia's eyes twinkled with the excitement of this new game – but she played her part with relish.

'What are you going to do to me?' she cried out, managing to inject a pretence of fear into her voice.

Still saying nothing, Roger quickly retrieved her blouse from the floor and used that to bind her second ankle to the bed, so that she was effectively pinioned down.

Only then did he stand back and answer her questions.

'I'm going to ravish your beautiful body,' he announced. 'Now that you are tied up and helpless, I am going to have you time and time again, until you scream out for mercy.'

Cynthia feasted her eyes on the sight of Roger's huge, throbbing cock standing proudly against his flat belly. Although the prospect of having it rammed up her hot cunt was actually more than welcome, she nevertheless did her best to enter the spirit of the play-acting. She opened her eyes wide in mock horror.

'Oh, please. You can't put that great thing into my tiny, tight little hole,' she pleaded. 'It's far too big. You'll split my belly wide open.'

Roger took his stiff cock in his hand, rubbing it up and down and waving it at her.

Cynthia watched his fingers moving rapidly over his engorged shaft, and feared that the beautiful weapon would shoot its delicious cream before it got into her.

'You'll have to put it into my mouth,' she suggested. 'It's far too big to go into my cunt.'

Roger grinned wickedly. 'I might do that after I've given you a good fucking,' he promised. 'But first I am going to ram this so deep inside you it will make your eyeballs pop.'

With this, Roger began to advance upon the supposedly helpless woman, still waggling his erect prick like an offensive weapon. Cynthia began to make little whimpering noises – although whether they were of excitement or feigned terror, Roger could not be sure.

Roger reached the edge of the bed and threw himself on to it, jumping into position on top of Cynthia's prostrate body. Still holding his massive prick in his hand, he guided the tip of it down to the open crack of her creaming cunt and pressed it into position before lunging forward with a savage thrust of his hips.

His distended length slid into her deep, hot wetness without a trace of resistance. Roger's stomach slapped against Cynthia's, his heavy balls making a wet smacking sound against her crotch where her copious juices had dripped from her oozing slit. Cynthia let out a shrill cry and went into a shivering convulsive fit, her eyes rolling wildly and her mouth hanging slackly open. Saliva frothed out of the corners of her lips and ran down to her chin.

Roger thrust into her savagely, making no attempt to control himself or his own imminent release. In seconds, he had reached bursting point, and now making his own wild screaming noises, he pumped his lust into her belly. Feeling weak and spent, he flopped against her, his head on her soft breasts.

'Bite them,' Cynthia murmured. 'Bite my breasts. Sink your sharp teeth into my soft tits. Nibble at my nipples.'

She began to squirm her belly against his, uncomfortably aware that in the excitement of the sex game, Roger's own needs had taken over and he had failed to satisfy her. It was not what she paid for.

'I've got a better idea,' Roger said, forcing himself to sit up. He slid his bottom along Cynthia's stomach until his limp prick lay between her creamy tits. 'Now, here's something for you to nibble on instead.'

Cynthia responded to the invitation with total enthusiasm, raising her head from the bed and sticking out her wet tongue to lick the sticky end of his wilted weapon. With her hands still tied, she reached down and cradled its spent softness in her cupped fingers, lifting it gently into a more accessible position.

Roger wriggled forwards until he was sitting directly on the soft cushion of Cynthia's well-padded tits. He bent over, quickly untying her wrists and stuffing a pillow beneath her head, propping it up.

Cynthia set about her unexpected treat with gusto, licking his balls with slurping, wet strokes of her tongue and tasting the tangy juice of her own secretions. Her hands now free, she scooped up the whole soft bundle of cock and dangling balls and pulled them gently towards her mouth, her tongue lashing the entire apparatus with the speed and agility of a snake.

Roger thrust his hips further forwards, reaching back at the same time to slip one hand between Cynthia's burning thighs and probe for her dripping crack. Inserting first two and then four bunched fingers into the slimy cavern, he rolled his wrist around in a circular, pumping action which soon had Cynthia's legs vibrating and kicking wildly with excitement.

Cynthia's mouth was drooling with saliva as she continued to lap vigorously at his cock and balls. Roger's prick began to inflate again from the effect of the warm and wet caresses – a little bonus soon noticed and appreciated by Cynthia, who withdrew her lashing tongue and sucked the slowly stiffening member deep into her mouth. Using her lips, she pressed and squeezed the semi-flaccid flesh while she pulled in little gasps of breath that sucked it further into her throat.

These oral ministrations soon had their desired effect. Cynthia started to gag as Roger's cock regained its former pulsating glory. Roger began to feel the thrill of genuine sexual desire flowing through his loins again – for what Cynthia might lack in terms of youth or beauty, she more than compensated for in sheer enthusiasm.

Pulling back, Roger let his engorged cock nestle in the valley between her breasts for a few moments, giving Cynthia the choice of whether she wanted to continue sucking it or not. He kept up his own plunging attention to her gushing cunt, confident that now his prick was primed up again, it would stay that way until needed.

Cynthia took advantage of the brief respite to analyse her own desires. She appreciated Roger giving her the choice, although it presented her with something of a dilemma. While she would be more than happy to continue sucking on his delicious cock, her cunt was undeniably hungry and her inner being screamed out for the sheer physical release of orgasm. It was a question of which end had the greatest need.

Her cunt won out, finally. 'Fuck me,' she grunted, a plea rather than a command. 'Fuck me until my whole body explodes.'

It wasn't the sort of invitation any man could turn down. Roger slid down her belly and thrust her thighs apart with his knees. His stiff cock found its own way to her gaping crack like a laser-guided missile, and one forward lunge sheathed it deep into its silo housing.

Cynthia went into a series of minor convulsions almost immediately, thrusting up wildly with her hips as Roger slid his throbbing tool in and out of her well-oiled passage with slow, deep and totally penetrating strokes.

Cynthia's cunt began to milk at his cock, a slowly building series of clenching, squeezing spasms that seemed to suck up his inner juices all the way from the deep reservoir of his balls. Roger groaned softly as the older woman wrapped her arms around his back, hugging him to her tightly as she gave in gratefully to her rising orgasm and allowed it to pulsate through her entire body.

Finally, as Cynthia's arms contracted around him with a force that almost took his breath away, Roger surrendered to the inevitable. He didn't so much shoot his load as have it pumped out of him – only to feel it all sprayed back over his belly and balls as Cynthia's sexual dam burst and gushed forth a boiling torrent of liquid.

Chapter Fourteen

Amanda resisted the temptation to yell out 'Hi ho Silver' as she grabbed a handful of mane and spurred her mount into movement with a kick of her heels. The mare shied briefly, obviously not too sure about its bareback rider, then obediently broke into a gentle trot.

A strange little shiver started up between Amanda's thighs almost at once. The next few minutes were going to be tough, she realised. She tried to stall the mounting tension by forcing herself to think of all the nasty things she would like to do to Jack and his gang.

The horse seemed controllable enough, and quite content to proceed at a trotting pace. That was one little blessing, Amanda reflected, since she suspected that anything over a canter would soon have her coming like a North Sea gusher. Pulling on her mount's mane in lieu of reins, she was just about able to get it to change direction. She headed back towards the Flatfield Farm area, confident that the anti-hunt brigade would have left the place by now to do a bit of banner waving.

Mental concentration was not a total answer, Amanda soon realised. The friction and stimulation against her pelvic area was too strong to be ignored. Amanda gave up after the first orgasmic wave rippled through her belly and decided to just sit back and enjoy it.

Amanda's panties were already soaked through by the time she reached the farm. She pulled her mount to a halt, reviewing the scene and thinking carefully about her plan of action. Although part of her was a little squeamish about unleashing havoc on the place, the fact remained that the owner of the place obviously had to be in league with Jack's nasty little bunch, and therefore deserved an equal share in the punishment. Amanda's eyes fell upon a field of tall barley. It would make a fine start.

In the distance, the faint sound of baying hounds could be heard. Amanda kicked her mount into motion again, heading for the barley field. The hounds would be expecting a trail to follow. So it made sense to give them a strong one, Amanda thought. Gripping the horse tightly with her knees, she took one hand off its mane and tore at the thin material of her blouse. The material ripped easily, as though the foul fox-scent chemicals had already started to rot the fabric. Tearing it into little shreds, Amanda began to drop little scraps to the ground. Even a one-eyed poodle with a head cold ought to be able to follow that trail without any difficulty.

She trotted into the waving barley, guiding the

mare in a winding, figure-of-eight pattern across the field and then back again. Amanda smirked with satisfaction. When the hounds and their attendant riders had done their work, there wouldn't be many of the proud stalks still standing.

Next stop was the chicken area. Amanda rode around it several times, dropping scented scraps of cloth in a dozen strategic places. With luck, the birds would be laying addled eggs for a month after a pack of noisy, frantic hounds had frightened the wits out of them. Amanda proceeded to the milking sheds, and then on to the fields where the cows were pastured. Thoughtfully, she opened every gate as she passed it, giving the animals total freedom to escape the hound pack. A minor stampede in the general area would probably do just as much damage as the dogs and riders.

One more trot round the perimeters of the farmyard and that seemed to be that, Amanda thought with satisfaction. Unless . . .

She pulled the horse to a halt in front of the farmhouse and dismounted. Walking up to the front door, Amanda tried the handle. She was in luck. Just as she had hoped, the country code of leaving doors unlocked seemed to be a fairly general habit.

Amanda ran through the house in a delirious madness, climbing over the furniture, dropping scraps of her blouse next to every breakable object she could set her eyes on. Finally, she ventured upstairs to the bedrooms and covered them before returning to the kitchen. Her eyes fell upon a tall Welsh dresser, loaded up with expensive-looking crockery, china and glassware. Tearing off her last tattered sleeve, she tucked it carefully behind a china ornament on the top shelf before stepping out into the yard again, leaving the door wide open behind her.

Amanda was now naked from the waist up, having shredded her blouse completely. There was only one way to continue laying the trail. Shrugging philosophically, she peeled off her skirt and ripped it into thin strips before struggling back on top of the horse with the help of a handy upturned bucket.

Like some latter-day Lady Godiva, she set off again in the direction of Jack's garage and the village of Amesford. However, Amanda personally doubted that Lady Godiva had had quite so much pleasure out of her ride. Certainly nothing in the history books suggested that she had experienced minor orgasms every two or three minutes during the course of her naked protest!

Leaving the perimeter of the farm, Amanda pulled her mount in briefly to look back and review her work. The pack of hounds were in plain view now, and had reached the barley field. Even from a distance, Amanda could see the rippling waves of canine vandalism as the frantic dogs rushed through the swaying stalks in pursuit of the scented trail. Amanda watched their destructive progress for a few seconds with a satisfied smile playing about her lips. More than pleased with her efforts, she set off again on the next stage of her quest.

Amanda reached Jack's garage. It was, unfortunately, closed but there were several highly polished and gleaming second-hand cars for sale on open display in the courtyard. Amanda glided the horse around each in turn, carefully wiping each bonnet and roof with a strip of her scent-impregnated skirt. The combined damage of dozens of sharp little claws ought to have quite an effect on their resale value, Amanda thought. Behind the garage was a large allotment, all laid out neatly with rows of vegetables. Clearly, Jack had a little sideline in fresh garden produce. A few moments of trail laying ensured that the pursuing pack would shortly be reducing the whole area to a muddy shambles.

Amanda was now down to just one last strip of cloth, and she wasn't quite ready to bring her trail to an end. Dismounting again, she tied the last strips to the end of the mare's long, flowing tail so that it just brushed against the ground. Stripping off her panties, now dripping with a heady mixture of come and fox scent, she climbed back on to her trusty steed.

Almost immediately, she realised her mistake. Fully clothed, the clitoral stimulation of riding was enough to reduce her to a randy wreck. Completely naked, the hair to hair contact of her pubic regions with the horse's back increased the stimulation tenfold. Amanda could feel the wetness pouring out of her as she rode on towards the village. The frequency of her orgasmic spasms increased with every step, until she was virtually in a permanent state of orgasmic tremor. Her legs felt like two dangling lumps of jelly, quivering and twitching with each new shock wave that shuddered down from her crotch area.

Losing control by the second, Amanda could only cling on to her horse's mane with both hands and pray that she would find her own way through the village. Unfortunately it chose to take a short cut through a bridle path which it obviously knew, and suddenly Amanda found herself riding through rough countryside. The horse, coming upon familiar territory, recognised a particular stretch where the riders who frequented its stables invariably urged it into a canter. Deprived of any firm control or orders to the contrary, the mare obliged automatically, breaking step and taking up the pace.

Amanda rose high in the air and jarred down again on to the horse's back with a shock that travelled right up through her pelvis and into her spinal column. Somehow, that shock finished her off. After countless minor orgasms, the big one built up into a sudden, surging wave which ripped through her entire body and exploded into a nerve-shattering climax. Amanda screamed out as a total sensation of all-consuming sexual pleasure washed through her, making her tremble and shiver like a plague victim. Weak, and totally exhausted, she could only flop across her steed's broad back and throw her arms around its neck for support. Hanging on for grim death, she managed to focus her eyes for just long enough to see that the horse was heading back in the general direction of Paradise.

Amanda practically fell off the horse's back as it neared the club grounds. Using the last of her strength, she gave it a hearty slap on the rump which sent it galloping off in the direction of Flatfield Farm.

She trudged wearily up the drive, across the lawn and towards the club's outdoor swimming pool. Luckily, it was empty. Thankfully, Amanda dived in, rubbing her body with both hands and thrashing about as much as her depleted energy reserves would allow so that the chlorinated water could wash away the last traces of the fox scent. Amanda reminded herself to arrange for the pool to be drained and cleaned in the morning.

From the safety of the pool, Amanda watched as a howling, baying pack of hounds tore through the front gates, bounded across the lawns and took off again in pursuit of her abandoned steed. Some minutes later, a rather bemused group of riders arrived, realised that they were about to trespass on private property and backed away, wondering where their dogs had disappeared to.

Amanda was still floating lazily on her back in the water when a police car turned into the drive and drove towards the house. As the car stopped, and the driver climbed out, Amanda recognised Constable

Harris, who had come to her aid before over the Anti-Vice League demonstration at the club.

Amanda waved to him. 'Hi,' she called, brightly.

Constable Harris looked far from bright as he walked over to her. In fact, he looked distinctly pissed off.

'Oh boy, you've really done it this time, haven't you?' he said, standing on the edge of the pool. 'Stealing a horse, malicious damage, indecent exposure, breaking and entering, causing a public nuisance – and a few more charges they haven't got names for.'

Amanda didn't seem too worried. She was pretty sure that Jack and his cronies would not be too keen to press charges. As for the rest of it, well, she could always sweeten up David Harris, she was sure. After his seduction by the gorgeous Caroline on his previous trip to the club, he had shown himself to be more than a little susceptible to a bit of police corruption.

Amanda started to clamber out of the pool, pointing to a pile of towels on a nearby table.

'"Would you be a darling and pass me one of those towels, please?' she purred, sucking in her breath and puffing out her chest to make her tits stand out even more prominently.

Constable Harris averted his eyes. 'Miss Redfern, you are not going to screw your way out of trouble this time,' he warned.

Amanda looked at him innocently. 'I really don't know what you're suggesting, officer. I was merely going to suggest that you come into the house while I make a statement.'

Harris shook his head fervently. 'No way. The only time I'll set foot inside this place again is in the company of half a dozen homosexual chief inspectors.'

'OK, have it your way then.' Amanda squatted down on the grass, still bare-assed naked. 'We'll talk here, then.'

Constable Harris's mouth opened and closed a few times in a passable imitation of a goldfish. His eyes darted from side to side, in case there was anyone watching.

'I can't just stand here in full uniform talking to a totally naked woman,' he protested.

Amanda smiled sweetly. 'Well I suppose you could always take your clothes off and pretend you're in a nudist camp,' she suggested.

Harris drew himself up to his full height. 'Miss Redfern – as an officer of the law, I order you to cover yourself up immediately.'

His action had thrown the tight front of his trousers into sharp relief, revealing the growing bulge under the blue material. Amanda pointed to it and giggled.

'You're getting a hard-on,' she pointed out bluntly. 'Either that or you carry your truncheon in a very strange place.'

Harris began to perspire. 'Miss Redfern, are you going to act responsibly, or do I have to drag you down to the police station as you are?'

'That won't be necessary,' said a deep baritone voice suddenly.

Amanda and Constable Harris whirled round to confront the mysterious Mr Smith, who had somehow managed to sneak up behind them both without a sound.

He walked up to the policeman, producing something from his pocket and flashed it briefly under his nose.

'All charges against Miss Redfern will be dropped,' Smith said in a commanding voice. 'You may safely leave the matter in my hands, constable.'

To Amanda's amazement, Harris turned on his heel and walked away without a word. Returning to his police car, he drove away.

Smith picked up a towel and draped it around Amanda's body. 'Shall we go inside?' he suggested, although it sounded more like a direct order.

Chapter Fifteen

'I expect you could do with a good stiff drink after your ordeal, Miss Redfern,' Smith said as they walked in to the house.

Amanda managed a smile, despite her sense of total confusion.

'Believe me, that's about the only stiff thing I could cope with right now,' she murmured.

Smith shot her a strange look. 'I hope you don't think I'm trying to proposition you, Miss Redfern,' he said, a little awkwardly. 'The very last thing I want or need is to actually get involved in any of the sexual activity that seems to go on around here.'

The man seemed genuinely embarrassed. Amanda clutched his arm, giving it a friendly squeeze.

'Look, just relax. Don't be so stuffy. And call me Amanda, please. I hate all that Miss Redfern stuff.'

They had reached the bar. There was no one on duty. Amanda took it upon herself to serve drinks for both of them, then joined Smith at one of the tables. She sipped her vodka martini, eyeing Smith over the top of the glass.

'So – what exactly is going on, Mr Smith, or

whatever your real name is?'

Smith tried to bluster. 'I haven't the faintest idea what you're talking about.'

Amanda wasn't having any of that. She was determined to get to the heart of the mystery once and for all.

'Spy cameras, snooping about the grounds and climbing trees, bugged telephones, rescue helicopters, and now your apparent ability to give orders to policemen,' Amanda recounted. 'So, let's try again. What's going on, and what are you actually doing here?'

Smith's eyes narrowed. 'You're a very perceptive young lady . . . Amanda,' he said, his voice softening but still cautious. 'You're right, of course. I'm not here just as a casual visitor.'

Smith broke off and actually managed a faint smile. He extended his hand over the table. 'Martin – Martin Pugh.'

Amanda accepted the proffered handshake. 'My first guess was that you were some sort of private eye,' she said. 'But it's a bit deeper than that, isn't it?'

Pugh nodded. He reached into his pocket and withdrew the same small plastic wallet that he had shown to Constable Harris. He opened it, flashing the official-looking card inside. Amanda was impressed.

'As you see, I am with the Security Services,' Pugh admitted. 'Which particular department isn't important. What is important is that my business here is of vital importance to national security, and merely showing you this card places you under a Grade Two security oath. Should you repeat anything that I reveal to you, you could be found guilty of treasonous activities and face a very severe prison sentence.'

Amanda managed a rueful smile. 'I wish I'd never asked,' she muttered.

Pugh smiled comfortingly. 'So do I,' he said in a kindly voice. 'But since you did, and as you had already started to put together potentially disruptive theories about me, I have no choice but to take you into my confidence. I have already satisfied myself that you are innocent of any direct involvement in what might be happening here. It would seem you are in fact about to become a victim, if my guess is correct.'

Amanda was already starting to piece the jigsaw together in her head.

'It's this sex clinic thing, isn't it?' she asked.

Pugh nodded again. He motioned to Amanda's glass. 'Finish your drink. There's something I want to show you up in my room.'

Amanda threw down the last of her vodka martini. She stood up, forcing a grin. 'If I didn't believe you, I'd say that was one of the corniest old chat-up lines in the business,' she said.

She followed Pugh up to his room. He slid a briefcase out from underneath the bed, taking out a video cassette, which he slipped into the playback unit. Before switching it on, he looked directly at Amanda.

'What you are going to see contains some extremely explicit material,' he warned her. 'I assume that it is safe for me to regard you as a young woman of extremely broad-minded tastes?'

'Oh, I think it's safe to say that a few blue movies aren't going to make me blush,' Amanda agreed.

Nodding, Pugh thumbed the remote-control button. On the monitor, a full-scale orgy scene clicked into view.

Amanda watched with prurient fascination as the camera closed in on a woman, probably in her late thirties. She was kneeling on a carpeted floor, sitting back on her haunches with her thighs spread wide apart and a huge rubber dildo clasped tightly in her hand. Slowly, she brought the swollen, bulbous head of the gigantic false prick to her fleshy cunt lips and rubbed it into the glistening crevice of her fanny, coating it with her own slimy secretions. Then, taking the twelve-inch monster in a two-handed grip like some sort of sacrificial sword, she raised it high in the air and then plunged it down into her cunt as though she were committing sexual hara-kiri.

The woman's eyes opened wide with a mixture of shock and pleasure as the huge rubber shaft tore into her belly. Her mouth dropped open, her tongue pushing out a wash of spittle which dribbled down her chin. She continued to work the dildo in and out of her cunt for several seconds, pulling it this way and that, up and down as it slid between her gaping cunt lips. After a while, she withdrew the cock-shaped object from her cunt and raised it to her mouth, dripping with her own flowing juices. Lovingly, almost reverently, she pushed it between her red lips, working it slowly into her mouth until her cheeks bulged around its exaggerated thickness.

Then it was back to her cunt again, still using the two-handed, dagger-like grip and the violent gestures which made the whole operation look like some weird, masochistic ritual.

A naked man stepped into the picture, standing in front of the woman with his stiff prick a few inches from her mouth. Still thrusting the dildo furiously in and out of her sopping fanny, the woman reached forward with her mouth receptively open, eager to take the real cock between her lips. The man stepped back slightly, teasing her, forcing her to reach for her fleshy, gently throbbing prize. Finally, the man stepped forwards again, seizing the woman's long black hair and pulling her face on to his cock with a savage, almost sadistic gesture. Pumping his hips, he fucked her mouth for nearly a minute, finally pulling his cock out at the last moment and pumping thick gobbets of sperm into her face.

Pugh stopped the tape. 'Well?' he said to Amanda.

Amanda shrugged, not quite sure what was expected of her.

'It's pretty sordid – nasty even,' she conceded. 'But

basically, it's just another porno movie, surely?'

'Not quite,' Pugh told her. 'The woman you saw there just happens to be the wife of a government minister who holds a fairly high, and extremely sensitive, cabinet position.'

He fast-forwarded the film, stopping it at another scene which showed a naked man crouching like a dog, licking at two exposed pricks while another man savagely fucked his arse from behind.

'And that man is a diplomat from a Middle East embassy in London,' Pugh informed Amanda. 'These are just two examples of the potential dynamite your friend Roger Vennings and his partner have in their possession.'

He switched off the video. 'As you may already have gathered, Vennings has been using the cover of his sex clinic as the basis for a blackmail racket. They specialise in entrapping powerful and influential people, many of whom are politically sensitive. I expect you're too young to remember the Christine Keeler affair, aren't you?'

'I saw the film *Scandal*,' Amanda put in brightly.

'Then you know that affairs like this can bring down governments,' Pugh said. 'Not only that, they can be turned to the advantage of some of the most ruthless and possibly insane people in this world.'

Amanda shook her head incredulously. 'You're not telling me that Roger has got himself involved in international espionage,' she said in disbelief. 'He's basically just a small-time con man looking for a quick buck.'

'Oh, I agree,' Pugh answered her. 'At the moment. That's why I have to close him down now, before he, or somebody else, realises the true potential of the situation he has inadvertently set up. To be perfectly blunt, my department has already identified three people hooked into this sex and blackmail racket who could, if put under sufficient pressure, make it possible for high-tech military secrets to be passed to one of the most dangerous regimes in the world today.'

Amanda was silent for a moment, taking in the full significance of these revelations.

'And I suppose that you are only telling me all this because you need my help,' she ventured finally.

Pugh nodded emphatically. 'I am going to need your fullest cooperation,' he confirmed.

'Do I have any choice?' Amanda asked.

Pugh smiled thinly. 'About twenty-five years in Holloway as an accessory if you refuse,' he said bluntly.

It didn't take a lot of thinking about.

'I guess you just got yourself a deputy,' she told Pugh. 'Do I have to swear an oath of allegiance, or anything like that?'

'That won't be necessary,' he told her. 'I'll just settle for your silence and the full facilities of this club to set a trap for our blackmailing little friends. I rather thought we could use the Hunt Ball as a cover for our operation – what do you think?'

Amanda sucked her breath in through her teeth.

'I think it's going to be one hell of a night,' she observed.

Chapter Sixteen

Charles was exceedingly worried, tormented by inner fears that he was suddenly turning into a closet homosexual. For nearly twenty-four hours now, the only sexual image that he had been able to think of was Bernard's tight little arsehole, and it was causing him severe inner anxiety. Even worse, he had actually considered going back to the kitchen for another helping of that particular dish on more than one occasion.

What he needed, Charles had decided, was a good heterosexual screwing. The problem was, finding one. Sally seemed to have gone off the boil completely, her every free minute completely monopolised by the sexually recharged Andrew.

He had tried digging out his private collection of porno magazines and wanking over various images of naked women – naked women making love to other naked women and naked women masturbating themselves while watching other naked women making love to other naked women.

None had helped. Whatever half-hearted erection he had managed to gain invariably wilted as soon as he touched his own cock. The only thing that produced a really stiff hard-on was the thought of fucking a little chef's arse.

The idea of doing this for the rest of his life seemed boring in the extreme.

Charles wondered whether he could hold out until the evening, when he might make some excuse to go off sick and persuade one of the club's girls to give him a good servicing in exchange for the promise of free drinks over the bar for a couple of nights. While the plan had its definite plus points, it left an uncomfortably long time to wait, and his need was right now.

However, as the only real possibility, Charles occupied his thoughts with finding something to do to fill in the time until this plan could be put into operation.

A sauna and shower might be nice, he thought suddenly . . . and at that very same instant, a revelation struck him with the force of a lightning bolt. Freda!

Thinking of a sauna had triggered off associated thoughts on the one female in the building who had been left out of his equations. Although she was a trifle on the Amazonian side for his particular taste, Freda was undeniably woman-shaped, with tits, a cunt and all the other requisite parts for a serious fucking session. Even more importantly, she was reported to be permanently horny and would, apparently, fuck anything on two legs.

196

His confidence suddenly and magically restored, Charles headed for the massage parlour.

As it happened, Freda was herself reviewing her sex life at that very moment, and coming to similar conclusions about her recent mating activities. Her most recent session with Roger and Letitia had triggered off a chain of reflective thoughts and doubts which had left her wondering whether she was doomed to spend the rest of her life being a sort of regular fall-back for every bizarre group sex combination other people could dream up. It seemed to Freda that it was many years since she actually had a man of her very own, who just wanted to make love to her on a purely personal level, without either someone else watching, someone else taking part, or someone else taking over halfway through the proceedings. It might be nice, Freda considered, to have a single man who would actually fuck her from start to finish in a reasonably straight fashion – and even perhaps do it again afterwards.

So Charles was in fact stepping into a seething hotbed of unrequited passion as he ventured into the massage room hoping for nothing more complicated than a quick screw.

Freda mouthed a silent prayer to ancient Norse gods as he strolled into her life. At first glance, Charles had all the basic requirements for a partner in a meaningful relationship. For a start he was male, the right side of fifty, not bad looking and surprisingly normal in his general appearance. In fact, Freda thought, he seemed almost shy, perhaps even somewhat inhibited. That was certainly something she could put right.

Desperate to get things off to a promising start, Freda dug deep into her fairly basic knowledge of the English language and attempted communication.

'What you wanting, plis?' she asked, with a beaming smile.

As usual, Freda had her crisp white pseudo-nurse's uniform unbuttoned to the waist so that her delectable and mind-boggling breasts were on full display. Like many men before him, Charles was so taken with the sight of those huge and creamy orbs that his mouth went quite dry.

'I . . . I was wondering . . . if you might consider letting me make love to you,' he managed to stammer out at last.

Most of the words went over Freda's head, but she latched on to the single word 'love'. Her mighty heart surged. It was too good to be true, yet it seemed that her prayers had been answered. Still, it seemed sensible to check.

'Lof? You want lof?' she asked Charles, a trifle incredulously.

Charles nodded. 'If that's all right by you.'

Freda's joy knew no bounds. Pausing only to strip off her uniform like a snake sheds its skin, she advanced on Charles like a female spider stalking its mate. Totally mesmerised by the sight of her lush body, Charles failed to notice the rather strange gleam in her eyes as she swept over him like a tidal wave, her muscular arms wrapping around his neck and hugging him in a lung-crushing embrace against her soft breasts.

Freda's ripe, full lips slobbered over his face, kissing his lips, nose, eyes and ears.

'I gif you lof,' Freda breathed, passionately. She dragged Charles to the floor of the massage room, still kissing him with total abandonment. Her strong fingers tore at his shirt, saving the precious time that would have been taken up undoing buttons by simply ripping the material away from his chest and shoulders in tattered shreds. The waistband and zipper of Charles's trousers quickly went the same way, the ruined garment was tossed aside as Freda stripped off his shoes, socks and underpants.

Moaning like a cow in labour, Freda threw herself across the now naked Charles, her weight pinning him to the floor.

She kissed him full on the mouth again, her hot and highly mobile tongue snaking into his mouth to stir their joint saliva into a froth. Still moaning with passion, Freda turned her attention to his chest, licking each small nipple in turn and planting kisses in a random pattern all the way down to his bellybutton.

Pinned down as he was, there wasn't much Charles could do, either to add to or control the pace of Freda's lovemaking. Wisely, he decided to merely lay back and enjoy it.

And enjoy it he certainly did. Charles shivered with pleasure as Freda's hot mouth devoured his body, finding strange and unfamiliar places where the brush of her lips or the warm wetness of her tongue could make his flesh quiver and his heart pound in his chest. Freda rammed her blonde head between his thighs, licking his groin on either side of his balls, the tip of her long tongue sometimes darting down until it nearly touched his arse. Her huge, soft breasts waggled deliciously against his bare belly, the stiff, prominent red nipples tracing lines of fire across his flesh.

Charles felt his cock swelling as though it were being pumped up with a pressure hose. In a matter of seconds, he had a throbbing erection which was physically painful, as heated blood was superfed into an organ which just couldn't take any more.

His high-pressure hard-on was not lost on Freda, who eyed it with undisguised hunger. She quickly abandoned his thighs for more tasty fare, kissing his swollen balls then running her tongue up the pulsing underside of his stiff shaft with a slow, lapping stroke, finishing it off by a momentary suck of its shiny purple helmet. Charles let out a little grunt of pleasure, encouraging the obliging Freda to repeat the manoeuvre another half a dozen times.

Finally tiring of these hors d'oeuvres, Freda moved on to the main course. Pursing her full, soft lips, she began to kiss his cock all over, moving her head slowly up and down its engorged length so that she did not miss a single delicious inch.

Only when the entire weapon was glistening with traces of her saliva did Freda unpurse her lips. Grasping his quivering flagpole in one fist, she pulled it upright and slid her lips over its bulging head, sucking and licking at it like a fruit lollipop.

Charles watched the tip of his cock sliding in and out of her red lips with a thrill of pleasure. He wanted to move his buttocks from the floor, pump his hips and drive his cock deep into Freda's inviting mouth, but he bided his time, letting the Swedish girl take things at her own pace. It was not a bad decision. Freda took her hand away from the shaft of his cock now that it was safely installed between her lips. Reaching down to his balls, she began to tickle them gently with her fingertips as she continued to nibble and suck on the head of his cock.

Charles writhed in ecstasy at the dual sensation. There was an electric tingling feeling running up from his balls right into his belly which seemed to make his body jerk and twitch of its own accord.

Finally, just when Charles thought his aching cock was about to burst, Freda opened her mouth and plunged her head down upon the swollen thickness of its long shaft. She sucked greedily for a few moments until she started to gag, then came up for air again. She looked up at Charles, a beaming smile on her face.

'I lof you goot – no?'

Charles could only nod weakly, returning the

smile. He didn't want to waste any precious time on conversation. What he wanted was that wonderful hot mouth to swallow his stiff prick once again.

Freda, however, had other ideas. With an athletic bound, she threw her body around until she was in a top-to-tail position with Charles and then straddling his chest with her long, muscular legs. Freda flopped down, pressing her oozing cunt into Charles's face as she turned her own oral attention back to his dancing prick.

Charles gasped for air as Freda's hot fanny closed over his lips and nose. Her musky, feminine smell seemed to invade his whole being as he inhaled her odour and tasted her flowing juices in his mouth. He gulped, sucking down her slimy secretions as she wriggled her buttocks furiously, grinding the soft lips of her gaping slit against his face. Charles's tongue snaked into the dripping crevice, lapping up the fresh flow of juice and probing the soft folds of the inner ribbed walls of Freda's cunt.

The Swedish girl moaned softly, dropping her own wet mouth over his rearing prick, swallowing him completely until her lips were pressed into the wiry folds of his pubic hair. They lay together like two limpets, sucking desperately at each other until their lungs were bursting, before coming up for air by unspoken mutual consent.

Freda moved again, lifting herself and swivelling around with his cock still lodged in her mouth until she was kneeling on the floor between his stretched legs. She looked up at him, her eyes conveying a look of total love and dedication as she sucked his cock slowly, letting him see her mouth and lips moving up and down on the stiff shaft, and her huge tits jiggling between his thighs. Charles felt the muscles in his stomach contract with the sheer erotic intensity of it all, watching her lush red lips wrapped around his cock and feeling the gentle massage of her tongue and mouth around its throbbing thickness.

Freda gobbled him for several minutes, somehow being able to judge when he was nearing the point of orgasm and controlling it, prolonging the sweet ecstasy to the point of near-torture. Finally, when she sensed that he could hold out no longer, she let his stiff prick pop out from between her lips, rose up on to her knees and edged her way over him, holding her dripping cunt over his quivering cock.

She sank, slowly, on to the meaty shaft with a deep sigh of satisfaction. Charles groaned with pleasure as the soft, hot walls of her cunt seemed to close around his prick, sucking it into a moist, welcoming sheath that might have been precision designed to accommodate it.

While, admittedly, not having quite the tightness of the chef's arsehole, Freda's cunt was nevertheless a little marvel of nature in its own right. Charles shivered with sensual delight as Freda manipulated inner muscles to consume and cosset his prick, swallowing and seducing it at the same time.

There was no other way to describe it, Charles

thought. Freda's cunt was actually making love to his cock – kissing it with a hundred pairs of hot little lips, stroking and petting it with a dozen trembling fingers, hugging it in an embrace which was alternatively tender and torrid. It was a total and unique sensation which he had never felt with any woman before. The ridiculous thought surfaced in his mind that his cock and Freda's cunt were somehow destined to be together – like two lovers kept apart throughout time and eternity until this moment of rediscovery.

For Freda, it was a feeling of being utterly filled for the first time. Charles's beautiful cock was inside her – yet it also seemed to envelop and swallow her. With a dreamy smile on her face, Freda held out her arms to Charles as he, too, reached up to embrace her. She pulled him up to her, burying his face between her warm and wonderful tits as she rode his cock towards their mutual climax.

Charles whimpered, with a sense of almost child-like wonder, as he nestled into the comforting softness of Freda's magnificent breasts and felt his inner juices being sucked out of him. He came – not with a violent spasm, but with a prolonged pumping action which seemed to drain his whole body until it was completely empty. He began to cry softly, with the sudden knowledge that he had given something of himself away for ever.

Freda's heart surged within her mighty chest. She hugged him tightly, this man-child who was hers, totally, at last. She had taken his seed and given birth to him at the same time. The boiling gush of her orgasm was merely the afterbirth.

They lay together afterwards for nearly an hour. Finally Freda stood, reaching down with her powerful arms to haul the exhausted Charles to his feet.

'Come,' she breathed, gutturally. 'We go to my room to make lof.'

Nodding helplessly, Charles let her take his hand and lead him to his fate. There was nothing else, never again. He knew this, and it made him feel ecstatically happy and inestimably sad at the same time.

Chapter Seventeen

Sally broke the bad news in the morning, when Amanda came down for her breakfast coffee.

'We've got a problem,' she announced bluntly, seeing no reason to break things gently.

Amanda groaned. 'Tell me the worst.'

'Apparently Charles has eloped with Freda,' Sally said. 'So now we have no masseuse, only one barman, and the Hunt Ball is tonight.'

Amanda digested the information thoughtfully. Losing Freda was no immediate problem. The club could get by for a couple of days without her services. The sauna and exercise room would still be in operation, and somehow Amanda doubted that the horse and hound brigade would want to do much more than eat, drink and generally cavort the night away. The real problem was Charles. There was no way that Andrew would be able to cope on his own.

'Could we get in a couple of temporary staff for the night?' she suggested tentatively. 'Surely there's an agency or something locally.'

Sally shook her head. 'Not round here, there's not. I might be able to pull in a couple of sheep-shearers or a whole turnip-digging crew, but there's no way we could find an experienced barman by tonight.'

There was a long silence. 'Well, what do you think?' Sally asked, finally.

'I think it's going to be one hell of a night,' Amanda muttered, conscious even as she spoke that they were the very same words she had said to Martin Pugh the previous night.

Thinking of Pugh brought her other problem to mind – namely dealing with Roger and Letitia and their nasty little game. It also suggested a possible solution to both.

'I'm going upstairs to see our Mr Pugh,' Amanda said, finishing her coffee.

Sally looked at her in surprise. 'Who?'

'Pugh.'

'Who's Pugh?'

Amanda fell in. Of course, Sally still thought of him as Mr Smith. There didn't seem much point in trying to explain, and besides, she had been sworn to secrecy.

'Don't worry about it,' Amanda said, heading for the door.

Amanda knocked gently on Pugh's bedroom door. He opened it immediately. Too immediately, Amanda thought, and then realised that he must have been alerted by her footsteps coming up the stairs. He was certainly a most suspicious and fast-acting man.

Pugh smiled as he recognised his attractive visitor.

'Ah, Amanda. What a pleasant surprise. Come to see some more dirty movies, have you?'

'Bit early in the morning for me,' Amanda said, falling into the easy banter. 'Actually, I need to talk to you about tonight.'

'Come in.' Pugh stepped aside, ushering her into his room.

Amanda sat down on the edge of the bed. 'The thing is, Mr Pugh, I need to know how you plan to set up the trap you talked about last night. You did say you needed my complete cooperation, so I need to know exactly what you plan to do, and what you expect of me.'

Pugh sat himself down beside her. 'Martin,' he said. 'Just call me Martin. And in answer to your question, I have to admit that I haven't really formulated any hard-and-fast plans yet. To tell you the truth, I was going to play it a bit by ear.'

'What you really need is to be in a prominent position where you can see and hear just about everything that's going on,' Amanda suggested to him.

Martin nodded thoughtfully. 'Yes, that would help, no doubt.'

'Like behind the bar, for instance,' Amanda prompted.

Martin's eyes narrowed. 'What's going on in your devious little mind?' he wanted to know.

Amanda feigned innocence. 'Going on? I'm sure I don't know what you're talking about.'

Martin laughed. 'It seems to me that we've had

this conversation before, but with our roles reversed. I'm supposed to be the mystery man with nefarious little plots, remember?'

Amanda realised that it was no use trying to hedge around with Martin Pugh. She came straight to the point, explaining her problems.

'So I thought it might help us both out if you posed as a temporary barman,' she concluded, looking at him with a hopeful expression.

Martin considered the idea carefully. It did, he had to admit, have certain advantages. He would be on the spot, with an ear and an eye to everything that was going on. And, as a bonus, it was well known that people tended to open up a few of their secrets to barmen – particularly when they had had a few. So, seen from that viewpoint, it wasn't a bad idea at all. However, there was an obvious downside.

'But I have no experience of working behind a busy bar,' he pointed out.

Amanda shrugged. 'Nothing to it. Besides, I thought they trained you security boys to cope with all types of emergency situation.'

Martin smiled thinly. 'There's quite a bit of difference between making a Molotov cocktail to shaking up a gin sling,' he said.

Amanda could see that she had him half-interested. 'Then you'll do it?' she prompted.

Martin made one of those split-second decisions for which he had been expensively trained. 'Why not?' he agreed.

Amanda clapped her hands in glee. 'Terrific!' she exclaimed. 'I'll go and tell Andrew to expect you later on for a bit of basic training.'

She stood up to leave. Martin reached out, holding her arm. 'Just one thing,' he said. 'Your friend Venner and his partner. Neither of them have seen me before, so they won't suspect a thing. We are going to keep it that way, aren't we?'

Amanda nodded emphatically. 'Too right,' she muttered. 'After what you've told me, the sooner I get them both out of my hair the better.'

She danced off happily, to tell Sally that the immediate problem was solved.

Returning to the breakfast room, she had a bit of a shock seeing the two people in question sitting there, deep in conversation with Andrew and Sally. She put a brave face on, and moved over to join them.

'Morning Roger, Letitia. I didn't realise you were back,' she said guardedly.

'Mm – we got back late last night,' Roger said. 'We were both tired, so we went straight to our room.'

Letitia's green eyes flashed. She gave a wicked smile. 'Yes, we both had a rather busy day,' she put in. 'Besides, we needed to get a good night's rest. We have some clients coming down for treatment this morning.'

Amanda's ears pricked up. 'Clients? Anyone important?' she asked.

Roger eyed her with instant suspicion. There was

something in her tone that alerted him to possible trouble.

'Why did you say that?' he snapped. 'Anyone important? What exactly do you mean?'

Amanda flushed, realising that she had been indiscreet. She blustered, trying to cover up as best she could.

'Well, of course – I know all clients are *important*,' she said. 'But I just wondered if there was anyone who needed any special sort of treatment ... anything like that.'

Roger seemed to be satisfied. 'No, nobody out of the ordinary,' he said, letting the matter drop there.

Amanda tried another tack. She was, after all, supposed to be helping Martin, and anything she could find out would be of some use to him.

'These treatments – are they individual or group sessions?' Amanda asked.

Again, Roger flashed her a penetrating look. 'Group therapy, but why are you so interested all of a sudden?'

Amanda shrugged carelessly. 'Just idle curiosity,' she lied. 'I just thought that as we are going to be working together, I'd like to know a bit more about what actually happens at these sessions. In case a potential customer asks me any questions, that sort of thing.'

Roger looked thoughtful. 'I suppose you've got a point,' he conceded at last. 'So what are you asking – if you can come along and join in?'

Amanda balked slightly at that one. She wasn't sure that she wanted to get too involved.

'Well, let's say come along as more of an independent observer,' she suggested.

Letitia chose to put her oar in.

'No, we can't have that. The whole point of these group therapy sessions is the total involvement of everyone. It's a gestalt thing – the power of the group against the inhibitions of the individual. Anyone standing back from it, being detached, ruins the whole effect.'

Roger nodded. 'Letitia's right. Anyway, I wouldn't have thought that a girl like you would have any inhibitions about a little group grope.'

Amanda realised that she had suckered herself in past the point of no return. There was nothing left to do but go the rest of the way.

'You're probably right,' she agreed. 'Yes . . . why not? I'll come along and join in.'

Roger grinned, his suspicions washed away. 'That's the Amanda I remember,' he muttered. 'Good girl – I think you'll enjoy it.'

Pushing his chair away from the table, Roger stood up.

'I guess we'd better go and make sure all the equipment is set up properly,' he said to Letitia, who got up to join him. He turned his attention back to Amanda. 'Right, so we'll see you in the gymnasium in about half an hour.'

Amanda nodded, with far more enthusiasm than

she actually felt. 'I'll be there,' she promised.

As they left the breakfast room, Sally looked at Amanda with a sulky pouting expression. 'You could at least have wangled us in on this session,' she complained.

Amanda laughed out loud. 'My God, Sally, you two are the last people on earth who need their sexual inhibitions loosened,' she observed.

Sally was not pacified. 'No, but it might have been fun,' she pointed out, still looking disappointed.

'You've got work to do,' Amanda reminded her. She turned to Andrew. 'Oh, by the way, I've sorted out your spare barman problem. Martin Smith will be down to see you for some basic training later on.'

Noting the surprised look that crossed Sally's face, Amanda decided on a quick and discreet exit to avoid lengthy explanations.

'I'll fill you in on the details later,' she said, getting to her feet. 'Right now I'd better go and get all undressed up for the party.'

Chapter Eighteen

There were six people crammed into the changing room of the gym, not counting Roger and Letitia. Four men and two women. Amanda estimated that most of them were in their middle to late forties, although one of the men was considerably younger. And not at all bad looking, Amanda realised. She wondered, briefly, why he needed to use the facilities of a sexual rejuvenation clinic. At first sight, he looked quite sexy and obviously healthy enough.

Roger regarded his little party with a smile of satisfaction. He started the ball rolling by introducing everyone by their first names. Amanda promptly forgot them all except the one that interested her – Damian. It was a nice name, she thought. It rather suited the tall, rather aristocratic figure of the young man who had taken her fancy.

'Well, the first thing we do is to take our clothes off,' Roger announced. 'There is no shame attached to the naked body. Actually, it's a rather beautifully designed and functional piece of equipment in which we all house our essential beings. A life-support system for our individual personalities, if you like.

Nobody should be ashamed of the place where they live. It's what we *are* that counts, not what we merely perceive ourselves to be.'

It was a nice, thoughtful little speech, Amanda reflected. No doubt Roger had rehearsed it a thousand times over, and it was probably as shallow as everything else in his shabby little con trick, but it seemed to work well enough. The other members of the group visibly relaxed, and began to take off their clothes following the lead set by Letitia and Roger.

Amanda noticed that Letitia concentrated her attention on the male clients, while Roger worked his own peculiar charm on the females. She smiled inwardly, impressed despite her inner doubts about the smoothness and subtle psychology of the operation.

Not surprisingly, Letitia's lush, full body was the centre of attention, although Amanda noted with a certain sense of satisfaction that Damian's eyes strayed to her own more than passable figure more than once.

Letitia moved through the group dispensing tiny yellow tablets.

'Swallow these. They will help you feel more relaxed,' she informed everybody.

Amanda regarded the pill dubiously when it came to her turn. 'This isn't the aphrodisiac pill – that was white,' she hissed to Letitia in a whisper. 'What is it?'

'Perfectly harmless, I promise you,' Letitia assured her. 'Nothing more than a simple tranquilliser.'

Letitia watched Amanda carefully until she had

swallowed the yellow tablet.

'Right, now we are ready to move on into the encounter area,' she announced to the group finally.

Roger opened the changing-room door, ushering everyone through like a mother hen with a brood of chicks. Stepping through the door, Amanda was at once struck with the total transformation of what had been the gymnasium.

Her first impression was of a blinding white light, and the strange sensation that the room had no proper shape. Or, rather, it had no constant shape. Instead, it was like a series of shimmering, shifting curves which seemed to be constantly changing in front of her eyes.

Picking out Roger at the head of the group, Amanda moved up to him.

'What have you done to this place?' she demanded.

Roger pulled her slightly aside from the main group.

'Impressive, isn't it?' he said proudly. 'Certainly not bad for a two-day conversion. We had to improvise a little, of course.'

'But what have you actually done? How did you achieve this weird spatial effect?' Amanda wanted to know.

'Mostly the lighting,' Roger said carelessly. 'Actually, the room is filled with translucent plastic bubbles, like huge balloons. There are also hanging drapes of different materials – silks, muslin, net curtaining, that sort of thing.'

217

'But why can't I see anything clearly? Everything is so vague and misty, like moving, swirling shapes.'

Roger grinned. 'That's the special high-intensity lighting,' he explained. 'All the materials in this room are coated with a special light reflective paint, so the intensity of the light affects the eye, blurring and blending everything into one total shade of white. Without proper contrast, the human eye finds it difficult to differentiate between one section of the room and another, so your brain registers just a confused blur. It's all perfectly scientific,' he finished, as though that should satisfy everyone from a three-year-old child to a doctor of quantum physics.

'Oh,' Amanda said weakly, having never had much of a mind for science.

'Anyway, just keep walking slowly through the room and appreciate all the sensations with your body and mind,' Roger added. He moved ahead of her again to guide the main group.

Damian approached her somewhat shyly. 'Hello,' he said simply. 'It's all very strange, isn't it?'

Amanda nodded in agreement. 'Very disorientating. And almost frightening in a way. Would you mind very much holding my hand?'

'Of course not,' Damian agreed eagerly. 'After all, that's what all this is supposed to be about, isn't it? Touching, tactile stimulation, sharing our bodies.'

His warm, firm hand closed over hers. Amanda felt strangely like a virgin schoolgirl on her first date. But it was a nice, comforting feeling. She returned the warmth of his grip with a gentle squeeze.

'So, let's take a gentle stroll through the silk,' she muttered. 'Meander through the muslin.'

Hand in hand, they stepped into the white, swirling confusion of shapes and forms. Everything shifted and changed even more as they moved, their bodies brushing against loosely hanging sheets of material, and the slight air movements of their passage were enough to cause further small eddies of motion. The floor felt soft and yielding under Amanda's feet. Probably a large air mattress, she figured. Altogether, it was a highly pleasurable sensation – like stepping into a slightly more sophisticated version of those 'house of fun' attractions at old-fashioned fairgrounds. The fine sheets of material brushing against her bare flesh were highly sensual, causing her to shiver with a sense of erotic pleasure.

Even as her body responded to the tactile stimulation, Amanda was suddenly aware that there was something else rather strange happening inside her head. She began to feel distinctly detached from reality, almost detached from her own body as if her mind were floating around somewhere outside it. It was not a frightening, or even unpleasant feeling, but Amanda tried to fight it out of instinct. As the light-headedness increased, Amanda suddenly realised that she had been drugged. Those little yellow pills had contained something a bit more powerful than merely a tranquilliser. Amanda imagined that it was probably a very mild dose of

LSD, or something similar.

They reached a clear area, where the lighting was a little more subdued and it was possible to distinguish things more clearly. Amanda could recognise the solid wall of the far end of the gymnasium, and the large white air-mat which was laid out on the floor. Roger, Letitia and the rest of the group were already sitting down, facing each other in two short rows.

'Ah, Amanda and Damian. Come and join us,' Roger called out to them. He indicated a couple of spaces at either end of the two rows.

Amanda felt a brief sense of panic at letting go of Damian's comforting hand. But somehow the effects of the drug were hypnotic, giving Roger's commanding voice an increased power, a more compelling authority. Meekly, she moved to the place indicated and sat down, as Damian also took up his designated position.

Roger and Letitia stood up, each moving along the line. Roger sat down again opposite Amanda, who felt a slight pang of jealousy as Letitia chose Damian to be her partner.

'Now we are going to explore the subtleties of touching each other's bodies,' Roger explained. He gazed directly into Amanda's eyes. 'So – touch me, Amanda.'

'Where, exactly,' Amanda said, a little stupidly.

'Everywhere . . . anywhere,' Roger said. 'We are both going to seek out the delights of each other's flesh, each other's body. Just follow my lead.'

With that, he stretched out his hands gently towards her, resting his fingertips lightly upon her bare shoulders.

Amanda followed suit, not really understanding the point of the exercise and feeling more than a little self-conscious. They sat together like that for several seconds, hardly moving.

'Now, can you feel it?' Roger murmured, both for Amanda's benefit and the whole group. 'Can you feel the sheer sensual pleasure of warm flesh? Can't you sense a thousand tiny vibrations of life beneath the surface of the skin? Can you not draw that warmth of living flesh through the skin of your fingertips and into your heart? Feel the tiny pores of my flesh – the pump and trickle of my blood along veins and capillaries – the delicate mixing of a million chemical reactions going on inside my body.'

'I can certainly feel your shoulders,' Amanda said, helpfully.

'Concentrate more,' Roger said, a trifle testily, 'Think about what you are doing. Use your senses in combination – touch with smell, sight . . . even imagination. For a start, just concentrate upon the simple transfer of heat from one body to another.'

Amanda's drugged mind responded to the suggestive power of Roger's voice. She struggled mentally, attempting to channel all her thoughts and feelings in the way he was suggesting.

For several minutes, she felt nothing different. Then, finally, and as suddenly as if she had just crashed through a mental barrier of some kind, it happened. She was suddenly and acutely aware that the smooth flesh beneath her fingertips was part of a living, complex organism. There were a thousand tiny little movements, waves, pulses of power. She sensed the heat of blood, the moistness of living tissue.

Through practice, Roger obviously knew instinctively that she had passed through the barrier. His fingers began to move for the first time, in slow, gentle circles which seemed to send out ripples as on a still pond.

'Now, concentrate on enjoying the touch of my fingers at the same time,' Roger whispered softly. 'Two sensations, but only one pleasure. You exploring my naked body and me touching yours.'

Spurred on by her sudden and surprising sense of awareness, Amanda forced her mind to take on this new challenge. She was aware that her mind was being stretched, forced to focus on two different sets of feelings and merge them into one single act of consciousness. She moved her hands slowly over Roger's body, feeling the very maleness of him, the life-force which drove him and the burning urgency of flesh. At the same time, she could feel the movement of his fingers stroking her own body, moving across her flesh like tiny, living creatures. The experience was totally fascinating, and she was temporarily disappointed when Roger took his hands away from her body and broke contact.

He stood up again. 'Now we shall each choose another partner,' he announced. 'And then repeat the exact same procedure before taking it on a couple of stages further.'

Amanda was on her feet in a flash, and made a dash for Damian before anyone else got there before her.

'Hi, again,' she breathed, as she sat down in front of him.

The way Damian's eyes twinkled was enough to tell Amanda that he was more than happy to be her partner. Just as Roger and Letitia had instructed them, they began by resting their fingertips on each other's shoulders.

This time the barrier went down much more quickly, to Amanda's delight and surprise. In a matter of moments, she was virtually sharing Damian's body as he caressed hers. Her senses seemed to overlap, dissolving into each other. She could almost see Damian's hands on her flesh, almost taste the slightly salty moistness of his skin. Her fingertips were like delicate and sensitive probes, picking up the subtle vibrations of another living human being and translating them into a new form of knowledge, a secret form of the most intensive intimacy.

Time seemed to go into stasis. Amanda neither knew, nor cared, whether a minute or an hour had passed. She was lost in Damian's body, marvelling in the new knowledge of muscle, and sinew, and tissue which was undeniably masculine, yet revelling in the full glory of her own sexuality at the same time.

For sexuality had most certainly been released. Amanda was acutely conscious that Damian's touch was arousing her in a way that few men had ever managed. Her whole body seemed to be gradually building up a powerhouse of repressed sexual desire like a little inner dynamo. Yet it was not the normal animal desire for the sort of sex Amanda would have recognised. Her inner being was aching, not for the penetration of a cock, but for the merging of two bodies – a sort of sexual fusion.

Temporarily breaking off her dream-like state, Amanda glanced down into Damian's lap, wondering whether her touch was having the same effect on him. His prick was certainly responding, yet it was not a really throbbing erection. It had a somehow lazy, self-indulgent and contented stiffness – like a well-fed and plump pet cat enjoying being pampered by its loving mistress.

She glanced down the line of the other group members. More overtly sexual play was certainly taking place now, as the erotic intensity of the group encounter built up. Amanda noticed that Letitia was in a state of particularly high arousal, her red hair thrown back and her lush lips open enticingly. Her partner – a grey-haired man in his fifties – was lovingly playing with her full, soft breasts, stroking the creamy orbs with slow, caressing strokes and stimulating her erect nipples with his thumbs. For her part, Letitia was stroking his stiff cock with the fingertips of one hand while her other cupped his balls in her palm.

Amanda turned her attention to Roger, who had also chosen one of the oldest women for his subject. She was dreamily stroking the insides of his thighs as he ran his fingers up and down the oozing folds of her slit, not quite penetrating beyond her fleshy labial lips.

Most of the other couples seemed to be at about the same stage of sexual titillation and arousal without actually doing anything serious about it. In the middle of the group, two men who had chosen to sit opposite each other were happily masturbating each other with slow, almost furtive strokes. Amanda assumed that their particular sexual problem was one of orientation rather than libido.

But these digressions were unwelcome. Amanda snapped her mind back to Damian, and concentrated upon her own exquisite feelings. Within seconds, she was back in a state of pent-up desire, feeling her heart pounding inside her breast and a dull and empty aching feeling deep in her belly.

It was all like a slow, agonising yet delicious torture. Sexual tension was somehow hovering on a strange new brink between sensitivity and desire. Amanda felt that her own body had somehow betrayed her, turning against her mind and putting it on a frequency that it could not quite understand or cope with.

Paradoxically, it was the sheer power of her feelings

which also started to bring Amanda out of her dream-like state. With something of a revelation, she suddenly recognised the insidious and potentially dangerous nature of Roger Venner's little set-up. She remembered Martin's words to her, 'These are just two examples of the potential dynamite your friend Venner and his partner have got their hands on.'

Amanda saw it all now – realised that Roger and Letitia had accidentally stumbled upon something beyond their full understanding and ability to control. Drugs, disorientation techniques, Roger's undeniable hypnotic powers and the powerful lure of free and unhibited sex – together they made a dangerous mixture.

She glanced down the line of bodies again. Roger had three fingers rammed up his partner's cunt now, thrusting deeply into her foaming passage with short, savage strokes as she slavishly fondled and worshipped his swollen cock and balls.

Letitia had sidled up closer to the grey-haired man, her legs over his, and their bellies nearly touching. He continued to play with her ripe breasts as she held his rigid cock in a firm one-handed grip and rubbed its swollen head up and down against her erect clit.

Another few moments and the tactile love-play would give way to full-scale copulation, Amanda knew. From then on it was but a short step to a group orgy and the concealed video camera would be running, faithfully filming every indiscretion, each act of sexual depravity. And a whole new batch of innocent people would be sucked into a web of blackmail and sexual debauchery.

Somehow, Amanda new that Damian did not deserve to become embroiled in all this. Although she hardly knew him, or what his motives were for seeking out the group in the first place, she instinctively felt that he was essentially a decent, well-meaning man.

Amanda snapped out of her trance-like state. Bounding to her feet, she reached down and grabbed Damian's hand.

'Come on – we're getting out of here,' she hissed, urgently. Despite his initial resistance, she managed to haul him to his feet. Out of the corner of her eye, Amanda saw Roger look up suddenly and glare at her, his face clouded with suspicion. Amanda forced a smile in his direction, making an overtly sexual signal to suggest that she was taking Damian somewhere a bit more private to take their love-play one stage further.

Roger seemed to accept it. He grinned knowingly for a second then returned his full attention to his elderly partner.

'Just follow me,' Amanda whispered to Damian. Still leading him by the hand, she followed the line of the gymnasium walls until she found one of the emergency fire doors and threw up the safety bar.

Outside, in the familiar environment of the corridor, Amanda was able to think more clearly again. She still felt a little spaced out, but assumed that it was just the lingering effects of the drug.

'What happens now?' Damian asked, as he too began to return to reality.

Amanda was still holding his hand. It felt good. She still felt good. In fact, she still felt a powerful need to continue touching him and have him touch her.

But not under group conditions.

'What happens now is that we go up to my room,' she murmured.

The gleam in Damian's eyes told her that he considered that to be a pretty good idea.

Chapter Nineteen

Meanwhile, still in the breakfast room, Andrew and Sally continued to sulk at their exclusion from Roger and Letitia's little sex party.

Remembering an earlier encounter with Letitia, Andrew thought of her thick, soft lips pressed around his rigid cock and sighed deeply.

Sally flashed him a questioning look.

'What are you thinking, love?'

Andrew snapped back to reality, recovering himself with admirable composure.

'I was just reflecting, my sweet,' he said ruefully. 'Just realising that nobody seems to want our little games any more. I suppose they think we're just a pair of over-the-hill swingers who are past it.'

Sally regarded him with affection, tinged with sadness.

'Still, we've had some good times, haven't we?' she said, trying to cheer him up. 'We gave the buggers a good run for their money, didn't we?'

Andrew smiled, remembering some of their wilder sexual exploits. 'Yep, we certainly did that,' he agreed. 'Still, it's just you and me now, girl. Charles has gone,

Amanda doesn't want to play, and the younger folk don't want to include us in the sex games.'

He slipped his arm around Sally's broad back and squeezed one of her big breasts lovingly. Sally dropped her hand to his lap, patting his cock tenderly.

'We could still show these smart-arse kids a thing or two,' she murmured. 'There's a bit of life in us two old dogs yet.'

Andrew seemed to brighten up. He looked thoughtful.

'I wonder,' he mused, finally. 'I wonder if there are any of our crazy little games that we never actually got round to playing?' He gave Sally's tit another squeeze, 'Let's see . . . we screwed in the sauna.'

'And we copulated in the cellars,' Sally put in. 'We managed to play pornographic pool in the games room.'

'. . . We shafted in the solarium.'

'And we sucked each other off in the swimming pool.'

'Do you remember giving me a blow job over a beer barrel?' Andrew recalled.

'How about when you diddled me in the dining room?' Sally put in. 'Remember that?'

Andrew racked his brains for that one, finally shaking his head and giving Sally a rueful smile. 'Not me, old girl. That must have been Charles.'

Sally's face fell. 'Yes, you're right,' she said at last. 'Sorry about that.'

Andrew grinned. 'Still, who cares?' he said

generously. 'We both enjoyed ourselves, that was the main thing. I just wish there was something really special we could have saved up – just for ourselves.'

They both fell into thought again, racking their brains for past experiences and new ideas. Suddenly, it came to them both simultaneously. They looked into each other's eyes, grinning madly.

'Of course,' Andrew blurted out. 'The one thing we always said we would try but never got round to.'

Sally's eyes flashed fire. 'You're right, my love, we never fucked in the freezer,' she almost shouted.

They fell silent for a few seconds, eyeing each other mischievously.

'Well?' Sally said at length.

'I'll go and get the blankets and a double sleeping bag,' Andrew announced, his voice vibrant with excitement once again.

A fine mist of frozen air hissed out of the freezer room as Andrew pulled open the heavy steel door. He shivered as an icy blast engulfed him. Perhaps it wasn't such a bright idea after all, he thought.

Behind him, Sally had no such misgivings. She was hurriedly stripping off her clothes and draping them over the basement's single central-heating radiator.

'We'll need some warm clothes to get straight into when we come out,' she said. 'Have you laid the blankets down yet?'

Andrew shrugged off his misgivings. Hell, they

had always said that they would try anything once. He threw two heavy blankets down on the freezing floor of the cold store and stepped back to take off his own clothes.

Sally arranged them carefully over the radiator. She giggled. 'I guess this must be the craziest thing we've ever done,' she said.

Andrew nodded, starting to shiver. 'That's for sure,' he agreed. He looked Sally straight in the eye, his face suddenly serious. 'You do know that I always loved you, no matter what different partners we had, or what we did?'

Sally squeezed his arm. 'Of course I do, you silly old sod,' she said, with deep affection. 'Just as I've always loved you.'

Holding hands like two lovers in a suicide pact, they stepped into the freezer room. Andrew dropped a small lump of wood into the bottom of the heavy door.

'Just to make sure we don't get locked in,' he explained. 'I'd hate this to be our final freezing fuck.'

He pulled the door behind him as Sally sank down on to the blankets. Dropping down, he cuddled into the comforting warmth of her plump body.

Sally's huge breasts quivered as the icy cold hit her body, making her shiver.

'Jeezus – it's colder than I imagined,' she admitted. 'I reckon we're going to have to make this a quickie.'

Andrew pressed his body over hers, trying to share his own residual body heat. It was partially successful. There was a faint glow of warmth between their bellies, even if the cheeks of his arse felt like they were being pricked by a million icy needles. Andrew suddenly wondered for the first time whether it was possible to get a hard-on under such arctic conditions. He hadn't thought about it before.

Sally reached up to him, wrapping her fleshy arms around his back. She pulled his face down to hers, pressing their cold lips together and insinuating her still warm tongue into his mouth. Her hands slid under his belly, reaching for his cock and balls.

It felt distinctly odd, holding the icy, half-hard weapon which was usually hot and throbbing with pumping blood. For a moment, she too feared that it might prove impossible to coax the chilled member into life, but then she was rewarded by the feel of his prick twitching slightly at her touch.

Andrew buried his face into her soft breasts as he felt his cock begin to stiffen. It was a curious sensation, feeling the familiar heat of sexual arousal in his loins yet at the same time having his entire body turn slowly to a block of ice. He began to shiver convulsively – a combination of the cold, his own sexual stirrings and the bizarre fascination of their situation.

His prick reached its full proportions remarkably quickly. To Andrew, it felt as though his cock had never been stiffer – although whether it was rigid with cold or particularly powerful desire he wasn't too sure. All he knew for sure was that he had never had such a strong incentive to ram his cock into a hot cunt as fast as possible. Yet he also felt a sense of responsibility to Sally, aware that he should spend some time, at least, helping her towards a state of arousal.

He crushed his lips against hers again, sucking her tongue into his mouth and nibbling on it gently. He thrust his own tongue between her lips, licking their soft and fleshy undersides, flicking over her teeth, probing the nobbled ridges of her palate.

Their escaping breath turned to fine vapour in the freezing air, the saliva which dribbled from their meeting mouths froze on their lips and faces. Andrew pressed his body down against Sally's soft belly, rocking his hips gently so that the tip of his erect cock rubbed against the lips of her cunt. It was hurried and basic foreplay, but it seemed to be having some effect. Sally's steaming breath began to come in little short gasps, and she thrust her hips up to meet him, her cunt hungry for more contact with his rigid prick.

Andrew shivered again, the icy prickling on his back and buttocks now becoming more of a dull aching pain. He realised that he was starting to lose sensation in his toes and fingers, and knew that it would not be long before hypothermia began to set in.

It was now or never, Andrew told himself. Together, they needed to release the heat of sexual energy which would warm them both and carry them through the next few moments.

He lifted his arse, reaching down with his frozen fingers to guide the tip of his cock to Sally's soft and inviting cunt. Without bothering to check whether she was hot and wet enough, he slid his cock straight into her enveloping shaft with one fast lunge.

A wave of sensation flooded over him, causing him to gasp out a throaty cry of indescribable pleasure. It was as if he had just slipped his cock into a boiling, bubbling cauldron of creamy soup. Andrew marvelled at the sheer burning intensity of his wife's cunt. He had never experienced such liquid fire, such an incredibly powerful sensation of being sucked into a sexual volcano. The liquid heat was everything. It surged into his cock and into his mind. A total experience – a new knowledge of the total essence of woman, and cunt, and the warmth and comfort of sharing two bodies.

Andrew threw himself into the thermal spa of Sally's receptive fanny. He bathed in it, swam in it, completely immersed himself in the soothing torrent of heat. Plunging in and out of her like a demon, Andrew fucked frantically, eager to release his own meagre emission of liquid fire.

He came in a sudden, savage convulsion that jolted them both. Sally squealed, wrapping her legs up around his back and pumped herself against him furiously, clamping and squeezing her cunt against the sides of his cock to trigger off her own imminent orgasm.

She exploded wetly, also amazed by the seemingly

boiling temperature of her own juices as they splashed out on to her thighs. A small cloud of steamy vapour rose around them both.

The freezer room was not the place for lazy or relaxed post-coital indulgence. Andrew jumped to his feet, shivering and trembling like a man with the plague.

'Come on, old girl, we've got to get out of here,' he said, reaching down to pull Sally to her feet.

They ran, gratefully, out into the comparative warmth of the basement, pressing themselves against the radiator as they hurriedly donned their warmed clothes. Finally dressed, and with their body temperatures beginning to return to something like normal, they looked at each other and began to giggle.

'Well, girl, we finally did it,' said Andrew, his eyes twinkling. 'I guess that finally puts the lid on our little repertoire of sexual adventures.'

Sally reached down to squeeze his soft cock through his trousers.

'Not quite,' she murmured, a roguish smile playing at the corners of her lush lips. 'I thought of one last little fling while we were in there – and I reckon it's something we could both do with right this minute.'

Andrew looked more than interested. 'So what is it?' he wanted to know.

Sally grinned. 'You never got to bugger me in a hot bathtub, did you?' she said.

Andrew was already one jump ahead of her.

'I'll race you,' he said, making a sudden break for the door.

Laughing like a couple of kids, they ran out of the basement and headed for the warmth and comfort of their apartment.

Chapter Twenty

Amanda and Damian had long since reached the safety and security of her room and seated themselves on the edge of the waterbed, still holding hands.

The gentle motion of the bed pleased and surprised them both, as the drug, which was still coursing through their bodies, took the sensation, somehow amplified it, and turned it into a heightened experience of physical pleasure and wellbeing.

It had seemed only sensible to lie down full length and make the most of the experience. Now, half an hour later, they continued to lie side by side, floating in a dreamy world of pleasure.

Damian spoke for the first time since their escape from the gymnasium.

'Why did you pull me out of there?' he asked. 'It was almost as if something frightened you. Did you think we were in danger or something?'

Amanda raised her head from the bed to look into his eyes.

'I think we *were* in danger, Damian – although not the sort you're probably thinking of.'

His eyes looked puzzled. 'I'm not sure I understand.'

Amanda drew a deep breath, wondering how best to explain to him. She wasn't actually sure whether it was a good idea to try and explain at all, since she still had no real idea of what Damian had been doing at the session, how involved he might already be, or indeed, anything about the man at all. Yet instinctively she trusted him, and felt sure that there was nothing devious or sinister about him. He appeared to be a man who was totally up front, with nothing hidden behind his apparent innocence.

'Look – how much do you actually know about these sessions?' she asked, trying to feel her way into the situation delicately.

'This was my first time,' Damian answered readily enough. 'I didn't know what to expect, really.' He broke off to smile somewhat shyly. 'I must admit I didn't imagine meeting someone as nice as you.'

'So what made you want to come in the first place,' Amanda wanted to know, conscious that she was prying into his private life and feeling a trifle awkward about it.

Damian's face clouded over. He shifted awkwardly, obviously embarrassed.

'I have a little problem,' he muttered sheepishly. 'I thought these sessions might help me.'

There was silence for a while. Amanda couldn't quite bring herself to ask him directly what the problem was. In the end, it was Damian who offered the answer of his own free will.

'I feel kind of embarrassed about it, but you've

been so nice to me, I suppose there's no reason why I shouldn't tell you,' he went on. 'The thing is, I was engaged to be married up to a few months ago. Everything was fine until we went to an all-night party and I got drunk and passed out in one of the bedrooms. Sometime during the night I woke up again and went downstairs to find my best friend screwing my fiancée on the living-room floor. Something happened after that experience which I don't understand.'

'What happened, Damian,' Amanda prompted, feeing more than a little sympathetic.

Damian took a deep breath, as if the rest was just too embarrassing to share. 'After that, I found that I couldn't get a proper erection,' he said, in little more than a whisper. 'Not with any girl, even when I really fancied her.'

'So you thought this clinic might help you?'

Damian nodded. 'And I think it was helping me . . . or you were,' he said. 'I was getting quite hard when we were touching each other, you know.'

Amanda smiled. 'I noticed,' she said. 'To tell you the truth, I was getting pretty hot myself.'

Damian looked pleased with himself. Amanda smiled inside. It was really funny how strong the male ego was, she thought. Even when faced with the possibility of impotence, the mere thought that he could turn a woman on was enough to give a man a sense of his own sexual power. However, it was a minor point. She returned to more important things.

'Where did you hear about this clinic?" she asked.

Damian shrugged. 'A friend of mine at work mentioned it.'

'And where do you work?' Amanda felt that she was starting to get to something.

'I'm a civil servant,' Damian told her. 'I work for the Department of International Trade. We issue shipping and export orders and licences – that sort of thing.'

It all fell into place. Amanda realised that Martin had been on the right track. Roger and Letitia were on the verge of breaking into something really big. Sucking Damian into the web might have been the final piece of the set-up. Had they been able to put some sort of blackmail pressure on him, they could have persuaded him to turn a blind eye to a couple of dodgy export orders, perhaps even issue a fraudulent licence to break an existing embargo.

She turned to Damian, her face suddenly very serious. 'Look, Damian – there's not a lot I can actually tell you, but take my word for it, you were in real danger back there,' she assured him. 'You'll have to take my word for it, and you'll have to trust me, but you must promise me that you won't make any attempts to rejoin that clinic.'

Damian wasn't too sure about that. 'But what about my problem?' he said, looking rather miserable.

Amanda smiled. 'We were doing pretty well on our own, weren't we?' she asked.

Damian nodded his head enthusiastically. 'Not half,' he agreed.

'Then why don't we continue the treatment from where we left off?'

Without waiting for an answer, Amanda swivelled round on the bed until she was sitting cross-legged and facing him. Damian struggled into a sitting position opposite her, gazing into her eyes expectantly.

'So, where were we, exactly,' Amanda mused. She placed her palms on his chest, her fingers just brushing his small brown nipples. She smiled gently. 'This is the Amanda Redfern school of therapy,' she announced. 'Just follow my lead.'

Reaching out, Damian cupped his hands under the swelling softness of Amanda's lush breasts, enjoying the creamy smoothness of her skin, marvelling at the firm but pliant flesh of the delicious twin orbs. His thumbs rubbed against the pink buds of her nipples, soon teasing them into a redder tautness. He rolled the stiffened nubs around in tiny circles, delighted to see the instant and dramatic effect his touch had on her.

Amanda ran her fingers gently up and down the warm insides of his thighs, her long fingernails raking briefly against his delicate and sensitive balls.

Damian pressed forwards, his mouth seeking hers. Their lips closed together softly, gently, in a long, lingering kiss that was without passion yet incredibly sensual. Amanda realised that the effects of the drug

243

had not yet fully worn off, and was glad.

She returned her attention to his thighs, continuing to stroke them with slow, feather-light strokes. Sliding her fingers beneath the soft sac of his bulging scrotum, she lifted his balls gently on her fingertips, tickling them with her nails. Her efforts were rewarded with a perceptible twitch, and Damian's soft cock slowly began to swell and harden.

In a matter of moments, his prick was as she remembered it from their earlier encounter. Almost full-sized, but not quite as rigid and throbbing as it should be. It was something Amanda now wanted very much to rectify, since even in its semi-aroused state, Damian's weapon was a pretty awesome piece of equipment.

Amanda's fingers strayed to the lips of her cunt, which were already beginning to moisten. Rubbing her fingers against her slippery slit, she transferred them back to Damian's cock, rubbing the slimy secretions over its bulbous head and along the semi-stiff shaft. Thus lubricated, it was easier to perform a gentle and smooth massage, using only the lightest possible touch. Under her delicate ministrations, the already sizeable prick grew another two or three centimetres in length, and pulsing veins announced that it was certainly beginning to stiffen with pumping blood.

Amanda moved forwards, uncrossing her legs and rising on her knees so that she could straddle Damian's thighs. She pressed herself against his stomach, feeling his taut prick straining against her soft belly. Rocking herself gently from side to side, she rolled the stiffening weapon between the warmth of their bellies, giving it a stimulating and erotic massage.

It gave a sudden, violent jerk, quickly followed by a series of smaller, fading throbs. Amanda felt the sudden stickiness of his come on her belly and pulled away, more than a little disappointed.

Damian's face was a study in sadness and embarrassment.

'That's the other part of the problem,' he murmured awkwardly. 'Premature ejaculation.'

A wave of pity washed away Amanda's disappointment and frustration. She had set out to do a job, and she wasn't going to be beaten now, she told herself. So maybe Damian's little problem wasn't quite as simple as she had first imagined. Well, there was always more than one way to skin a cat.

Amanda slid down the bed, dropping her head into Damian's lap. Her soft lips gobbled up the subsiding lump of soft flesh, her hot tongue lashing it from side to side inside her wet mouth.

She began to pump away at the soft cock with her lips, mouth and tongue, sucking and licking for all she was worth. Grasping his balls in her hand, Amanda squeezed them into a tight little parcel, gently clenching and unclenching her fist as though to inflate the soft tube of flesh that was attached to them.

Gradually, Amanda felt life returning to the flaccid apparatus in her mouth. Pulling back so that her lips were only just enclosing the stiffening shaft, she glanced up at Damian, rolling her eyes expressively to let him see how she was doing.

Damian propped himself up on his elbows, his eyes transfixed by the sight of Amanda's lush red lips wrapped around his prick. To be able to watch himself being sucked off was a thrill in itself, since most of his sexual experience to date had been all rather furtive, self-conscious and ridden with inhibitions.

Sex, in Damian's little world, had been something done in darkened rooms – a quick, strictly missionary-position coupling which was invariably associated with some sort of guilt feeling or suggestion of 'dirtiness'. Now, he had a beautiful young woman sucking his cock in broad daylight, obviously thoroughly enjoying it and quite happy to let him watch her doing it. Damian felt a little shiver of excitement ripple through his loins. His rapidly stiffening prick throbbed with sudden new life.

Amanda felt the object of her attentions growing to its full size once again. She shifted her position, wriggling down in the bed so that she could give Damian the added thrill of a deep throat job. Holding her breath, she sucked his rigid love shaft in until it was lodged in her gullet. Holding it there, she constricted her throat muscles to apply a gentle massage to its entire swollen length.

Damian groaned out loud as his cock seemed to

swell to bursting point. He watched almost unbelievingly as Amanda pulled her head back slowly, letting the underside of his cock slide over her extended and gently waggling tongue. She licked the swollen head for a few seconds, then sucked the meaty tube back into her throat, repeating the oral massage technique. Her soft lips pressed into the wiry bush of his pubic hairs, her mouth clamping around his throbbing prick until she had to pull back again to gasp for air.

It was probably about time to ease off on the heavy stuff, Amanda figured. After Damian's first effort, she wasn't sure how long he could hold out or how well he could control his second ejaculation. Although she had no objections to having him come in her mouth, Amanda was conscious that her cunt was now running with slimy love juice, and aching to be filled with hot cock.

With the merest hint of reluctance, she allowed the pulsing shaft to slip out of her mouth, planting wet kisses on its glistening helmet before abandoning it temporarily.

Amanda sat up on her haunches to admire her work. Damian's cock was back to its former glory again, standing proudly erect like a flagpole and throbbing gently. Sliding herself up over his thighs, Amanda manoeuvred herself into position until its blunt head was pressed against her thick and slippery labial lips. With a sigh of satisfaction, she lowered herself slowly on to the fleshy spike.

Damian's cock slid effortlessly into her well-lubricated shaft, stopping only when it encountered the restriction of Amanda's cervix. Amanda wriggled her buttocks, savouring the delicious sensation of the thick shaft sloshing around in her gushing tunnel. She rose slightly, holding this position so that the very tip of Damian's cock just filled the mouth of her cunt, throbbing gently against the stiff little button of her clitoris. Then, abandoning herself to the joy of total penetration, she collapsed upon its full length, grunting slightly as she was plugged to the hilt.

She felt Damian's body writhe beneath her, as he pushed his hips up from the bed, thrusting against her downward stroke as she rode his prick. Juice poured from Amanda's brimming cunt, running down Damian's erect shaft like hot oil. Amanda speeded up her tempo, her knees flexing like a pair of steam pistons as she bounded up and down like a demented jack-in-the-box upon the fleshy pivot of his prick.

Damian was also putting his heart and soul into the spirited fucking session – pumping and thrusting against her with all his might as he tried to drive his sword even deeper into its welcoming sheath.

Their earlier positions were soon reversed. Far from worrying about Damian coming too soon, Amanda realised that she was fast approaching the point of orgasm, even though Damian now seemed to have gained his second wind. She attempted to slow things down, but it was already too late. Amanda felt the old familiar tinglings deep in her belly and let herself go. She rode the first delicious spasms with all the pleasure of a child on a fairground ride – completely abandoning herself to the thrill of pure sensation.

Damian felt the hot gush of Amanda's orgasm spray down on to his belly, and it spurred him on to even greater efforts. He could hear the sloshing of his plunging prick as it slammed in and out of Amanda's sopping cunt, smell the heady aroma of her love juice and feel the quivering vibrations which seemed to travel the length of her enclosing shaft. He pumped away like a demon, pressing his hands down upon the bed for more leverage as he bucked his hips furiously, feeling that he could fuck like this forever.

Amanda shuddered violently as the secondary wave of her orgasm tore through her body. She fell sideways, pulling Damian over with her and encouraging him to climb up into the dominant position.

Damian responded eagerly, his body and mind surging with the wonderful knowledge of his newfound sexual stamina. As Amanda flopped on to her back and lay there weakly, he fucked away like a mad thing until his own release finally came.

With a roar of triumph, Damian slammed into Amanda's belly with one last pumping stroke and shot his hot discharge into the very mouth of her womb.

Exhausted, he flopped down, rolling off Amanda's

body to lie on his side, his heart pounding, and his lungs pumping for air.

Amanda smiled weakly. 'For a first lesson, that was pretty impressive,' she murmured.

Damian grinned back. 'I really don't know how to thank you enough,' he said, his voice choked with emotion. 'How can I possibly ever repay what you have just done for me?'

Amanda reached down to pat his soft cock with her fingertips.

'You just lie there quietly until you've got your strength back,' she said. 'I'll think of something.'

Chapter Twenty-one

It was well into the afternoon when Amanda and Damian finally decided by mutual consent that his sexual problems were well and truly cured. After saying goodbye to him, Amanda decided to have a general check around to find out how preparations for the evening's little shindig were coming along.

First stop was the kitchens, to see how Bernard was doing with the catering arrangements. Reaching the kitchen door, Amanda was surprised to see that the lock had been forced. Alerted to possible trouble, she walked in to the kitchen to find Bernard sulking furiously, his painted mouth pursed into a camp little pout.

He glared at Amanda balefully as she entered. He had not forgotten the hostility of their earlier meeting.

'What do you want?' he demanded petulantly.

Despite his attitude, Amanda forced a smile. It was obvious that he was on the verge of throwing a tantrum, and the last thing she could afford was for him to blow a fuse and storm out – as highly strung and temperamental chefs are notoriously prone to do.

'I just came to see how you were getting on,' Amanda said, in as friendly a tone as she could manage. 'And to offer any help, if you needed it.'

Bernard looked quite shocked at this second suggestion. He dismissed Amanda's genuine offer of help with a rude outburst.

'I thought I had made myself quite clear, Miss Redfern. I do not allow women to mess around in my kitchens.' He gave a little shudder at the mere thought.

Amanda shrugged. If that was his attitude, then what the hell? she asked herself. Let him get on with it.

Turning to leave, she pointed to the door with its broken lock.

'What happened?'

Bernard screwed his little face into an expression of aggrieved pain.

'I've been broken into,' he complained bitterly.

Amanda winced. 'Oooh – painful,' she commiserated.

The little chef's eyes narrowed to slits of hate. 'It seems just typical of this disgusting place,' he fumed. 'How an artist like myself is supposed to work in such a shambles of an establishment, I just don't know. It's lucky for whoever did it that I didn't catch them at it.'

'Hoping to catch someone with their pants down, were you?' Amanda asked facetiously. She couldn't resist it, having been wound up by his petulant and aggressive attitude.

'Well, don't get your knickers in a twist about it,' she added, hoping to calm him down before he exploded. It was the wrong thing to say.

Bernard flew into the full tantrum that had been simmering beneath the surface. 'I just hope this ball of yours turns out to be a horrible flop,' he ranted, in a childish whining voice.

Amanda turned her back on him. 'Yes, well, you'd know all about flopping balls, wouldn't you sweetie?' she said in an affected lisp. She flounced out of the kitchen, leaving the temperamental little chef to his own devices.

She headed directly for Martin Pugh's room. Somehow, Amanda suspected that he had something to do with the broken lock on the kitchen door. And even if he didn't, perhaps he ought to know about it.

She knocked on his door.

'Who is it?' Pugh sounded a little nervous.

'It's me, Amanda,' Amanda said. 'Can I come in?'

There was no refusal, so she took the silence to be an invitation. Turning the handle, she walked in to the room to find Martin busy with what looked vaguely like a schoolboy's home chemistry set. He had set up a Bunsen burner and several racks of test tubes on the bedside cabinet, and was busily mixing chemicals in a large flask.

Amanda should have been surprised, but found herself surprised that she wasn't. Somehow, she had come to expect just about anything of Martin by now, in the light of everything she had discovered so far. Spy cameras, disguise kits, telephone bugging equipment – somehow a portable science laboratory didn't seem particularly outrageous.

'Don't tell me, you're practising mixing up cocktails for tonight,' Amanda observed sarcastically.

Martin smiled faintly. 'Analysing one little cocktail, certainly,' he agreed. 'As a matter of fact, I am just finding out exactly what goes into this so-called aphrodisiac mixture our friends use in their food preparations.'

'So it was you who broke into the kitchen. Bit crude, wasn't it?' Amanda asked.

Martin looked apologetic. 'Sorry about that,' he said, rather sheepishly. 'I did try to pick the lock professionally, but this is a very old house and the fittings are pretty rusted up. So I had to resort to rather more primitive measures.'

As he spoke, he poured a few drops of a clear chemical liquid into the flask and shook it up. The contents immediately turned a bright shade of blue. Martin let out a little whoop of triumph. 'Got the bastards,' he said with glee. 'There are enough traces of illegal drugs in this stuff to satisfy any police forensic test. So even if I don't get any more on Vennings and his little bunch, I can get them five to ten years for drug trafficking.'

He placed the flask down on the bedside table.

'Right, I suppose I'd better get ready for my *real* job,' he said to Amanda.

Martin caught her off guard. 'Oh, what's that?' Amanda asked, mystified.

Martin grinned. 'Bartender in a house of ill repute,' he said. 'I guess it's about time to report for basic training.'

'I'll take you down and introduce you to Andrew,' Amanda said. She paused, looking at Martin gratefully. 'Listen, I want you to know I really appreciate your pitching in to help me out like this.'

'Forget it,' Martin said generously. 'As you said, it will give me a chance to keep and eye open . . . and besides, I'll probably be coming to you for some wages at the end of the night, when this business is all tied up.'

'Oh, of course I'll pay you the going rate,' Amanda offered, caught off-guard again. 'I didn't mention anything about money because I thought it might offend you.'

Martin smiled roguishly. 'I wasn't thinking about money,' he said. 'I thought I might take my salary in kind, as it were. Perhaps you could introduce me to one of your escort girl friends or something.'

Amanda looked flabbergasted. For some reason, she had never thought of Martin having normal sexual desires.

He caught her surprised expression and laughed.

'Well, don't be quite so amazed,' he said. 'Not everyone in the security services is recruited from the old pouffe network at Oxford and Cambridge, you know. Some of us are quite happily heterosexual.'

Amanda felt embarrassed. 'Yes, of course. I'm sorry,' she mumbled. 'It just never crossed my mind. It must be quite frustrating for you, being surrounded by all this sexual activity and not getting your share.'

Martin nodded. 'Yes, it does make things hard – in more than one sense of the word,' he agreed.

Amanda glanced at her watch. It was only five o'clock. The Hunt Ball wasn't due to get under way until eight. She looked at Martin in a completely new light. He wasn't at all bad looking, she realised. A bit older than the type she generally went for, but in the peak of physical condition for his years. And she did owe him a favour, after all. Amanda was a firm believer in always paying one's debts.

She toyed with the buttons on her blouse. 'Listen . . . about these wages of yours,' she murmured. 'Do you need a little sub to keep you going until payday?'

Martin's eyes twinkled. 'I must admit, the thought had crossed my mind.'

Amanda was already opening her blouse, exposing the tops of her swelling breasts. Martin licked his lips in anticipation as the pair of delights were exposed to his gaze.

'From where I'm standing, this looks like more of a bonus than a sub,' he said, by way of a compliment.

Amanda laughed. 'Us crime-fighters have to stick together,' she said, peeling off her blouse and making a start on her skirt fastening.

Martin's eyes reviewed her body admiringly, noting the proud, firm shape of her full breasts, the tautness of her stomach and the silky blonde triangle of her delightful cunt as her skirt slipped to the floor. His hands flew to his trouser belt.

'I'd better get these off before things get too painful.'

Amanda regarded the highly promising bulge in his underpants as he dropped his trousers. For what had basically been a spur-of-the-moment decision, something told her that she was going to do rather well out of the deal. A second later, when Martin's pants joined his trousers on the floor, this initial observation was confirmed.

Martin's stiff prick sprang into the air as he slipped the tight elastic of his underpants over it. Quivering slightly, it jutted out from his firm, athletic body at an angle of about seventy degrees. Although not particularly thick, it was longer than average, with a particularly large and bulbous helmet.

'Hey, with a weapon like that, you should have been in the Special Branch,' Amanda joked. She moved forwards to fondle the enticing tool, hefting it in her palm as though she was checking it for weight. The stiff shaft jerked at her touch, a small bubble of seminal fluid seeping out of its tip.

'I hope you approve,' Martin said with a smile, as Amanda continued to fondle and admire the rigid weapon.

Amanda gave the throbbing shaft a gentle squeeze. 'Consider me impressed,' she purred. 'Now I know why all the women fell for James Bond.'

Martin laughed. 'Oh, him,' he said dismissively. 'A

strict amateur.' He nodded down at his cock, nestling in Amanda's hand. 'I go one better than him – this little piece of equipment gives me a 008 rating.'

'And what's that?' Amanda wanted to know.

Martin grinned. 'A licence to thrill,' he said. He draped his arm around Amanda's naked shoulder, pulling her towards him. 'All joking apart, Amanda, I've fancied you like crazy from the first moment I set eyes on you.'

Amanda looked down at his pulsing prick, still swelling in her hand.

'I can't honestly say the same,' she retorted. 'Although I must admit that you're growing on me.'

Amanda pushed Martin to the side of the bed, still holding tightly on to his cock. As she held it, she could feel the swollen tube of flesh pumping erratically in her hand, the knobbly veins pulsing with heated, pressurised blood.

Pushing him down on to the bed, Amanda sat beside him and began to pump his love shaft up and down with a slow, regular rhythm, jerking and squeezing it at the same time. Martin groaned softly, his fingers straying between her thighs to seek out the moist entrance to her gorgeous honeypot. Turning sideways, he buried his face between her magnificent tits, nuzzling into their warmth, fleshy softness.

Amanda opened her legs, allowing Martin to slide two fingers into her hot little cunt. Martin plunged his fingers deeply into the welcoming hole, twisting them round in a spiral action which made Amanda shiver with pleasure. They continued to masturbate each other for several minutes, with a gentle, unhurried pace which kept them both at a safe plateau of sexual excitement without passing the point of no return.

At last, Amanda felt her cunt begin to ooze with the hot juices of passion as Martin's thrusting, swivelling fingers did their work. Her hot little clit was stiff and throbbing, the slimy, wet depths of her love canal ached to be filled with a stiff cock. She rose from the bed, preparing to climb upon his lap and impale herself upon the point of his quivering love arrow.

'No, not yet,' Martin muttered, huskily. 'You're the most beautiful young woman I've been fortunate enough to know for years, Amanda. I want to make love to all of you, fuck every delicious inch of your wonderful body.'

Putting his words into action, Martin jumped up from the bed and pushed Amanda gently back into a sitting position. Pressing himself against her, he slid his cock into the deep valley between her swelling tits. Grasping each soft mound in his hands, he squeezed them together gently until his rock-hard shaft was completely encased in a sheath of warm, soft flesh. Rocking his hips slowly, he fucked Amanda's tits lovingly, thumbing each quivering and stiff little nipple with light, circular strokes.

Amanda stuck out a wet tongue, licking the swollen head of his prick each time it rose to within striking range. Martin sighed with appreciation, pushing higher until the tip of his cock brushed against Amanda's soft, parted lips. She responded gratefully, withdrawing her probing tongue and delivering soft, sucking kisses instead. Finally, as Martin thrust more insistently towards her face, she opened her mouth and let the first two or three inches of his cock slip between her wet lips.

She would quite happily have taken his lovely cock deep into her mouth, but Martin had other ideas. Pulling away slightly, he reached down and slid his hands under Amanda's armpits, urging her to her feet. Amanda followed his lead submissively, allowing him to pull her to her feet, turn her round and reposition her to satisfy his latest whim.

Martin turned her completely round until she was facing the bed, then bent her over. Moving behind her, he slid his prick between her buttocks and urged her to squeeze her legs tightly together.

Amanda looked down at her crotch as Martin's long prick seemed to grow out of her blonde bush. She contracted her thigh muscles, squeezing the hot tube between them. She reached down to fondle it, imagining that she was a man wanking himself off.

This little fantasy, together with the erotic stimulation of his hard cock pressed against her clitoris, gave her an unexpected little buzz of sensual delight. She continued to play with her new prick like a child with a toy, as Martin slipped his hands under her dangling breasts and began to squeeze them gently.

Martin's knees pressed into the back of her legs. Amanda felt her legs being bent and gently lifted up on to the bed. She was now in a crouched, kneeling position, with her pert little arse sticking up provocatively.

Martin released his grip on her legs and grasped the soft cheeks of her arse firmly in both hands, his hard fingernails digging into the firm but pliant flesh. He adjusted his position, sliding his stiff cock back under her thighs until the hot, throbbing tip was resting under the fleshy lips of her dripping slit. Martin rocked slowly from side to side a couple of times, waggling his cock against the oozing crack until it was slippery with her viscous juices.

Amanda was hungry for his cock now. Martin's subtle and masterful love play had aroused her to a peak of excitement, and she could not wait any longer to feel his throbbing hardness deep inside her belly. Reaching between her thighs, she grasped the stiff weapon firmly and guided the blunt tip between her labial lips and into the frothing entrance to her cunt. With a little twitch of her arse, Amanda drove herself back on to the intruding rod and shivered with pleasure as she felt it slide smoothly into her well-lubricated canal.

Martin heaved against her, his belly slamming against the firm cushion of her buttocks. His fingers crept around to the insides of her thighs, pulling her back on to his already deeply buried prick. He started a forceful pumping action, thrusting his hips forwards with short, aggressive strokes which seemed to jolt Amanda all the way up to her womb.

'Ooh yes . . . oh yes please,' Amanda murmured, thrilling to the expert touch of a master lover. An older man he might be, but Martin Pugh had all the advantages of experience and technique on his side.

'Do you want me to give it to you?' Martin grunted, between gasps for breath. 'Do you want me to really fuck it to you?'

Amanda bucked her arse against his jabbing prick. 'Yes, yes,' she moaned. 'Ram it up me, shove it up as far and as fast as you can.'

Knowing that she was on the edge, Martin let himself fully go for the first time. Abandoning his earlier restraint, he pumped his throbbing cock into the slimy recesses of her quivering, clenching cunt as Amanda began to make little whimpering, animal-like sounds in the back of her throat.

With a consummate sense of timing, Martin paced his own rising orgasmic curve to the very instant that he felt Amanda's internal muscles go into a spasm of pulsing contractions. Only when he felt the first hot and liquid gush of her love juice did he relinquish all mental control over his body and let it follow its own blind path towards release. With a final surge of energy, he slammed into her with deep, driving strokes until his heavy balls slapped against her thighs.

Amanda let out a whooping cry of triumph as she felt him shudder into her one last time, and spurt his hot seed into her own flowing torrent of come.

Afterwards, Amanda drew in a long, deep breath. She looked at Martin with a new light of respect in her eyes.

'You're one hell of a man,' she breathed in awe.

Martin smiled, but without a trace of arrogance. 'And you're quite a woman, Amanda,' he murmured, with total sincerity.

Their eyes met and exchanged a strange look of promise – almost commitment. It was Martin who finally backed away from the unspoken bond, averting his eyes so that Amanda could not see the embarrassment in them.

Even so, she somehow sensed his withdrawal and felt a pang of disappointment.

'There's something . . . isn't there?' she prompted. 'What is it, Martin?'

He turned to face her again, and she could see the confusion in his expression.

'I didn't expect it to be like this,' he muttered uncertainly. 'I'm sorry.'

Amanda didn't understand. 'Sorry? For what? That was wonderful.'

Martin nodded sadly. 'Too wonderful,' he agreed. 'And, unfortunately, something which I fear we might ultimately regret.'

Amanda thought she understood, at last.

'You're married, aren't you?' she prompted, in a quiet voice.

Martin shook his head. 'No,' he said. 'I was, but she was killed – by someone trying to get at me.'

'Oh,' Amanda said, and fell silent for a long while. Finally, she voiced her thoughts. 'And you don't think you can afford to get involved again, is that it?'

Martin sighed deeply. 'Something like that. My life just isn't compatible with those of normal people.'

Amanda slipped her arm around his shoulder, hugging him. 'We seemed pretty compatible about two minutes ago,' she reminded him.

Martin nodded. 'I know – that's the trouble,' he said, detaching himself form her embrace and standing up.

Wisely, Amanda stayed silent, allowing him to dress quietly and get ready to leave. Inwardly, however, her thoughts were racing. Above everything else, one thing seemed crystal clear.

Martin Pugh didn't seem to realise what a thoroughly dogged and determined sort of person Amanda Redfern could be when she had set her mind on something. He was in for something of a surprise, she promised herself.

Chapter Twenty-two

Bernard's foul mood had evaporated, having plotted, planned and finally executed his revenge on Amanda. He surveyed the tables laden with food for the Hunt Ball with a sense of satisfaction. Every single dish had been spiked with a double dosage of the aphrodisiac mixture. When the guests had finally consumed that little lot, all hell would break loose, Bernard was sure.

Amanda's precious Hunt Ball would certainly go with a bang, in more ways than one, he reflected, unable to keep a vindictive leer off his face. That would teach the interfering and rude little bitch for insulting him.

Just to make sure, he set about opening all the salt and pepper pots, adding a further liberal dose of the mixture to their contents. Finally satisfied with his efforts, he began to load the dumb waiter with dishes to transport the prepared food to the dining room.

Amanda finished her shower, made herself up and slipped into an elegant, tight-fitting black evening dress. Appraising herself in the mirror and liking what she saw, she sauntered downstairs to the bar to greet the first of her evening guests.

The bar was already crowded. Glancing round, Amanda recognised at least a dozen of her escort agency friends, all with well-dressed men firmly in tow. With a warm glow, she spotted Beryl, a particularly dear friend who had shared in more than one swinging sexual threesome with her in the past. Amanda hadn't seen Beryl for nearly a year. She hurried over, eager to renew their friendship.

As usual, Beryl was regaling her male escort with her fund of inventively crude jokes. She was just launching into the one about Moby Dick and his girlfriend as Amanda approached. Not wishing to interrupt, Amanda waited in the background until she had finished.

'So Moby Dick finally gets sick and tired of Captain Ahab hunting him all around the world,' Beryl was recounting. 'Finally, he decided that it has got to be either Ahab or him and goes to see one of his girlfriends.'

'Listen, you've got to help me get rid of this Ahab bastard,' says Moby. 'I'll distract him into coming after me while you swim up alongside his ship and blow water out of your blow-hole until you sink it.'

'Right,' says Moby's girl, and swims off to do as she's told, spurting fountains of water until the ship finally starts to sink and all the crew jump overboard in panic.

'Right, what do we do now?' she asks Moby.

'Now we eat the bastards,' says Moby, gulping down the ship's cook.

His girl friend shakes her tail. 'No way,' she says. 'I've told you before, Moby, I don't mind giving you a blow job, but I'll be fucked if I'll swallow the seamen.'

Beryl's companion burst into peals of laughter as she reached the punchline. Amanda merely smiled, having heard it before.

'I guess the next one is the tale of the octopus with eight pricks,' she said quietly, in Beryl's ear.

Beryl whirled round at the sound the familiar and welcome voice, her eyes lighting up as she recognised her old friend.

'Amanda, how wonderful to see you,' she gushed, throwing her arms around Amanda's neck and embracing her warmly.

Amanda smiled, gently detaching herself. 'Easy, Beryl, we don't want to give your companion the wrong impression, do we?'

Beryl laughed. 'No chance of that,' she said with conviction. 'Charlie here knows only too well how I like my sex – don't you, Charlie?'

Her companion nodded. 'Frequently,' he put in.

Amanda smiled. 'You haven't changed much, then,' she observed. 'Are you two staying the night?'

'Is that an invitation?' Beryl inquired. 'I thought all the guest rooms were fully booked.'

'You're not a guest, you're a good friend,' Amanda told her. 'We'll sort something out – even if you have to sleep in my bed.'

A stupid grin spread across Charlie's face. 'I'm all for that,' he said with great enthusiasm. His eyes roved over Amanda's lush body and the creamy breasts which overflowed from the low-cut evening dress.

Beryl gave him a sharp dig in the ribs. 'Forget it, Casanova,' she said. 'If Amanda is offering us her bed, it's a ten-to-one shot she has somebody else's bed in mind. Right, Amanda?'

Amanda smiled, thinking of Martin's strong and sinewy body. 'Something like that,' she agreed.

'Well, it's good to see that neither of us has changed,' Beryl observed with a smile. 'I thought you might have turned into a respectable businesswoman, Amanda.'

'No chance,' Amanda responded at once, but her tone failed to carry total conviction. Her eyes strayed to the bar, where Martin was busily pulling pints and living up to his unexpected new role.

The gesture was not lost on the observant Beryl, who followed her gaze.

'So you finally discovered the advantages of maturity in a man,' she murmured, correctly interpreting the situation.

It wasn't a subject Amanda wanted to discuss, or even dwell upon.

'Come on, let's get a drink,' she suggested, leading the way towards the opposite end of the bar where Andrew was serving. Ordering a round of drinks, she steered Beryl and Charles to a nearby table. 'Look,

I've got to circulate,' she explained. 'There are a lot of old friends here, and I need to do my welcoming hostess bit for a while. I'll catch up with you later, if that's all right.'

With a last fond squeeze of Beryl's arm, Amanda moved away. She had already spotted Giles in one corner of the room with a small group of the hunting fraternity.

'Hi,' she said brightly, approaching them.

To her surprise, Giles was civil enough, but oddly cool and distant.

'Ah, our charming hostess,' he said, going on to introduce her to his friends. They too were polite, but Amanda could sense an underlying hostility.

Perhaps it had something to do with her involuntary sabotage of the last hunt, she realised. Discreetly, she made her excuses and drifted away again, only to see Roger and Letitia making a beeline in her direction. Neither of them looked very happy.

Sensing that something was wrong, Amanda glanced around hastily, trying to find someone handy to engage in conversation. There was no-one within striking distance. Roger closed the gap between them and grasped her firmly by the arm. There was a smile on his face, but his eyes were cold and angry.

'Amanda, my dear,' he hissed. 'We want a little word with you.' Gripping her tightly, he steered her towards a quiet corner of the room.

Amanda winced with pain. 'Roger, you're hurting me,' she complained. 'What's wrong with you?'

Roger's eyes narrowed to slits. 'Believe me, Amanda, I'll hurt you a damned sight more if you interfere with my plans,' he threatened. 'Letitia and I were not at all happy with the way you stole one of our clients this afternoon.'

Amanda bluffed it out. 'He was turning me on,' she explained. 'What did you expect me to do – start fucking right there in front of everybody else?'

Roger's grip tightened even more. 'I'm just warning you, Amanda,' he spat viciously. 'Stay out of my business or you'll be bloody sorry.' He ended his little speech by digging his fingernails into the flesh of her arm, causing her to make a little squeal of pain.

Amanda wrenched herself free at last. 'I need a drink,' she said, turning on her heel and heading for the bar. She went directly to Martin.

'Roger is suspicious about something,' she whispered over the bar. 'The bastard just threatened me.'

Martin thought for a second. 'Maybe we'll have to make a move sooner than I anticipated,' he said finally. 'There's not much I can do while I'm stuck behind here. I'm going to have to count on you, I'm afraid.'

Under normal circumstances, Amanda was not the bravest person in the world. But Roger had threatened her, and it made her angry. Besides, she needed to prove something to Martin, show him that she was the sort of woman who could stand up under pressure.

'What do you want me to do,' Amanda said, her

270

voice firm and unwavering.

Martin looked at her with a new sense of admiration. 'That's my girl,' he said, and Amanda almost preened under the implied compliment.

'Now listen carefully,' Martin went on. 'I need that red record book you told me about. I couldn't get it yesterday because I think they were carrying it around with them. My guess is that they were out making a few collections.'

'So you want me to sneak up to their room and see if I can find it?' Amanda asked.

'Right.' Martin nodded. 'They've only just come down, so you should be safe for a while. Use your pass key, get into their room and find the book as quickly as possible, then get out again fast. Understand?'

'Got it,' Amanda said. She turned away from the bar. Martin called after her.

'And Amanda – be careful, don't take any risks,' he added. 'I wouldn't want anything unpleasant to happen to you.'

His concern gave her a warm glow inside. It helped to cancel out the equally cold feeling in the pit of her stomach.

Amanda headed for the door, glancing nervously behind her as she exited. She failed to notice Letitia's eyes firmly fixed on her, or the discreet nudge in Roger's ribs as she made her exit.

Ducking into the reception area, Amanda took out the pass key from behind the desk. Holding it tightly in her hand, she moved towards the stairs.

Behind her, in the bar, Bernard flounced into the room and called out at the top of his effeminate little voice.

'Food is served in the dining room,' he announced, with an evil gleam in his eyes.

Chapter Twenty-three

Amanda let herself into the room and headed directly for the bedside cabinet where she had found the record book hidden previously. Snapping on the table lamp, she opened the drawer and rummaged inside.

Letitia's black leather costume and whips were still there, but the red book was missing.

Frantically, Amanda checked the contents of the drawer, in case she had missed it. There was no mistake. The book had definitely gone. She tried the other drawers in turn, with an equal lack of success. She was so intent on her search that she failed to hear Letitia slip into the room behind her.

'Is this what you're looking for?' Letitia said quietly.

Amanda whirled round as though she had suddenly received an electric shock. Letitia stood, framed in the doorway, the red book in her hand. Her face was slightly mocking, but totally menacing. She closed the door slowly and silently behind her.

'I knew you were up to something,' Letitia hissed. 'You're stupid, Amanda, you should have kept your nose out of things that didn't concern you.'

Amanda's brain raced, zipping through the options open to her. She considered the most obvious and direct alternative of trying to overpower Letitia and escape through the door, but rejected it. Something told her that the athletically built girl would be more than a match for her in a show of strength, and it didn't take much intelligence to realise that with so much to lose, Letitia would be a pretty dirty fighter.

Instead, Amanda retreated, placing more distance between them. It was a mistake, giving Letitia the advantage.

The redhead ran forwards, quickly snatching the vicious black leather bullwhip from the open drawer. Retreating back to the door, she flexed the weapon with her supple wrist, her eyes fixed on Amanda with a baleful glare.

'Well, I guess it's time to find out what you actually *do* know and what you've pieced together,' Letitia said, in a low and menacing voice. She flexed the whip again. 'This little persuader ought to loosen your tongue a bit.'

Letitia drew back her arm slowly. Her wrist jerked. Amanda squealed out in pain as the vicious lash snaked out to deliver a sharp sting to her bare shoulder. Glancing down, she could see that the end of the whip had made a small red weal against her white flesh, not quite hard enough to actually break the skin.

'That was just a tickle,' Letitia said. 'Just to let you see how expert I am with this thing.'

The whip cracked again, but Amanda felt no pain this time. Instead, she felt her dress suddenly sag in an odd way. Looking down at her shoulder again, she saw that Letitia had managed to target the very tip of the vicious lash at one of the shoulder straps of her evening dress. Its tearing, destructive power had been enough to rip the thin strap completely away from the main fabric of the dress.

Letitia chuckled gloatingly. 'See what I mean?' She made the whip arc out yet again, destroying the strap on the opposite shoulder. Deprived of support, the expensive dress began to slide off Amanda's smooth shoulders.

Instinctively, she raised her hand to stop the dress slipping to the floor. A vicious crack of the whip and a sharp, painful sting on her wrist persuaded her otherwise. Helpless, Amanda let the dress slide down to her feet in a crumpled heap. As usual, she wore no bra.

Letitia eyed her lush body appreciatively, her green eyes flashing emerald fire and her full lips drawn up in a sneering, vicious smile.

'I suppose you realise by now that I could mark you for life with this thing?' she hissed, with sadistic pleasure. As if to back up her claim with some hard proof, she sent the end of the lash snaking towards Amanda's defenceless body again. Amanda screamed in agony as the sharp leather cracked against her naked belly, leaving a thin red scar from which a trickle of blood began to seep.

Letitia lowered the whip, but Amanda could see that it would take a mere flick of her wrist to bring it into operation again.

'So,' Letitia said quietly. 'It's time for a little chat. I'm going to ask you some questions and you're going to give me some answers. Only they'd better be the answers I want to hear. If not, I'm going to work on your beautiful tits.'

Amanda's blood ran cold at the sheer evil and sadism of the woman. Up to this point, she had half imagined that Letitia was something of a victim in this entire messy business – perhaps sucked in against her better judgement by Roger's strange power over women. Now she realised that this was far from the truth. Letitia was a scheming, cold-blooded and thoroughly nasty piece of work. The pair of them fully deserved each other.

'Why did you start poking your nose in to start with?' Letitia demanded. 'What made you start snooping around in our room? We knew someone had seen the book, because they put it back upside-down.'

Amanda could see no point in trying to lie at this stage. In any case, the basic truth was innocent enough. She explained the need to borrow Letitia's dominatrix uniform and the accidental discovery of the red book.

Letitia digested the information and thought about it for a few seconds.

'So what did you imagine the book contained?' she asked, finally.

Amanda shrugged. 'I didn't think anything,' she said. 'I didn't really read what was inside.'

Letitia's hand and arm moved in a blur. The stinging end of the lash cracked against the side of Amanda's soft breast. Amanda screamed out in pain and anguish, forcing herself to look down even though she expected to see blood and raw, shredded flesh.

Instead, there was just a small red spot. It had been a token strike – nothing more.

'One lie – one last warning,' Letitia said coldly. 'So, no more of either.'

Amanda gave up, hopelessly. She had no doubts that Letitia was just waiting for the excuse to really hurt her. Bluff hadn't worked. There was only the truth left.

'All right, so it didn't take much working out to realise that you and Roger had a nice little blackmail racket going,' Amanda conceded.

Letitia nodded thoughtfully. 'So why did you come back here tonight?' she asked. 'Thought you could cut yourself in on the deal, did you?'

For the first time, Amanda saw a glimmer of hope and latched on to it quickly. Letitia herself had provided a totally plausible lie. All Amanda had to do was to play along with it to gain valuable time. Sooner or later, she was sure, Martin would start to worry about her and come to the rescue.

'OK, so it was worth a try,' Amanda said, trying to sound like someone who has been caught out at last. 'All that easy money going, I thought I'd like to get my share. You would have done the same, wouldn't you?'

The final line was the clincher, just as Amanda had hoped it would be. She eyed Letitia carefully as she thought it over. Finally, the redhead's lips curled into a thin smile.

'Sure, but then I would have been a bit smarter about it,' she conceded, having apparently swallowed Amanda's story hook line and sinker.

Amanda pressed her advantage. She shrugged. 'Yes, well – I'm the traditional dumb blonde. Still, you can't blame me for trying. This is my club, after all. Surely I ought to get a share?'

Letitia thought this over.

'Well, you could certainly be very useful to us,' she agreed after a while. 'I don't suppose Roger would object to cutting you in for a small piece of the action – provided you fit in with our ideas.'

Amanda forced a smile. 'Hey, I fit in with anyone,' she said with faked enthusiasm. 'Little Miss Jigsaw Piece, that's me.'

Letitia suddenly grinned. She cracked the whip again, delivering a sharp sting to Amanda's bare buttocks.

It was not hard enough to really hurt, but Amanda let out a cry of surprise, rather than pain.

'What the hell was that for?' she demanded. 'I've told you what you wanted to know.'

Letitia's eyes glittered. 'The first part was work,' she murmured. 'This is for fun.' She flicked the whip again, raking the inside of Amanda's soft thigh. 'Let's see just how well you're willing to fit in. Get down on your hands and knees.'

Confused, and more than a little alarmed at the sudden new turn things were taking, Amanda obeyed. She had no desire to serve as further target practice in Letitia's vicious little games.

Letitia reached down with her free hand and lifted up her skirt. 'Now come over here and suck my cunt,' she commanded.

Amanda's response was immediate, reflex and instinctive. 'Kiss my arse,' she shot back.

Letitia did exactly that – but with the end of the lash. Amanda squealed with pain as the leather tip made contact with her bare buttock.

'Let's try that again,' Letitia said coldly. 'You crawl over here, stick your head between my legs and stick your tongue into my crack. And when you've satisfied me with a good tonguing, I'll expect you to suck up every drop of my juice and swallow it.'

Amanda didn't move. Letitia cracked the whip again, catching her on the shoulder. 'I like to be obeyed,' she murmured. 'Now get over here and start sucking my cunt like you've never sucked before.'

Amanda shuddered at the horror of her two alternatives. Either she did Letitia's vile bidding, or the sadistic bitch would turn her body into a mass of bloody jelly. Either choice was equally repugnant to her.

Letitia's arm began to move again, spurring

Amanda into action. She began to crawl across the carpeted floor towards her tormentress.

Letitia smiled wickedly, spreading her legs further apart and hoisting up her skirt even higher.

'That's it, Amanda. Now you're showing some sense,' she said. 'Come and eat pussy, my little precious.'

Silently, Amanda crawled forward until her blonde curls were touching Letitia's knees. She looked up, to where Letitia's flaming bush of pubic hair poked through a pair of black split-crotch panties. Nestling in the middle of the furry mound, the gaping slit of the girl's cunt was already glistening and dripping with love juice.

Slowly, very slowly, Amanda raised her head towards the pouting crack. Letitia made a faint growling noise in her throat at the feel of Amanda's hair tickling the soft insides of her thighs. As Amanda drew close to Letitia's cunt, she opened her mouth wide, as though to suck upon it like a split watermelon.

Instead, she clamped her teeth into the softest and most tender part of the girl's thigh and bit with all her strength.

Letitia let out a wailing scream of sheer agony as Amanda's teeth broke the flesh and drew blood. The whip dropped from fingers that had suddenly gone numb as the pain racked through her body.

Amanda was on her feet in a flash, scooping up the whip as she rose. Grasping it about a foot down from the heavy, knotted leather handle, she swung it like a club against the side of Letitia's head. The redhead collapsed as though she had been poleaxed. She was out cold.

Amanda stood over her unconscious form and drew a long, deep breath. She waited until all her fear had been washed away on a soothing tide of relief before stooping down to lash Letitia's wrists tightly together with the leather thong of the whip, drawing the knots more tightly and painfully than was strictly necessary. When that job was done to her satisfaction, she rummaged through the drawers until she found a couple of pairs of tights and used them to bind the girl's ankles.

Amanda picked up the red book and Letitia's shoulder bag from the floor. Rooting through the bag, Amanda found the single set of room keys and took them out, feeling a sense of relief. She had given Letitia and Roger only one set of keys between them, and she held the only pass key. That meant that Letitia would be safely locked away with no chance of rescue.

There was also a battery-operated dildo in the shoulder bag. With a wicked thought in her mind, Amanda took it out. She looked down at the securely bound Letitia, who was just regaining consciousness.

Amanda smiled sweetly as the girl's green eyes flickered open.

'You wanted me to suck cunt,' she murmured. 'Now I'm going to give you a chance to suck cock.'

She stuffed the dildo deep into Letitia's slack

mouth, binding it in place with a pair of elasticated panties. It would make a highly effective gag, she thought.

Satisfied that the girl was now completely helpless, Amanda put on her dress again and fixed the shoulder straps temporarily with a couple of safety pins. She could go back to her own room and change before returning downstairs.

She moved towards the door, pausing briefly to look back at the gagged and bound girl on the floor.

'You'll like ten years in Holloway,' she told her. 'Only I think you're likely to get your cunt sucked a little bit more than you bargained for.'

Letitia glared at her with undiluted hate as Amanda left, making sure the door was securely locked behind her.

Chapter Twenty-four

Roger collared her the second she strolled back into the bar. Amanda had only just come through the door when she felt his tight grip on her arm from behind.

'Where's Letitia?' he hissed in her ear.

'She's still in her room,' Amanda replied, truthfully enough. 'I think she's planning to stay there for a while.'

Roger propelled her into a corner, allowing her to turn round and face him directly.

'So what went on up there?' he wanted to know. 'Was I right? Were you trying to muscle in on our little scam?'

Amanda saw no reason to disillusion him. It was obviously the conclusion that both he and Letitia had come to, and for now it made sense to stick to the same story.

'Letitia and I came to a little deal,' Amanda told him.

Roger's eyes narrowed. 'And you're going to be happy with that? No more interfering?'

Amanda smiled innocently. 'Oh, I can assure you that I'm perfectly happy with the eventual outcome of our negotiations,' she said. 'Letitia did think she held the whip hand for a while, but I finally tied things up to my satisfaction.'

She pulled herself free from his grip. 'Now if you don't mind, I'm going to get myself a drink.'

Amanda headed for the bar. Seeing her coming, Martin ignored all the other customers clamouring for his attention and moved along the bar to meet her.

'What took you so long?' he hissed. 'I was getting worried about you.'

'Everything's fine,' Amanda assured him. It wasn't the time to go into details. She furtively produced the red book which she had been concealing, and slipped it across the counter. 'This should give you all the evidence you need. When are you going to pull Roger in?'

Martin slipped the book into his back pocket. 'Now I have this – right away,' he said firmly. 'Can you hold the bar for half an hour or so?'

'Sure.' Amanda nodded. She skirted around the bar and ducked in under the flap.

'See you later,' Martin said, and was gone.

From the business side of the bar, Amanda suddenly realised how busy the place actually was. There were several hundred people milling about – and a high proportion of them appeared to be extremely thirsty. She glanced along the bar at Andrew, who was rushing about like a blue-arsed fly, then back at the customers who were pressed three or four deep against the counter. It was patently obvious that the two of them were never going to be able to cope. Any minute now, there was going to be a riot.

It was time to call in the emergency troops, Amanda decided. She stared out through the milling throng, searching for a friendly face.

Finding Beryl, Amanda called her over urgently. 'Listen, Beryl, can you do me a favour,' she pleaded. 'Round up two or three of the girls and ask them if they'll help out behind the bar for a while, would you?'

Beryl grinned good-naturedly. 'Sure thing,' she said easily. 'I saw Chrissie and Fiona a couple of minutes ago. They just went into the dining room to get some food from the buffet. I'll go and fetch them.'

Beryl scurried off on her mission, while Amanda busied herself pouring double gin and tonic for the hunting fraternity.

Beryl was back within two minutes, with Fiona and Chrissie. Both girls still had traces of Bernard's oyster-and-cunt pie around the corners of their mouths. Lifting the flap, Amanda invited them behind the bar.

'Listen, I hope you don't mind helping out like this for a while,' she said. 'I'll make it worth your while later on.'

Both girls shrugged. 'Anything to help out,' Fiona said with a smile, and went straight into action, having served as a barmaid before in her chequered career.

Chrissie regarded Amanda dumbly.

'What do I do?' she wanted to know. Chrissie was not exactly brain of Britain.

Amanda gestured to the beer pumps and to the rows of optics. There's the beer, and there's the booze,' she said. 'Most of the prices are marked, but don't worry too much. Charge everybody one pound-fifty for each drink and you won't be far out.'

'Oh,' Chrissie murmured. She continued to stare at the beer pumps blankly. 'How do I work these things?'

Amanda took the girl's hand and wrapped it around the nearest beer handle.

'Just pretend that's a stiff cock,' she said. 'And pull it lovingly.'

Chrissie's eyes brightened. 'Oh, that should be easy,' she said with a giggle.

Leaving the two girls to it, Amanda went in search of Martin. She found him coming down the stairs, looking pretty pleased with himself.

'Everything all right?' Amanda asked.

Martin nodded. 'He put up a bit of a fight, but I can handle the Roger Vennings of this world. I've handcuffed him to the radiator in my room. He'll be safe enough there until the night's over.'

Amanda explained, quickly, about her own citizen's arrest of Letitia.

Martin's eyes sparkled with admiration. 'Nice piece

of work,' he said. 'We make a pretty good team, don't we?'

Amanda felt a warm glow of pleasure inside at hearing praise from Martin's lips and preened like a schoolgirl who has turned in a good piece of homework.

'Well, I'd better get back to the bar,' Martin said awkwardly, aware that Amanda was gazing up at him with slightly moist, adoring eyes.

Amanda grasped his hand. 'Sod the bar,' she said firmly. 'You've done your work for the night. Now it's time for play.'

Martin had the sense and decency not to protest as Amanda led him back towards the stairs.

Martin looked up at the room number on the door with surprise as Amanda prepared to open it with the pass key.

'This isn't your room,' he pointed out.

Amanda grinned. 'I know.' She opened the door and showed Martin through into the bedroom.

Letitia looked up at them with disappointment clouding her green eyes. When she had heard the sound of the key in the lock, she had fondly imagined Roger was coming to rescue her.

Martin looked down at the helpless girl, then back to Amanda. He looked confused.

'Amanda, what's going on?'

Amanda grinned savagely. 'Poor Letitia isn't going to get any straight sex for a long time where she's going,' she said, raising her voice so that the unfortunate girl could hear every word. 'So I thought it might be fitting punishment for us to screw right here in front of her – just to remind her what she is going to be missing.'

Martin grimaced. 'Amanda, that's perverse,' he said. 'Even a trifle on the sadistic side, don't you think?'

Amanda wasn't listening. She had stripped off the top of her dress, exposing the vicious red weals on her beautiful breasts where Letitia's whip had found its mark.

'Do you really think so, after what she did to me?' she asked Martin.

Martin saw the scars and scowled. 'No, maybe not,' he agreed.

Amanda undressed and lounged seductively across the bed as Martin stepped out of his trousers.

'Make it good, lover, you're performing for a very discerning audience,' she told him.

The second time around, Martin was less gentle but even more skilled in the techniques of sexual gratification. Amanda squirmed with sensual pleasure as he ran his tongue over every part of her naked body, kissing each little whip mark tenderly and teasing the rest of it into tingling sexual readiness. She caressed his stiff cock lovingly as he probed every sensitive little area with his hot tongue, licking her eyes, lips, ears and throat on his way down to more obvious places.

Amanda's eyes rolled with ecstasy as he buried his

face between her thighs and began to tongue the swollen lips of her cunt, sucking on her erect clitoris until it throbbed in response.

Yet, despite her personal raptures, she kept one eye closely on Letitia, who was watching the entire scene with an expression of total loathing. Perhaps Martin had been right, she thought, and this little scene was totally perverse. But then revenge brought its own delicious thrill, which more than made up for any slight feelings of guilt.

So when Martin's thick cock finally ploughed deep into her hungry fanny, Amanda's groans of pleasure were just that little bit too exaggerated, her sensuous thrashings just a shade overdone for Letitia's benefit.

Finally, when Martin had exploded into her brimming cunt and she had let out one last shriek of pure pleasure, Amanda rose from the bed and crossed over to the bound girl, gazing down on her with a look of total satisfaction on her face.

She unwrapped the panties and took the dildo out of Letitia's mouth.

'Enjoy the show?' she asked.

'Bitch,' Letitia spat at her. 'I wish I had torn your tits to shreds.'

'Too late for regrets now, love,' Amanda told her with a smile. 'You should always take your chances when they come.'

Amanda returned to the bed to dress. Martin zipped up his trousers and donned his black evening jacket. 'I'll be back for you later,' he told the girl on the floor as they prepared to leave.

'Wait,' Letitia called after them. 'Look, would it make things any easier for me if I handed over most of the money we've pulled in?'

Martin turned back to her, his eyes narrowing thoughtfully. 'I can't promise any deals,' he warned, 'but obviously any cooperation you give me now will go in your favour.'

Letitia nodded her head towards the air-conditioning vent up in the wall.

'There's over sixty thousand hidden in there,' she told him. 'Virtually all the blackmail money we've collected in the past month.'

Martin smiled. 'Not quite,' he observed. 'It seems your dear friend Roger has been holding out on you. He told me about another fifteen thousand tucked away in the gymnasium.'

Amanda had already crossed to the vent and was unscrewing the grille. She pulled out a large brown envelope and checked the contents before handing it to Martin.

'Naughty girl,' she admonished Letitia. 'You should have asked to use the club's safe.'

She tripped out of the door, motioning Martin to follow her.

As they returned downstairs, everything sounded perfectly normal. The sounds of the hired band playing in the ballroom drifted along the corridors, and there was a buzz of conversation and activity coming from the bar.

Amanda smiled with satisfaction. 'Looks like this Hunt Ball is working out pretty well,' she said to Martin.

It was something of a premature judgement. Bernard's aphrodisiac food had done its worst.

Chapter Twenty-five

'I've heard of dirty dancing, but this is ridiculous,' Amanda exclaimed in astonishment, as they walked into the ballroom.

Martin followed her shocked gaze on to the dance floor, which resembled a movie set for a Roman orgy scene. Under the pulsing strobe lights, at least fifty couples writhed together in various stages of advanced sexual passion, all vaguely in time with the band, who were still playing bravely on as though everything was normal.

The dance floor itself was littered with discarded cocktail-dresses, black tuxedos and white dress-shirts. Virtually every dancer was stripped naked, at least from the waist up, with a good dozen couples and individuals who had already gone the whole hog and were happily prancing about totally nude. The general impression was one of a small sea of moving, touching flesh.

Amanda tore her disbelieving eyes away from the dancers to the tables scattered around the edges of the floor. There, out of the glare of the lights, the majority of the guests had completely abandoned themselves to a full-scale sexual orgy.

On top of the tables and underneath them, on chairs and on the floor, and even standing up against the walls, naked people performed scores of different sexual acts, in varying permutations, configurations and numbers. Pairs, trios and larger groups humped and heaved at each other in a confusing mêlée of cunts and cocks, mouths and tongues, tits and arses. The wallflowers, the loners and the voyeurs seemed content to stand on the sidelines and merely look on, while idly masturbating themselves.

Amanda found her own gaze drawn to one particularly inventive group of people who had managed to arrange themselves into a sort of sexual daisychain. She watched with prurient fascination as the eight-strong group performed a sexual conga on the floor – sucking and fucking at each other in a set-up that ensured that each individual was engaged in at least two different sexual acts at any one time.

Those of more specific sexual persuasions had formed their own little area near the emergency fire doors. Martin's eyes bulged as he picked out two large, full-breasted women curled into a tight *soixante-neuf*, their mouths buried in each other's succulent cunts. Beside them, content with her own lonely pleasure, a younger woman sat watching the performance, ramming a long white candle, which she had robbed from a nearby candelabra, into her own juicy hole.

She seemed to sense Martin's eyes upon her, for

she looked up in his direction, rose to her feet and strolled over casually, still sliding the candle in and out of her dripping cunt as she walked.

'What's the matter? Why have you still got all your clothes on?' she demanded of Martin, completely ignoring Amanda.

With her free hand, she reached out to Martin's flies, trying to find his zipper.

'Come on, get your trousers off. Wouldn't you like to fuck me? Wouldn't you like to stick your big fat cock into my slippery little cunt?'

If Martin was at all tempted by the offer, Amanda's tight grip on his arm told him that accepting would be a definite mistake. He drew back, away from the woman's questing fingers.

The woman seemed to get the message. Shrugging, she turned away and headed into the middle of the dance floor, shouting out at the top of her voice.

'Come on, you load of useless wankers. Who's going to give me a good screwing? I'm fed up with fucking myself with this candle. I want a real cock inside me.'

Amanda tugged on Martin's arm insistently.

'What the hell's going on, Martin?'

Martin turned his eyes away from the candle-wielding woman's progress into the sea of flesh somewhat reluctantly. He would have liked to find out whether she got her wish or not.

His attention now firmly back on Amanda, Martin could only wave his hands in a gesture of total confusion in answer to her question.

'I haven't the faintest idea,' he admitted. 'But if the ballroom is like this, then what in the name of hell is going on in the bar?'

Amanda pulled at his sleeve.

'Perhaps we'd better go and find out,' she suggested.

With one last, still unbelieving glance back into the heaving ballroom, they beat a hasty retreat in the direction of the bar.

If anything, the scene in the bar was even worse, Bernard's powerful mixture had been strengthened threefold by the added effects of alcohol.

Amanda's two emergency bar staff recruits had long since given up any pretence of serving their customers with drinks. Instead, they were dispensing one hundred per cent proof sex, with Chrissie laid out on the bar top being energetically fucked by the deputy Master of the Hounds and Fiona giving out blow jobs to all-comers behind the counter.

Perhaps in keeping with the spirit of the Hunt Ball, or possibly because they just liked it that way, several naked men wielding horse whips rode around the floor on the backs of kneeling naked women, yelling out traditional calls such as 'yoicks', 'tally-ho' and 'up and at 'em'.

Amanda looked round for Giles in the sea of flesh, eventually finding him seated at one of the tables with a pleased if rather bemused expression on his face as her friend Beryl sucked frantically on his

magnificent cock. Far from being jealous, her partner
Charlie had taken full advantage of the mad sexual
free-for-all, and was busy sucking the huge tits of a
horsey-looking woman who straddled his lap,
bouncing herself up and down on his stiff prick as
though she was riding a Grand National winner to
victory.

With Giles so obviously occupied, Amanda gave up
any ideas she might have had about finding a sane or
sober explanation for the bizarre state of affairs.
Grabbing Martin by the hand, she steered him
through the mass of feverish sexual activity towards
the bar.

'We might as well help ourselves to a drink,' she
observed. 'Everybody else seems to be doing so.'

She pushed past a couple having a knee-trembler
up against the bar counter and joined a small queue
of people raiding the row of spirit optics. She poured
a couple of extremely large measures and handed
one to Martin.

'I guess there isn't a lot I can actually do,' she
mused eventually, after a healthy intake of hard
alcohol had helped to calm her confused brain.

Martin agreed with a noncommittal grunt, half
his attention on Amanda and the other half on a
group of four women who were clustered around
Phillipe the gardener's massive prick like the
handmaidens of the gods. With almost reverential
worship, they took it in turns to lick, kiss and suck
upon the monstrous and throbbing cock as its proud

owner lay happily taking his pick of naked breasts to fondle.

Chrissie slid into view directly in front of Amanda and Martin as they sipped at their drinks. She was being pumped along the smooth counter top by the rhythmic, thrusting action of a trouserless but otherwise immaculately dressed man whom Amanda recognised as Clive Brannart. He was plunging his stiff prick in and out of her yawning cunt like a steam piston.

Chrissie looked up and flashed Amanda a dreamy smile.

'Isn't this fantastic,' she said with great enthusiasm. 'I never realised that being a barmaid could be so much fun.'

Amanda reached down to hold her head, preventing further movement along the counter.

'Thanks, Amanda,' said Clive. 'When we're through, how about you and me . . .?'

Amanda shook her head and he smiled ruefully before returning his attention to the job in hand, his buttocks rising and falling in a blur of flesh as he stabbed into his now stationary target with renewed vigour.

'Chrissie, what the hell happened?' Amanda wanted to know. 'How did this bloody orgy get started?'

Chrissie's eyes were glassy as she tried to concentrate upon Amanda's face. 'I'm not really sure,' she managed to get out between grunts and little moans of pleasure. 'We had something to eat, and the next thing I remember is feeling incredibly horny. Next thing I knew, everybody else got to feel the same way and people started taking their clothes off.'

Amanda removed her hand. Chrissie began to jerk up the counter again, finally sliding out of Amanda's eye view.

'It's the bloody food,' Martin said suddenly. 'It's that aphrodisiac mixture. Somebody has made a mistake and put too much in.'

Amanda scowled, remembering her little run-in with Bernard earlier in the day.

'No, it's no mistake,' she muttered, finally twigging what was going on. 'The nasty little bastard did this deliberately. It's his way of getting back at me.' She was silent for a few seconds, thinking about things. 'I suppose there's not likely to be an antidote, is there?' she asked Martin at length.

He shook his head. 'Not from my analysis. Only time, basically. These people will probably continue to fuck themselves silly until it starts to wear off.'

'So there's absolutely nothing I can do?' Amanda asked, even though she already had her answer.

Martin grinned. 'Well I suppose we could always join in,' he said brightly. 'You know – if you can't beat 'em, join 'em.'

Amanda gave him a withering look. 'I do hope you're not serious,' she said icily. 'I like my sex in a bit of privacy.'

Martin smiled. 'Just kidding,' he assured her – although Amanda was not entirely convinced. 'I suppose we could always go and find Bernard, just in case he does have something that will help to make the effects wear off a bit sooner. If not, I could always arrest the little bastard on an attempted poisoning charge, if it would make you feel a little better.'

Amanda was looking out over the mass of humping bodies. With something of a surprise, she picked out Jack, the garage owner and anti-hunting group leader. With his convictions, and track record, it was a pretty safe bet that he was here with some nasty little scheme in mind.

'I've got an even better idea,' Amanda announced, suddenly realising that she could settle two old scores at the same time.

She pointed Jack out for Martin. 'See that man? He's the little shit who tried to gang-rape me,' she told him. 'What I would like you to do is to go and pull him in for me right now, and then bring him back over here.'

'Why not?' Martin said, agreeing more readily than Amanda had thought. 'I guess I still owe you a couple of favours.'

Martin vaulted over the counter, striding across the room to where Jack was attempting to get himself accepted by a mixed threesome. As Amanda watched, Martin grabbed the man in a savage half-nelson and began to frogmarch him back towards the bar.

'Now what?' he asked, when Jack was pressed tightly against the bar.

'Now we take him down to the kitchens,' Amanda

answered. There was a smugly satisfied grin on her face. Jack looked up at her, his face black with rage.

'What do you think you're doing?' he demanded angrily.

Amanda looked at him sweetly. 'I'm about to introduce you to the great love of your life,' she told him.

She turned to Martin. 'Will you bring him down to the kitchen for me?' A knowing smile began to dawn on Martin's face. 'You're not planning to do what I think you're planning to do . . . are you?'

Amanda said nothing, but her silence spoke volumes. Martin chuckled.

'My dear Amanda, you are even more vindictive than I thought,' he muttered with amusement in his voice.

Pushing the struggling Jack ahead of him, Martin followed Amanda out of the bar and towards the kitchen.

Bernard looked up as the unexpected trio burst into his kitchen – at first merely in surprise, but with a growing sense of alarm as he noticed the struggling Jack and the stern look on Amanda's face.

'What do you want?' he bleated, attempting to brazen things out.

Amanda said nothing, picking up a particularly large and sharp-looking kitchen knife from the table and brandishing it threateningly.

Bernard paled, all sorts of nasty possibilities flitting

through his mind. He backed away towards the larder, his eyes firmly fixed on the gleaming blade of the knife.

Amanda saw his fear and smiled to herself.

'Relax, Bernard,' she told him sweetly. 'We haven't come down to carve any little bits off you. It's more of a supper party, if you like.'

Amanda's eyes had already fallen on a couple of plates laden with the little chef's highly spiked aphrodisiac dishes. Bernard followed her gaze and his face registered a faint, but rapidly growing comprehension.

'You wouldn't,' he whined.

'Oh yes I would,' Amanda told him firmly. 'After what you did to my little shindig, I should think that's fairly poetic justice, wouldn't you say?'

Waving the knife menacingly, she gestured for him to sit down at the table.

'Now eat,' she commanded.

Never the bravest of souls, Bernard took one last look at the vicious blade in Amanda's hand and started to stuff food into his mouth.

'Now you, Jack,' Amanda murmured, as Bernard stuffed himself.

Martin pushed the man to another chair and forced him down into it. Amanda pushed a large plate of Bernard's specialities under his nose.

'Tuck in, Jack,' she invited him. 'Make a pig of yourself.'

Conscious of Martin's firm grip still on his arm,

Jack too began to force food into his mouth.

Bernard choked down a second helping of banana split and looked up at Amanda pleadingly. 'That's enough, isn't it?' he asked imploringly. 'This stuff has some pretty nasty aftereffects if you take an overdose.'

Amanda wasn't in the mood to be generous. 'A fat lot you cared about that when you dosed all my guests with it,' she pointed out. She waved the knife again. 'Have another good helping.'

Satisfied that Jack had eaten more than his fill, Martin released him and stepped back.

'Now what do we do with them?' he asked Amanda.

She shrugged. 'Nothing,' she said simply. 'Now we just lock them both securely in the food larder and let nature take its course. Or, in Bernard's case, should I say unnatural course?'

Jack was beginning to fall in. He looked at the simpering little chef with a mixture of horror and loathing on his face.

'You're not going to lock me in with this little faggot, are you?' he moaned.

Amanda nodded. 'That's exactly what I'm going to do, Jack. And with enough of Bernard's little mixture coursing through your system, you'll shortly be so bloody randy that you'd happily fuck a syphilitic warthog. My guess is by the time that stuff wears off in the morning, you'll be about ready to despise yourself for the rest of your life.'

She turned her attention to Bernard, with a disarming smile on her face. 'Bernard, of course, will probably enjoy the experience. But, of course, he will have his own little problems in the morning, since his companion for the night will probably be feeling extremely angry, violent and eager to take it out on whoever is handy. In addition, he will have the rather depressing knowledge that we shall be back to arrest him on a charge of administering illegal drugs and conspiracy to commit blackmail.'

She turned to Martin. 'Would you be so good as to escort our two lovebirds to their nesting compartment for the night?'

Martin grinned, his face tinged with more than a hint of admiration for Amanda's sheer artistry in retribution. Pulling Jack from his chair, he thrust him across the kitchen towards the larder as Amanda forced Bernard to follow suit at knifepoint.

Shoving the unlikely pair into the small larder, Amanda closed and securely bolted the door. She looked up at Martin.

'Thanks,' she said. 'Although to tell you the truth, I'm surprised that you agreed to help me quite so readily.'

Martin smiled warmly. 'Believe me, Amanda, this job is usually so damned depressing that I'm glad for the chance of a bit of fun,' he said. 'Meeting you has been like a breath of fresh air in my life.'

They looked at each other in silence for a while.

'Well, what do we do now?' Amanda asked eventually. 'Do we go back and watch the orgy?'

Martin shook his head. 'I think not.'

'So what, then?' Amanda grinned suggestively. 'You think we should have a little orgy of our own?'

'I thought you'd never get round to suggesting it,' Martin said, with great enthusiasm. 'I think we can safely leave everyone else to their own devices, don't you?'

'Absolutely,' Amanda agreed fervently. She glanced aside at the unfinished food on the table. Looking up at Martin again, she grinned roguishly.

'Fancy a little snack before we go up to my room?'

Martin laughed, knowing that she was only joking.

'Believe me, Amanda, you're one girl who most definitely doesn't need any special diet to get you going.'

He patted her tenderly on the rump as they walked out of the kitchen.

Chapter Twenty-six

The sounds of the orgy going on downstairs drifted through every room in the club as Amanda and Martin undressed and lay together on the bed.

Martin pressed against her, his fingers moving naturally towards the hot moistness between her legs, his lips closed around the swelling bud of her left nipple.

Amanda rolled away from him suddenly, turning on her side and staring directly into his eyes.

Martin looked surprised.

'What's the matter?' he asked. 'Don't you want me to touch you?'

Amanda smiled gently.

'I was just thinking of all that action you're missing out on downstairs,' she murmured. 'So I figured I ought to make it up to you somehow.'

Martin didn't quite understand until Amanda rolled over on top of him and reached down to take hold of his already stiff and throbbing cock. She guided it to the soft lips of her hot slit.

'So you just lie still and enjoy things,' she purred throatily. 'This one's on me.'

Martin let out a little gasp of pleasure as Amanda sank down on to his quivering shaft. Leaning forward over his broad chest, she plumped up a couple of pillows and tucked them under Martin's head, so that he could see through her dangling breasts to where his proud cock was buried between her thighs.

Pushing herself back, Amanda sat up, completely impaled on a thick spike of tumescent flesh.

'Just watch, feel and enjoy,' she said softly, beginning to clench and unclench her stomach muscles in a slow, sensuous rhythm.

Martin groaned softly at the delicious sensation of having his cock squeezed and massaged in such an exciting way. It felt as though he had plunged his prick into some sort of heated milking machine, which was now trying to suck and pump the very essence right out of his loins.

'My God, that's fantastic,' he breathed, voicing his pleasure and gratitude.

Amanda merely smiled, increasing her rhythmic contractions by gradual degrees until the inside of her love shaft was like a soft, warm hand – jerking him off internally.

Martin's own muscles seemed to twitch in time with Amanda's contractions as the tempo increased to fever pitch. Finally, he was unable to lay still any longer. Raising his hips from the bed, he stabbed upwards into her belly as he felt the trembling spasms preceding his ejaculation. With a final heave, he spurted into her and felt his creamy come being sucked deep into her pulsating tunnel of love.

Amanda flopped over him, her soft breasts crushed against his chest. She lay with her face pressed into his shoulder, her gasping breath hot against his neck. They lay there silently for several minutes, until Amanda had got her breath back.

'You know what you were saying about your job being so depressing,' she murmured, finally.

Martin nodded his head gently by way of reply.

'Well why don't you quit?' Amanda suggested tentatively. 'You must have put enough years in to get a decent pension – even a golden handshake.'

Martin sighed. 'Nice idea, Amanda,' he conceded. 'But what would I do? Much as I hate the job, I'm a man who has to be doing something – something that gives me a bit of a challenge.'

It was the cue that Amanda had been hoping for. 'You could always stay and help me run this place,' she said. 'We have £75,000 which we would use to really do the place up. Roger and Letitia aren't going to mention it since it would further incriminate them, and the blackmail victims aren't going to kick up a song and dance because all their dirty washing would come out in the open.'

Martin lay very still for a long time, thinking about it.

'Of course you realise that keeping that money would be technically illegal?' he said at last.

Amanda shrugged. 'Like I said – who's going to miss it?'

Martin took another few seconds off for consideration. It was, he had to admit, a very tempting proposition.

Amanda sensed that she had him on the run, and pressed home her advantage.

'We could always try to turn the Paradise Club back into a fully respectable establishment,' she went on. 'Make it what it ought to be – a sporting, health and leisure retreat for overstressed business people.'

As Amanda finished her little speech, the orgy downstairs went into a secondary and more boisterous stage. The sounds of wild screaming and ribald laughter rolled along the corridors outside their bedroom.

Martin began to chuckle, and finally to laugh out loud.

'Turning this place respectable? Now that would be a *real* challenge,' he managed to blurt out, finally.

'Then you'll think about it?' Amanda asked.

'I'll think about it in the morning,' Martin promised.

'Then I've got the rest of the night to finish persuading you,' Amanda said. She began to clench her stomach muscles again, massaging his soft and satisfied cock inside her. Looking into Martin's eyes, she winked.

'Just to make sure you give it some really hard thought,' she murmured.

Headline Delta Erotic Survey

In order to provide the kind of books you like to read - and to qualify for a free erotic novel of the Editor's choice - we would appreciate it if you would complete the following survey and send your answers, together with any further comments, to:

Headline Book Publishing
FREEPOST 9 (WD 4984)
London
W1E 7BE

1. Are you male or female?
2. Age? Under 20 / 20 to 30 / 30 to 40 / 40 to 50 /
      50 to 60 / 60 to 70 / over
3. At what age did you leave full-time education?
4. Where do you live? (Main geographical area)
5. Are you a regular erotic book buyer / a regular book buyer in general / both?
6. How much approximately do you spend a year on erotic books / on books in general?
7. How did you come by this book?
7a. If you bought it, did you purchase from:
      a national bookchain / a high street store / a newsagent / a motorway station / an airport / a railway station / other........
8. Do you find erotic books easy / hard to come by?
8a. Do you find Headline Delta erotic books easy / hard to come by?
9. Which are the best / worst erotic books you have ever read?
9a. Which are the best / worst Headline Delta erotic books you have ever read?
10. Within the erotic genre there are many periods, subjects and literary styles. Which of the following do you prefer:
10a. (period) historical / Victorian / C20th / contemporary / future?
10b. (subject) nuns / whores & whorehouses / Continental frolics / s&m / vampires / modern realism / escapist fantasy / science fiction?

10c. (styles) hardboiled / humorous / hardcore / ironic / romantic / realistic?
10d. Are there any other ingredients that particularly appeal to you?
11. We try to create a cover appearance that is suitable for each title. Do you consider them to be successful?
12. Would you prefer them to be less explicit / more explicit?
13. We would be interested to hear of your other reading habits. What other types of books do you read?
14. Who are your favourite authors?
15. Which newspapers do you read?
16. Which magazines?
17. Do you have any other comments or suggestions to make?

If you would like to receive a free erotic novel of the Editor's choice (available only to UK residents), together with an up-to-date listing of Headline Delta titles, please supply your name and address:

Name...

Address..

....

....

A selection of Erotica
from Headline